OPERATION RAFE'S REDEMPTION

Justine Davis

HARLEQUIN

ROMANTIC SUSPENSE

HARLEQUIN®
ROMANTIC SUSPENSE™

Recycling programs
for this product may
not exist in your area.

ISBN-13: 978-1-335-59395-5

Operation Rafe's Redemption

For questions and comments about the quality of this book, please contact us at CustomerService@Harlequin.com.

Harlequin Enterprises ULC
22 Adelaide St. West, 41st Floor
Toronto, Ontario M5H 4E3, Canada
www.Harlequin.com

Printed in U.S.A.

"Why, Mr. Crawford," she said, far too sweetly, **"if I didn't know better, I'd take that as a compliment. But I do know better, so I have to assume you're just being an ass."**

She didn't add "as usual," but it rang in the silence as if she had. Rafe didn't care. Only one thing mattered right now. But she had to realize it would be beyond foolish to go back—it would be downright dangerous.

"Don't be stupid. Flood is one step away from knowing who you really are."

"Considering how stupid Ogilvie is, more like ten steps."

"If Ogilvie's after Flood's help on his case, what could be better than warning him you're Foxworth?"

"There's no reason Ogilvie would know or guess. He's never seen me in person. And even if he had, it was never like this." She made a gesture that seemed to encompass herself from head to toe. "This is as much a disguise as if I were wearing a mask. I don't ever go to this much trouble."

But you used to.

Dear Reader,

Well, here it is. That book you've been waiting for, asking for (okay, demanding), for *years*. I've heard you all, and so did a certain Mr. Crawford, but a more stubborn man I've never met. I interviewed him several times and got very male grunts and nonanswers. Each time I sighed and said to myself it clearly wasn't time yet.

It wasn't all his fault, mind you. It was also mine because I've always had it in my head that Rafe's story would be the last Cutter's Code book, and I was having so much fun with the series I didn't want it to end. But it's been made clear to me by you, the reader (and my editor as well, bless her), that you want more.

But I still had to convince Rafe. And to do that, upon recommendation from a writer friend who understands this weird aspect of writing fiction, I turned to the financial genius behind the Foxworth Foundation. To which Charlie Foxworth said, "It's about time you talked to me."

Despite Charlie's help, which was considerable, I was still iffy. (Hmm, I'm thinking maybe the problem was more *me* than Rafe...) So I went to the real source, the heart of it all, and I interviewed the star himself. And so it was Cutter who finally handed me the key that opened the door.

However you feel about the story, know that I worked harder on it than almost anything I can remember. It's a true labor of love, for a dog—and a man—unlike any other, and my readers, about whom I feel the same way.

Thank you,

Justine

Justine Davis lives on Puget Sound in Washington State, watching big ships and the occasional submarine go by and sharing the neighborhood with assorted wildlife, including a pair of bald eagles, deer, a bear or two, and a tailless raccoon. In the few hours when she's not planning, plotting or writing her next book, her favorite things are photography, knitting her way through a huge yarn stash and driving her restored 1967 Corvette roadster—top down, of course.

Connect with Justine on her website, justinedavis.com, at Twitter.com/justine_d_davis or at Facebook.com/justinedaredavis.

Books by Justine Davis

Harlequin Romantic Suspense

Cutter's Code

Operation Homecoming
Operation Soldier Next Door
Operation Alpha
Operation Notorious
Operation Hero's Watch
Operation Second Chance
Operation Mountain Recovery
Operation Whistleblower
Operation Payback
Operation Witness Protection
Operation Takedown
Operation Rafe's Redemption

Visit the Author Profile page at Harlequin.com for more titles.

Justine here, repossessing this space in this rather special book. Not for a goodbye to a much-loved furry one, but for a thank-you to one that only exists in my imagination.

When I wrote the first Cutter's Code book, I had no idea I'd still have this furry rascal in my head and heart seventeen books later. Twelve years, to the month, later. Yet here I am, and here you are, for which I thank you.

And I thank all the people who have contributed their own stories, some sweet, some funny, but always about the sad ending that inevitably comes for all dog lovers, for this dedication space. Sometimes I think dogs' lives are so much shorter than ours because they lavish all that love on us from day one. That doesn't stop me from wondering, When they can breed for size, color, skills and temperament, why can't they breed a dog who will live twice as long? Heck, three times as long, and it still wouldn't be enough. But that's one thing I can promise about Cutter. There will never be one of those moments where we have to say goodbye because he has to leave us.

So this book is dedicated to all of the readers who have come along on this journey and who have fallen a little bit in love with a certain canine rascal named Cutter.

Chapter 1

"Seriously?"

Hayley Foxworth knew she was gaping at her husband, but what he'd just told her made her doubt her own perception about many things. And judging by the way he grimaced and shrugged, and the uncharacteristic puzzlement in his ice blue eyes, he was as blown away as she was by the phone call he'd just gotten.

"So it seems."

"Your sister," she enunciated carefully, "your I-don't-have-time-for-such-things sister, is dating a former senator turned power broker with…questionable ethics? And they're coming here? Tomorrow?"

"She's coming here," Quinn said, gesturing to include the Foxworth headquarters building. "He's coming to the city, probably to broker some of that power."

Hayley grimaced in turn. She'd put her long, autumn colored hair in a loose braid today, and now she tugged at it distractedly. She had an opinion, a strong one, about the man in question, Maximilian Flood, often referred to in opposing party quarters as Maxi-million. Her dog, Cutter, must have sensed her mood, because he nudged her hand with his nose. She gave him a quick pat on his dark head but kept her eyes on her husband.

"And she had Ty call and tell you?"

He nodded. "All he knew was that she'd said there was good reason."

"Sometimes," Hayley said with a shake of her head, "your sister plays it a bit too close to the vest. Are we supposed to meet Flood?"

"He said she didn't say."

"And you didn't ask?"

He shoved a hand through his dark hair. "More a case of I didn't want to know. You know Charlie," he said dryly.

"Apparently not," she retorted, "because I can't imagine her with someone like Max Flood. I always hoped someday she and Rafe—"

She broke off abruptly. She didn't want to put into words what she'd always hoped. Quinn's gaze locked onto hers.

"So did I," he said softly.

She drew in a long breath and let it out in an equally long sigh. A moment later she heard a small whine, and looked down to see Cutter looking up at her with an expression she could only describe as worried.

"I know, sweetie," she said as she stroked his head. And for once the sense of comfort the dog always gave was somehow lessened. As if the dog was distressed himself, and had no comfort to spare. He nudged her hand, then her leg, almost knocking her off balance. "Your only failure."

"Don't know if it could be called a failure when he never really got a try."

The dog's dark head moved again, first nudging her leg insistently, then his amber-flecked gaze shifting. Hayley looked that way just in time to see a tall, lean, dark-haired man leaving through the back door she hadn't even heard open.

"Rafe," she whispered, and Quinn froze. She hadn't even realized he'd been there, and apparently the former sniper had moved so quietly Quinn hadn't, either, which was saying something.

Cutter, however, had clearly known. Had been trying to tell them. She'd known the dog had gone over to the hangar to greet him when they'd first arrived, but she hadn't realized Rafe had apparently come back with the dog.

They stood there, staring at the now closed door, wondering how much the Foxworth operative—and their dear friend—had overheard. Anyone else, it wouldn't matter. But Rafe… The man they never mentioned Quinn's sister to, except when it was unavoidable.

"Do you think we'll ever know?" she asked. "What happened with them?"

"Not if he has anything to say about it," Quinn said.

"That's just it. He has absolutely nothing to say about it."

Quinn grimaced as he nodded in acknowledgment of the truth of that statement. "He's as stubborn as—"

"Your sister?"

Quinn let out an audible breath. "At least."

"Funny how the guy who can hide any trace of his feelings about anything else…" Her voice trailed off.

"Can't keep a lid on it when it comes to Charlie?" Quinn asked. "I've noticed."

"Well, at least you don't have to decide whether to tell him," she said with a wry twist of her mouth.

Quinn looked startled, then smiled at her. "Leave it to you to find the bright side."

"I just wish Rafe and Charlie had found it," she said softly.

Quinn reached out and pulled her close. Cutter walked over to the door Rafe had left through and plopped down rather dejectedly. Quinn held her for a long time, and she leaned into him in turn. Finally, as if he'd gotten some signal undecipherable by humans, Cutter got to his feet and headed for the front door. He raised up to bat at the control pad with a front paw, and the door swung open. Hayley knew where the dog was headed.

"He's probably the best thing for him right now," Quinn said. "We'd just make him clam up even tighter."

"Yes," Hayley agreed with a sigh.

She hated it when a friend was in pain and there was nothing she could do about it.

It was worse when that friend refused to admit he was in any pain at all.

She should have paid more attention in drama class.

That was Charlie Foxworth's uppermost thought as she looked out the window of the small, elegant private jet. But she hadn't, because she'd had no interest at all in the on-stage performances. No desire to be in the spotlight, with all eyes fastened on her, watching every move, every gesture.

The backstage stuff, now, yes, that had intrigued her. And was why she'd shifted to the stage crew almost right away. The process of building sets, of recognizing how to make something look like something else from an audience viewpoint, preventing any midperformance accidents like a prop missing, or a fake wall falling over. Making it all work behind the scenes—that was what had appealed to her. And still did.

But now here she was, having to act as if she were up front on that stage, having to keep up a facade, pretending to be someone she was not. Having to pretend to feel something she didn't feel. Having to appear infatuated with this man—years older than she was, even if he didn't look it—when in fact she loathed him.

And there was a lot more than applause at the final curtain at stake here.

It will be worth it.

She had no doubt about that. Putting an end to three years of searching, of hunting. Finally nailing the guy who had betrayed his word, his country, and most important to her, nearly gotten their team—and Hayley, the woman who had changed her brother's life—killed.

No, her doubts were more personal, as in how long could she keep up the pretense of being enamored by this guy, charmed by his practiced manner, impressed by his easy wielding of power. A power subtly emphasized by the presence of the man who now sat a discreet distance away, yet still facing them. The man who was watchful even now, as if he took no one at face value, even his charge's new…whatever she was. The man she'd seen that first night at the glitzy party, ever present, ever watchful, ever silent, always within reach but never intrusive.

He'd been introduced to her merely as Ducane, although she'd later heard Flood use the name Cort to address him. When she had noticed the wedding ring he wore and found herself wondering what kind of woman it would take to live with this kind of man, a jolt of realization hit her. They looked nothing alike, but there was something about him, some inner quality of strength, intensity and utter control that reminded her of the one man she was forever trying to forget.

"He's rather intimidating," she had said to Flood that night.

"That's his job," the former senator had said dismissively, confirming her guess that he was a bodyguard.

A wise decision, she'd thought, for anyone this high profile.

A necessity, for anyone this high profile involved in unsavory dealings under the surface.

And frankly, she found Flood's unctuous aide, Alec Brown, now seated in the far corner seat, a lot more bothersome. The man was always around, usually at Flood's elbow, and assessing what good anyone they encountered could be to them. Not that Flood didn't do the same, but he was much better at hiding it.

She'd also wondered how long she could put up with that spotlight Flood not only drew but craved, savoring every time he was recognized, photographed or approached with that deference he expected as his due.

"I didn't put in all those years in the Senate to simply fade away," he'd explained. "I have plans, big plans. I'd love to share some of them with you, Lita."

She'd chosen to use the first name Lita—along with Marshall for the last, randomly chosen—on her manufactured ID not just because it had a faintly ethnic sound to it that she knew would fit the man's carefully constructed public image, but because it had been her college roommate's name and she would instinctively react to it if she heard it, in a way she hoped would seem natural. She'd had to use the manufactured ID because if he ever found out who she really was, things could get very ugly very fast. He was many things, including dishonest, corrupt and immoral, but he was not stupid. And he would instantly put together the name Foxworth with that witness protection operation he'd been paid big to sabotage.

And if he did…

The guy sold crucial info to one of the largest drug cartels, to help them take out the top witness against them. Do you really have any doubts what he'd do to you?

No, she didn't.

She knew her brother was not going to be happy with

her following this lead personally, without even consulting him, let alone letting him in on the planning. Such as it was. But she'd already had her suspicions, the chance had so unexpectedly appeared, and they'd been hunting this guy for so long, she didn't dare pass it up. She'd had to move and move fast, and Quinn was just going to have to accept it. She'd waited to tell him in person, because it would be harder for him to argue her point face-to-face. Plus, they'd be on his turf, one of the deciding reasons for her. Once she'd found out where Flood was going, she couldn't help feeling it was meant to be.

Quinn could adapt on the fly, he was good at it, one of the best. They both were, because they'd had no choice.

She felt an echo of the old, long-ago grief. That day, when they'd learned a horrific act of terrorism had orphaned them, was etched so deeply into her mind and psyche that she knew it would never fade completely. She thought of it every time she got on an airplane.

Of course, she hadn't spent a lot of time on planes like this. True, she'd spent time on small planes, like the Foxworth plane Quinn had insisted they needed to sometimes reach more remote areas in the Northwest. The Piper Mirage had the benefit of being one of the first ever propeller-driven planes with a pressurized cabin, so she'd seen the attraction. The Northwest was full of mountains, after all.

But as useful as the plane Quinn's team member Liam Burnett had dubbed Wilbur was, this little jet was in another class altogether. Elegantly appointed, sleek inside and out, the six-seater private jet included a lavatory and what the manufacturer called a refreshment center, but she, after perusing the contents, would simply call a bar. At least on Max Flood's version of the aircraft.

Even as she thought the name he was there, back from pacing the small open space near that bar, his phone in one hand held up to his ear, a drink in his other hand. The "crucial" call he'd had to take ended now, he sat in the seat next to her.

"It's begun," he said, his booming voice unrestrained here in this place where he thought it safe, where he thought no opponent would overhear.

Little do you know, Mr. Flood.

"What has?"

"The speculation."

There was satisfaction in his voice, the sound of a master planner who was seeing yet another strategy come together. She recognized the feeling—she felt it herself when a major plan worked as she'd envisioned.

"Speculation?" she asked, although she suspected she knew what he meant.

"We were seen at the airport."

She had been right. He hadn't had a headline in at least three days, and that just wasn't acceptable.

"I have to keep up the high profile to maintain my ability to get things done," he'd told her that first evening when she'd asked him, with a shy flutter of eyelashes, how he tolerated being in the public eye all the time.

Get things done. Right. Like getting a payoff from the head of a huge drug cartel. Gotta pay for this jet somehow, right, Max?

She tried to rein in the voice in her head, because it made it harder to maintain the necessary facade. But she couldn't quite stop herself from wondering if he'd had the same tone of satisfaction in his voice when he'd seen all the sympathetic headlines after the death of his wife in a car accident a few years ago. By all accounts Alondra Flood had been a good, kind and smart woman, involved in several worthwhile charitable causes, including a couple that were important to Charlie as well. The marriage had seemed pretty solid, publicly at least. She had no idea if Flood had actually loved his wife, but she was certain he hadn't been above using her death to his advantage.

His phone rang again, and he excused himself as he got up and walked back to the more open space where he'd been pacing before. He might be flirting madly with her, and putting on the big show of wealth and influence, topping it off with this flight on his private bird, but he wasn't sharing anything of real importance with her. He was very careful, about everything. Which was only to be expected, after just a few days of knowing her. It was unexpected enough to end up here on his plane.

I have to fly to Seattle next week, for some meetings. He'd sounded as if he regretted leaving and looked at her as if she were the reason. He was very smooth.

It's a beautiful part of the country. I have friends there. She'd carefully avoided saying family. And as she'd hoped, he bit.

Then you should come with me. You could visit them while I take care of business.

She'd put on a show of being doubtful, gotten his assurance—so very charmingly—that he would not push her into anything she wasn't ready for, and she had finally agreed.

She hadn't expected the private jet. And she should have. She should have assumed all his talk about regulations to save the planet was bull.

Or at least, that those regulations did not apply to him. *Rules for thee, not for me...*

Yes, taking this man down would be worth the effort. And with the full might and resources of Foxworth behind her—she'd built a lot of them after all—she would get it done.

Chapter 2

I always hoped someday she and Rafe—
   So did I.

He couldn't get the exchange out of his head. None of his usual tactics worked. So Rafer James Crawford simply stood next to the helicopter named Igor and let it batter him.

He'd sensed, on some level, that they knew. Knew something, anyway. Not much got by Quinn, and even less got by Hayley. They might not know the details, but they knew enough. Enough to assess and, as much as they ever did to someone they cared about, to judge.

And they did care about him. He knew that, too. For a long time it had been an odd feeling, one he wasn't comfortable with. He didn't feel…worthy of them caring as much as they did, and he'd always told himself that if they knew the whole story, they wouldn't. But he also knew Quinn carried more than his own share of haunting memories around, and yet here he was, happier than

Rafe had ever seen him. Which Rafe was glad about; no one deserved it more.

But he himself didn't deserve any amount of happy.

Charlie did, though. She deserved to be happy. She worked as hard as or harder than any of them, in the areas none of them understood as well as she did. She had such a knack for knowing when and where to invest, and more importantly when to pull out. Among the many other things she had a knack for.

Including turning him inside out.

It had been a pipe dream from the get-go. It would have been so much easier if he'd stood strong, but he'd weakened, and instead of some vague whisper of unrequited longing, he was lugging around vivid images of something that never should have happened. He never should have let himself—

With tremendous effort, he refused to let his brain careen into the old memories. Memories he couldn't seem to shed.

It was crazy, with everything he'd been through, everything he'd done in his life, all without turning a hair, that she could still do this to him after all this time. He'd spent years in war zones, he'd plunged into battles with as little as ten minutes' warning, he'd made shots some considered impossible, others miraculous. He'd saved lives, a lot of lives, enough to make the fact that he'd done it by taking enemy lives bearable. It didn't haunt him, it had simply been a job he excelled at. It didn't keep him awake at night, because it had had to be done. It didn't send his mind careening down dark, ugly paths, because the fighters he'd saved got to go home to their families.

No, only one thing could do all that to him. One gorgeous brunette with more energy than an entire platoon and blue eyes deep enough to drown in. As he once almost had, before he'd pulled back, before he'd turned his back on the most wanted but least possible thing in his life.

It would be wrong, and not just because she's Quinn's sister. You have no right to a woman like her. And she has the right to a better man.

He leaned back against the chopper's solid side panel. The one that carried a carefully tended bullet hole, a souvenir of the mission where Quinn had met the love of his life. The mission that had almost ended up with them all dead thanks to the betrayal of a traitor they had yet to find, three years later. A case anyone would admit had gone cold.

But cold cases were a quiet cause of his. And he'd yet to give up on that one. Someday they would find the man who had sold them out, who had told the drug cartel where to find them. And he would personally see that the man paid.

But even that wasn't enough distraction at the moment. An image of Max Flood popped into his head. Smooth, polished, handsome, with just a touch of gray in thick, brown hair swept artfully back from a still young-looking face that Hayley suggested, long before this, had seen the edge of a plastic surgeon's scalpel. He'd had a rather meteoric rise at a startlingly young age, going from a two-term mayor of a midsize coastal city at twenty-five to a senator with apparent ease. But he had startled people when he'd declined to run for a fourth term in the powerful position.

At least, he'd startled people less knowledgeable and informed than Foxworth.

Rafe had a memory of being at one of the gatherings at Quinn and Hayley's home that he usually tried to dodge, but this last one just a few months ago had been to welcome Foxworth operative—and his friend—Teague Johnson's little sister home and into the fold, after she'd run away at age seventeen thinking her beloved big brother had been killed in action overseas. He remembered the news had been on in the den, and he'd retreated there for a bit of a break from the celebration. He'd found their consulting attorney, Gavin de Marco, there, watching a report on Flood's retirement from office.

They listed the causes he'd espoused, his wins in Congress—including a few that Rafe privately thought had done much more damage than good—and then spoke in hushed voices of the sorrow he'd endured after the death of his beloved wife a couple of years before. This, they concluded, was what had driven him to retire. Even Rafe had to admit he'd felt bad for the guy then, although the public display of grief had seemed a bit over-the-top. But maybe that was because he was a much more private kind of guy.

When the piece had concluded with some more rather fawning adoration, de Marco had snorted in unconcealed disgust.

"Not buying?" Rafe had asked, genuinely curious about what the world-renowned attorney thought of the man.

"He became a senator to build his power infrastructure. Now he figures he's got it in place, it's time to start pulling those behind-the-scenes strings."

"More power than he'd have as a single senator," Rafe had said, unsurprised and pretty much agreeing with the assessment.

He also remembered de Marco looking at him with a slight smile. "Exactly."

And Rafe couldn't deny that having a man on the level of de Marco, who genuinely had walked away from a career most in the world would envy to do what he thought was right, give him that approving look meant a great deal.

And now here he was, having to face the fact this scheming, backroom-style politician—because he had no doubt that de Marco had been right—was coming here to continue his wheeling and dealing.

And that Quinn's sister—he'd long ago found that think-ing of her that way helped a little—was coming with him.

With him. Because she was dating him.

A faint nausea rose in his gut, as if just the thought had literally turned his stomach. If that was who she wanted, the kind of man she wanted, then it only proved he'd made the right decision. This, finally, should crush this chronic problem of his once and for all. They had been hot, short and impossible. When reality had finally caved in on him, leaving him in shambles, he'd known that. He'd made the best decision and walked away, her protests ringing in his ears. He'd set her free to find someone worthy of her. And had braced himself for the day it happened.

He hadn't been braced for this. Couldn't quite believe it. Couldn't believe that Charlaine Foxworth would really, truly want that…that…

The string of invective that ran through his mind was not helpful. But right now he wasn't sure anything could help.

He slid slowly down the side of the helicopter until he was sitting on the ground beside it. His left leg protested the sharp bend, as it always did. He ignored it, as he al-ways did.

He heard the faint click of the hangar door as it was nudged open. When no one spoke he knew who it was. And looked up to see Cutter heading straight for him. The dog always seemed to know. And seemed, to Rafe at least, to spend a lot of time and energy trying to ease that chronic ache in his leg.

Among other chronic aches.

"You can't fix this one," he murmured to the dog, who sat beside him and rested his chin on that leg, looking up at him with those dark, amber-flecked eyes. "But you sure manage to make the leg feel better." He reached out to stroke the dog's dark head. "Or make me think you do."

He didn't remember exactly when he'd started talking to the dog so much. Crazily, he wanted to say it was when the animal had started demanding it with that unwavering stare. And it didn't really matter. It wasn't like the dog was going to tell anyone he'd been babbling like...like an almost normal person.

But that was all Liam's fault. The other Foxworth Northwest operative who was their in-house tech guy—and who had been hired by Quinn after he'd been caught trying to hack the Foxworth website—had one day mentioned how, as a kid, he'd often talked to the dogs his family raised just to test how things sounded. It worked, somehow, to say things to a living thing that paid attention to you, even if it didn't understand what you were saying.

Of course with Cutter, there was no guarantee at all that he didn't understand every word. And everything he didn't say, too.

He knew how rattled he was when he realized he was serious about that thought. But he wasn't sure how else to explain the dog's almost unnatural awareness of...well, everything. The rest of Foxworth had long ago progressed to simply accepting his instincts. He himself had learned better than to doubt the dog on a case, to doubt the uncanny accuracy of his judgment about cases, circumstances and people. More than once the dog's actions had tipped the case in the right direction, sometimes even blown it wide open.

So far, Cutter had never been wrong. About anything.

Including his other weird, unexpected skill of somehow knowing when two people needed to be together. As if love, or fate, or whatever, had a scent only he could pick up, or threads only he could see. Even Rafe, soured as he was on the subject, as absurd as he'd always thought the idea of soulmates was, couldn't deny that the couples the too-clever dog had brought together seemed rock-solid. Starting with Quinn and Hayley.

Cutter made a soft little sound as he nudged Rafe's hand, urging him to stroke again. Sometimes it simply amazed him how this creature he'd seen, when necessary, turn into a fierce, snarling attack dog, could be so gentle. How he could tell when people needed the comfort he could offer, comfort that somehow seemed to come simply from petting him. Comfort that eventually overwhelmed even Rafe's bone-deep skepticism, and he had to admit that stroking the dog's soft fur relieved…something. Whether it was the mental side, which then eased the physical, or the other way around, he didn't know.

He only knew it happened.

And as Cutter nudged him again, practically crawling into his lap now, he knew he'd needed it at this moment perhaps more than he ever had. Not because of the pain in his leg, but the pain inside, whenever he was face-to-face with the simple fact that Charlaine Foxworth existed.

Only when the image of the dark-haired beauty slipped back into his mind did he realize Cutter had done it again. He'd given him a side trip to take, pondering the dog's unexpected skills and the results, distracting him enough to get his breath back and at least reach for some equilibrium.

"Saving me again, boy?" he murmured.

Cutter whined slightly, something else he did rarely. In fact, did only when the person he was helping—because Rafe didn't even try to deny that anymore—was in a very bad place, physically or mentally. Or both.

This time he reached out and scratched the loving animal behind his ears, which he knew was a favored caress. It wasn't a long reach, not with the dog actually in his lap, now that his legs had straightened out into a more comfortable position. He bent his head to stare at the miracle worker. Cutter reached upward in turn and swiped his tongue over Rafe's chin.

The experienced former Marine, the battle-hardened warrior, the deadly accurate long-range sniper, felt his eyes sting at the simple, loving gesture. And had the thought that the human race would be a lot better off if people would learn from dogs.

Chapter 3

Charlie looked out the window again as the small jet flew westward toward the distinctive landscape that was the Pacific Northwest. It wasn't the water that would soon be in sight ahead that always caught her attention. In St. Louis, she lived within sight of the Mississippi, and no water in the country was more—just as, perhaps, but not more—significant than that. No, it wasn't the fjord of Puget Sound that struck her most, or the islands that dotted the chilly waters, or the towering evergreens along so many of the shorelines. It was the mountains that surrounded the area, the knowledge that some of those mountains were living volcanoes that could still erupt, and that one had not all that long ago.

She was used to the flats, sometimes seemingly endless, stretching out as far as the eye could see, marked by no more than an occasional slight undulation in the earth. With few exceptions, flat was the rule, and any break in it the exception and unusual enough to be considered a landmark. And there were tall trees, yes, but they were usually birch, maple and the occasional pecan tree. Not that there weren't maple trees here as well, but the landscape was dominated by the trees the state was nicknamed for. And very, very unlike what she was used to.

Very unlike what her brother, Oliver, had been used to, and yet…

She remembered so vividly the day he'd called her. He'd flown out here to set up a new Foxworth office, the first of a planned two on the west coast. It had taken longer than expected, but she'd put it down to the complications of working in a new territory.

"We're set," he'd told her. "Ready to go operative."

"Good. Any problems I need to know about?"

"No. The headquarters is done, the outbuilding nearly so. Met with Teague Johnson, and he's a good fit."

"We'll need more operatives."

"I know. I've…partially solved that."

"Somebody new?"

"In a way." She recalled the deep breath he'd taken then. "I'm staying, Charlie."

"What?"

"I'm going to do my bit from here."

"But you can't—"

"I love this place, sis. I have from the moment I got off the ferry on this side."

She remembered, through her shock, that he'd quickly written off the city of Seattle as a place for them and had widened his search, settling on a small town—or village, actually—on the other side of the sound.

"Quinn—"

"I know, it seems crazy to you, but it felt like coming home, just as much as coming home from overseas when I left the Army did. Maybe even more. All I could think was…so this is where I'm supposed to be."

That fanciful thinking from her practical, ever-efficient brother had given her pause. The certainty in his voice had put the cap on it. And less than two months later it was done—her brother had relocated, leaving her and their small staff to run the main offices of the Foxworth Foundation. And a little to her surprise, as technology progressed—and their resident genius, Tyler Hewitt, had been on the cutting edge of some of it—it had worked.

Quinn had built a great team there. No matter how she felt about one particular member, it was undeniable. The later, unexpected addition of Liam Burnett, the young hacker Ty had caught trying to breach his own considerable firewalls, to the team had completed the four-man roster.

Quinn being Quinn, he'd then quickly set about building goodwill and relationships, establishing the Foxworth mission in the area, and gathering others who believed in the idea of helping the little guy in the right fight the big ones who wanted to stomp him down. With each case that goodwill grew, with each success their pool of helpers widened. Because Foxworth didn't take any payment for their help, except the kind that couldn't be bought—the willingness to somewhere down the line help someone else as they had been helped.

And then, on their biggest mission up until that time, Quinn had encountered Hayley, and his life was changed forever, in the best possible way. So maybe it was meant to be. She was sure Hayley's frighteningly smart dog would think so. She wasn't much on imputing human characteristics onto animals, but that remarkable creature had made her think about it more than once.

A chill rippled down her spine as the thought of that mission, and what had nearly happened, crashed into her musings, erasing all else. She pushed back at the onslaught. Forced herself to remember instead the first time she'd met

Hayley. She'd purposely come on strong, knowing what her brother had probably told the woman.

So you're the one who thinks she can tame my brother?

I don't want him tamed. I love him as he is. And he loves me. So if you hurt me, you hurt him. Don't.

She'd known in that moment just how right it was, that her beloved brother had found a woman to match him.

The memory served its purpose, and the chill receded. She gave herself an inward shake. She needed to focus on her own mission, on why she was here. The man coming back to sit beside her again.

The man she suspected was the mole they'd been chasing for three years.

"Sure you don't want to blow off those friends and come with me?" he asked as he fastened his seat belt and indicated she should do the same, as they would be landing soon. "I could introduce you to a lot of movers and shakers."

She put on her best smile. "Oh, I couldn't do that. I haven't seen them since the last time I was here, over a year and a half ago."

"What was that trip for?"

"A wedding," she said, carefully omitting that it had been her brother's wedding. As far as Max knew, she had no family, and she intended to keep it that way. A man who would do what she strongly suspected he'd done wouldn't hesitate to use any leverage he could find, if there was something he wanted.

"And that's who you're going to go see?"

"Among others, yes."

Others. She had a lot of new others to meet. Teague's wife, Laney. Liam's wife, Ria. And Gavin's fiancée, Katie. She never would have expected Gavin to leave St. Louis, either, and yet here he also was, in this so very different place. All of them happier than ever.

A happiness she was certain she would never find.

And that fact could be laid at the boots of one person, and one person only. The one person she hadn't allowed into her thoughts about this trip. The one person she couldn't allow in, because it would shake her concentration.

Shake? How about destroy?

"—after you've finished your visit."

She snapped back to the present, a present that confirmed the thought she'd just had. Rafe Crawford was deadly to her focus.

And her heart.

The heart she would never again risk, because of him.

"That can wait," Quinn said.

"It needs to be done. I'll just pick up the parts—"

"They can ship them."

Rafe had to consciously relax his jaw muscles. "They're just down in Salt Lake City. Only take two, maybe three days."

"And they can ship the parts in the same amount of time. Try again."

Quinn was looking at him as if he knew exactly what was going on. And maybe he did know. Just because he'd never discussed it with him didn't mean Charlie hadn't. And it would be like Quinn to never mention it, even if she had. Unlike his interfering dog, Quinn was a big believer in letting nature take its course.

Then again, Hayley seemed like a mind reader half the time, so maybe that was where Quinn was getting this.

"All right," he said, his voice rougher than he would have preferred. "Then I'll be at the airport. Wilbur needs some attention."

This, at least, was true. The plane—that Liam had named after one of the Wright brothers, just as he'd named Igor after the man who'd pretty much invented helicopters—hangared at the small airport about thirty miles south, a few miles from the Naval shipyard, did need some regular maintenance done. A lot of the time they got the crew there to do it, but if things at Foxworth were slow, as they'd been in the three weeks since their last case, he did it himself.

"Is it that bad?" Quinn asked quietly. "That you can't even be in the same room with her?"

His jaw tensed again. "Maybe it's her…companionship I can't be around." It was a dodge, he knew it was, but it was better than admitting Quinn had been exactly right. There was no way in hell he could stomach seeing her with a man like that.

Be honest, if nothing else. With any man.

"Can't blame you for that," Quinn said, surprising him. "But he's not coming over with her."

But she came here with him…

With one of the greatest efforts of his life, he closed the door—no, mentally slammed it—on that twisted, beaten part of him. For good. Because if that's the kind of man she wanted, it just proved he'd done the right thing all those years ago.

"Are you ordering me to stay?" he asked flatly.

Quinn studied him for a long, silent moment. Then, finally, he let out an audible breath. "No."

Relief flooded him. He had such respect for this man, not just for the incredible soldier he'd been but for what he'd built out of his massive, personal grief—and what Quinn had done for he himself, pulling him out of a morass that likely would have been the end of him—that he would have obeyed. He would have hated every minute of it, but he would have done it. And he knew that Quinn knew that.

Which was likely the reason he hadn't, in the end, made it an order.

And so Quinn Foxworth saved him once more. This time from coming face-to-face with the one thing that haunted him more than anything he'd ever done—or not done—in his life.

Chapter 4

"So what is it you're hoping to accomplish here?" Charlie asked, trying to make her voice sound simply interested.

"Adjusting relationships, mostly," Max said with that wide, practiced smile. "These are people I've dealt with before, but things are different now."

"Because you're no longer in office?"

"Yes."

She considered her next words carefully, and put on her most innocently curious expression and as much concern as she could manage into her voice when she spoke. "Are you worried these people won't deal with you any longer, now that you're not…in an official position to help them?"

He smiled again, and this time it was as if she were a student who'd correctly answered a question. "That's exactly what I'm here to clarify with them. That without the constraints of office, I can help them more than ever."

For a price, no doubt.

"At least you left on your terms," she said, trying to sound proud of the fact that he had retired, not been booted out.

He flashed that camera-ready smile that he so often used. Be it friend or foe, that smile was always handy. Friend, and it was welcoming, grateful and all things warm. Foe, and it was amused, belittling and pitying. And the man had it down, she had to give him that.

Which one did you wear when you were selling out Vicente Reynosa? When you told the cartel when and where the only witness against them would be moved and by who? When you made the deal that almost got my brother and his team killed? When you almost got the only man I—

She cut off her own thoughts sharply. It did no good to think of that now. She was nearly certain she knew what the man beside her now was. And the more time she spent with him, the more certain she became that the connection Ty had found was real and solid.

They'd been down many dead ends in this search before, too many. They'd spent time and resources, had actually come across more than a couple of people who had done illegal or hideous things and ended up making them face their crimes, but none thus far had been the man they truly sought.

But her gut was telling her Max Flood was. She never claimed to have the instincts her brother had, both innate and honed by years in the military, but when it came to business and businessmen, as this man essentially was, her instincts might be even better. And if she were looking to make a genuine investment, one that would benefit the Foxworth Foundation's continuing work, she would rather stuff the money in a mattress. Better yet, under Cutter's bed, because he'd keep it far safer than Maximilian Flood would.

"I'm very glad you decided to come with me," he said with that charming smile, yanking her out of her ruminations. She'd best stop that, because the inward anger she was feeling was going to show. She called up the practiced mask she used in financial negotiations. She had to make him believe she was flattered, pleased to be here with him. Just as she'd had to occasionally convince a start-up or already successful business that Foxworth was exactly the quiet partner they needed.

"It was so kind of you to offer the ride in this lovely plane of yours. It's much more convenient and pleasant."

His smile widened. She bit back an additional comment about the state of commercial air traffic these days, because Ty's in-depth dive had told her he was not only on the board of one of the major airlines—added the week after he'd retired from the Senate, so clearly long planned in advance—but was a large investor as well. Hidden well, many layers deep, but that was the kind of thing Ty Hewitt excelled at; there had never been anything yet hidden so deep he couldn't find it eventually. One of the best things she'd ever done was to pull that guy out of the downward spiral he'd been in after his parents had been murdered and put him to work on bringing the people responsible to justice. That had resulted in a genius talent who was loyal to Foxworth to the bone.

The talent who had found, buried deep, the link between a shell corporation Flood was connected to and another shell that, even deeper down, was the "legitimate" front that washed the cartel's drug cash. The link of a sizable transfer of funds the week before Foxworth had set out to transport the one witness who could take down that cartel. And had.

But that hadn't been enough for Ty. He'd kept going. And eventually, on one of the several deep-dive searches he'd done, he'd made a connection that sealed the deal for her.

Charlie let a bit of the pleasure she felt over that show in her smile. If Max thought she was enamored already—which he likely would, given his assessment of his own charms—all the better.

"Once I'm through with these meetings, we can spend some time together," Max said, responding to that expression on her face.

"That would be lovely," she said. *I hope I spend it watching them take you away.*

"And of course, you'll come with me to the big party Friday night," he said, as if granting an award to a lesser being.

"I would be honored."

She managed to get it out fairly evenly, despite the faint nausea that churned at the idea. She could only imagine some of the people who would be there. As if being with Flood wasn't bad enough. Adding in some of the likely guests at that exclusive gathering, it would be enough to make her truly want to vomit. There might not be a shower long enough or sufficient soap to make her ever feel clean again if she had to spend too much time among those top feeders.

She let out the smile inspired by their uncle's long-ago phrase, which he'd coined to describe the ones at the top, who fed upon those below them, who in turn fed on the next level down, and then the next, until you got down to the last ones fed upon, the everyday folks who had no power or influence worth taking or using, the ones who were not users but only used.

The kind of people Foxworth now helped.

"You go have a good time with your country friends," he said, managing to keep it to just a touch of condescension in his voice, "then I'll introduce you to a different group of people."

He didn't say "better," but she heard it in his tone and read it in his expression. And she knew that to him, anything that wasn't wall-to-wall skyscrapers with a Starbucks on every corner was "country," and anyone who voluntarily lived there had to be what he'd call a hick.

"Sounds fascinating," she said. And meant it, in the same way watching a gathering of sharks was fascinating.

Yet again his phone rang, only this time they were close enough to landing that the pilot had given the seat belt notification, so he stayed put as he pulled it out and answered, although he gave her a sideways look. She wondered if his careful responses, mostly yes, no, and "It can wait until I land in a few minutes," were trimmed because of her presence, within earshot.

To show him she was paying no attention to his private call, she took out her own phone as if to make a last check for messages before they had to put them into airplane mode for the landing. As far as Flood knew, she was a mid-level advisor at a small financial firm; they'd stuck close to her real life experience so she could believably field any questions tossed at her. And if he had checked, as she suspected he or someone on his still sizable staff had, they would find a comfortably successful business that made good money for their clients.

There were no messages, and she'd known there wouldn't be, because this was not her actual daily use phone. That one, with her real name and contact list, was safely locked up at home, while she carried this one in the name of the non-existent Lita Marshall, with a list of contacts that didn't really exist, either. It had been carefully tailored, the business side populated with fake names that would ring through with a warning to Ty if dialed, and the personal side with almost all female names, since her story to Flood had been that she had no family left—she didn't want him to have that leverage—and was not in a relationship at the moment.

Any call to one of the numbers listed would take her someplace else, depending on the name. And any call she made to any of those private numbers would trigger an alert telling them what was incoming, and to speak as if she were truly Lita Marshall.

So she only had to remember the system she and Ty had concocted. Tina Hartford—the T.H. matching Ty's initials—would reach Ty's private number. Luna Bickford would reach Quinn, the initials she would happily tell him stood for Little Brother. Heather Cox was for Hayley's maiden name of Cole, and Lea Dallas was for their resident tech guy, Texan Liam Burnett, who'd worked well with Ty before. Teague Johnson was Marnie Johnson, the last name being common enough to keep, and the first name an anagram of Marine. The plan she hoped Quinn would go along with when she explained was, if anyone other than she herself called any of the guy's numbers, they'd react as a relative or significant other of the fake woman, and then get Hayley on the line to cover.

She refused to think about the other name Ty had insisted be included, and that she couldn't insist be excluded without explanations she did not want to and would not make. So she'd picked Raine because it seemed appropriate, and kept Crawford as a reminder not to ever let down her guard.

All of this preparation was, of course, useless until she had the chance to tell Foxworth Northwest about this new system in person, away from any of Flood's nationwide army of connections and informants. Ty had told her the man had an impressive crew monitoring and tracking all sorts of phone, internet, website and email activity. On one level it could be passed off as just being a good representative of his constituents, and knowing what they wanted and cared about.

But Flood's network went far beyond that, digging into things he had no business knowing. Violating privacy to an extreme that had brought this about, the switch in phones and her not telling her brother what was going on until she could tell him face-to-face. Once everyone was read in, then they could proceed.

To cover her actions, she actually wrote a text to "Tina" to let Ty know they were about to land. He answered quickly with Can't wait to see you! and a smiley emoji that was very un-Ty-like, but very fitting for the fictional Tina.

For a moment she allowed herself a bit of pride at what she'd helped build. That people who'd suffered as she and Quinn had—losing their parents at such a young age and then having to watch as the cause of it walked free after some backroom deal between people who didn't care who was hurt—that people who'd tried to fight for what was right and been outnumbered or out-influenced, that Fox-worth could help those people, meant so much to her. She and Quinn had found a calling few had in life, something that was more fulfilling than anything else she could imagine. It didn't make up for the loss they'd suffered, but it made the loss mean something.

And she'd helped build it.

You've got the money brain, Charlaine. Use it.

Uncle Paul had told her that when she'd graduated high school. He always called her by her full name, he said to honor her parents, his brother Charles and his wife, Elaine, for whom she was named. She appreciated the thought, even if she much preferred Charlie, if only for the assumptions it frequently led to, assumptions she then had the fun of blasting to pieces.

His advice had sent her on to college to learn just that—

how to make the sizable insurance payout their parents had made certain of, and that their slightly awkward but honest to the core uncle had refused to touch for himself even as he provided them a home, do nothing but grow in the long run. It just seemed to come naturally to her, that knowledge of what to do, where to invest and, probably more importantly, when to pull out.

And because of that, Foxworth had grown from one office helping a few people a year to five helping dozens, from small but personally crucial things to much bigger things. Like Quinn and his crew taking down a sitting governor for murder.

She was proud of him for that. But then, she was proud of him for just about everything he'd accomplished. Especially his priorities, and that he'd considered the recovery of a treasured locket holding the image of a child and her deceased mother, and getting it back to that child, just as important as any other case. She'd like to think she had a part in that, in making him the amazing man he was, since she'd been the closest thing he'd had to a mother since she'd been fourteen when their lives had been nearly destroyed.

And now she was going to hand him a gift he richly deserved. The name of the mole they'd been hunting for three years.

The man who was sitting smugly beside her right now.

Chapter 5

If he worked a little slower than usual, maybe even took a break now and then, he could stretch this maintenance work out to two or, if he did a full exterior cleaning, even three days.

Rafe rubbed his stubbled jaw as he considered it. He had been in such a rush to get away he hadn't bothered to shave. Now he looked up at the sleek little aircraft. He didn't mind flying in this. Airplanes, after all, essentially wanted to fly by design. And unless interfered with by an outside force—weather or man-made—or an inside one in the form of a bungling pilot or poor maintenance, it would fly. Even if that meant gliding to an unplanned and perhaps ungraceful landing.

Igor the helicopter, on the other hand, wanted to tear himself apart.

"With Wilbur, you enjoy the flight," Quinn, who flew them both, had once said. "With Igor, you enjoy having survived the flight."

Rafe did a mental inventory. He had both his go bags in the trunk of his slightly battered and surreptitiously powerful car. One a standard backpack with survival necessities, the other what he called his gear bag, and others called his arsenal. He could easily sleep on the plane. He was too tall to enjoy sleeping in one of the seats, even reclined, but he could sack out on the floor easily enough. It wouldn't be comfortable, but at least he could stretch out. He'd slept in worse places. Much worse.

As for eating, the stuff available in the airport lounge would get him by during the day, and it so happened the place whose retro decor made him smile wasn't too far away. He could easily live on Crazy Eric's burgers for dinner for a few days.

Maybe stretch it out into a week, huh, Crawford? You want to be sure she's not only not at headquarters, but not even in the state, maybe?

The self-directed derision made him regain his focus on the matter at hand. So, feeling he'd solved the immediate problem, he went back to work. The winterization process wasn't due until November, but that didn't mean he couldn't do a few things now. He knew Quinn, knew that he'd never take a plane out in any season without having checked it out completely himself, but he also knew Quinn counted on his help keeping the plane airworthy. Especially in winter when things like the deicing system, heater and carbon monoxide detector were crucial. Quinn was not one to let a little weather stop a flight that needed to be made, so Rafe made sure to have the oil changed out to a more winter-suited type, and that the fuel tanks were full to prevent the buildup of condensation.

But that was for weeks from now. Right now he just needed enough to do to keep him here until the threat was over. And that quickly he was back in the morass he'd just climbed out of.

Just when did you become such a coward?

He laughed silently, sourly, his head ringing with the bitter tone of it. He knew exactly when he, the guy they'd hung a boxful of medals on, had become just that, a coward. When he who had faced down battalions could no longer find the nerve to face down one single human being.

But knowing didn't help him get past it.

Nothing helped. And he was convinced now that it would stay that way. The only real solution would be to leave Foxworth. And he couldn't, wouldn't do that. Foxworth had pulled him out of a hole so deep he'd almost been lost forever. So he considered the pain, the embarrassment of admitting his own cowardice, simply the price he had to pay for this job with colleagues he trusted completely and for a man he admired beyond all others.

Determinedly he reached out and opened the top of the rolling toolbox.

"All right, Wilbur," he muttered aloud. "Let's get to it."

Cutter was the first to greet her when she arrived.

She knew Quinn or someone would have come to pick her up, but she didn't trust that Flood didn't have someone watching her. And so she'd rented a car on the city side—it seemed rideshare had yet to spread thoroughly on this more rural side of the sound—and taken the ferry over.

Normally she would have relied more on her admittedly prodigious memory than the vehicle's GPS to get her here from the landing, but for that same reason she'd taken the most convoluted route she could, until she was certain no one was following her. So it had taken her twice as long as it usually would have to reach the inconspicuous dark green building masked by a thick stand of almost matching evergreens. Those tall, majestic conifers she was so unused to back home, except perhaps when their much shorter cousins appeared for sale at Christmas.

She hadn't even gotten out of the rental before the front door swung open. She remembered how crazy she'd first thought it—that they'd installed an access pad on the front door mainly for the dog, who had learned what it was and how to operate it by batting at the pad with his front paws in a matter of a minute. It had been her first inkling that what they'd told her about the dog—which from a distance, without having ever met the animal, had seemed like something out of a fanciful kid's movie—was actually true.

She'd been even more doubtful about them seeming to accept that the dog had some sixth sense about finding people who needed Foxworth help. But after about the fourth or fifth case file she'd read, she'd had to admit every person he'd brought to them had been a prime example of the reason they'd started the foundation.

Her feet had barely hit the gravel of the parking area before Cutter was through the door. The dog seemed to remember her, even after the twenty months—nearly two years!—it had been since Quinn and Hayley's wedding. He came charging out of the headquarters building, dark head up, reddish-brown tail wagging in welcome. She'd never had a dog herself, so didn't quite understand why the sight made her want to smile.

And when he skidded to a halt in front of her, tongue lolling happily as he looked up at her expectantly, almost smiling—gads, she was getting as bad as they were, attributing human characteristics to a dog—she wasn't able to resist bending to pat him on the head.

With a little snap it came back to her the moment her fingers touched the soft fur. That unexpected warmth, the soothing feeling of…comfort, somehow, as if everything would be all right.

She'd noticed it when she first met the animal, and Hayley had told her pretty much everyone felt it, and that was why she'd gotten Cutter certified as a therapy dog to visit local hospitals and nursing homes. That had gotten Charlie thinking about therapy dogs, and why they seemed to work. Which had in turn led her to making a sizable Foxworth donation to a local charitable group who trained and arranged for them to work with injured veterans. In a moment of whimsy, she'd done it in the name of Cutter Foxworth, and had sent the resulting donor acknowledgment to Quinn as a joke. Her brother hadn't laughed. He'd merely told her with a nod, "Good idea."

"You are the most interesting creature," she murmured to the animal, who sat giving her a rather intense look with those dark eyes that seemed flecked with tiny spots of gold. Just as she remembered from that last day she'd been here in this surprisingly lovely, peaceful place.

She hated that it had been so long, but the wedding—that beautiful, heartfelt ceremony so full of love and joy—had been a strain for her, and she'd needed some recovery time after she'd had to table her own feelings about the best man.

Except the one time when she hadn't been able to keep her emotions on a leash and had let out a snide, "You're the best man he could get?"

His quiet retort had chilled her. "I'm nobody's best man."

That exchange, in the moments before the ceremony had actually begun, could have been overheard by anyone there had it been any louder. And that alone had enabled her to rein it in. Not for anything would she ruin this day of joy and beauty for her beloved brother.

Not even to dig at the man who'd walked away from the possibility of the same thing for them.

The man whom she dared hope was not here now.

"I'm sure there's a reason you didn't want us to come get you?"

She straightened quickly to look at the tall, strong, dark-haired man approaching. The man with icy blue eyes that always made her heart give a little kick, they looked so much like Dad's. Sometimes, when she hadn't seen her brother in person for a while, she forgot just how impressive he was.

"Glad to see you, too, brother mine," she said, smiling to see him despite the circumstances.

He smiled back at her and enveloped her in a warm hug. Then he put his hands on her shoulders and held her where he could look into her face. His smile faded. "What is it, Charlie?"

She drew in a deep breath and let the words tumble out. "I found him, Quinn. I found him."

Chapter 6

Rafe was ankle deep in parts and tools and oil when his Foxworth phone sounded an in-house communication. His first reaction was to freeze in place. He just stood there for a moment, his jaw tight as the signal echoed in his ears. The three-bladed prop, looking like what it was, ready to chew the air—or anyone in its way—on command, took up the edge of his vision. It was a long moment before he turned away.

Then he started toward the wheeled tool chest that stood open next to the sleek nose of the small aircraft, where he'd set the phone. He had the sudden, stupid wish that it was at the far end of the over six-thousand-foot runway. Three times what the Mirage needed to take off, but a small fraction of the distance he was wishing for now.

He set down the socket wrench he held with much more care than the tough tool needed. He grabbed the rag from atop the chest and wiped at his oily hands. Thought about buying another minute or two by washing his hands before picking up the unwelcome device.

Always on a tether, always reachable, never alone.

With a sharp reminder that that tether was his connection to the man who had saved him from what likely would have been a steady downward spiral, he dropped the rag and tapped the phone's screen. A text message came up. Short, blunt.

Return to HQ. Now.

Quinn was never wordy with these things, but that was brusque even for him. Possibilities started to slam into his mind, each one worse than the one before. He assumed Quinn's sister had arrived. Had she brought Flood with her, after all? Was he supposed to come meet the power broker and—he almost gagged on the thought—be polite?

Or was something else going on? Had she brought bad news? Some kind of financial trouble for Foxworth? As sharp as she was in that area it was hard for him to believe she'd made a mistake of any size. But then it was hard for him to believe she ever made serious mistakes.

Except one.

Yes, her biggest mistake was ever thinking you were something you aren't.

But then, she'd always thought that. Even when they were kids. She'd thought he was…like them. Steady, strong and basically balanced.

He knew better.

It was hard for him sometimes, to even remember those early days. Back when the Foxworths had lived down the block, when they ran into each other at various locations and functions. It seemed a dream now, those long-ago days before a terrorist had blown up so many lives, including Quinn's and Charlie's. Charles and Elaine Foxworth had always been kind to him, welcomed him into their home. Back when life had been simple, and admittedly pretty easy.

At least at their home; his own had been decidedly less comfortable. His mother had done her best, but a single mom's life was never easy. Had it not been for Charles Foxworth he would never have known what the influence of a stable and loving husband and father could be.

When they had both been killed in that horrible terrorist attack, he'd vowed to do something, and as soon as he'd been old enough he had. He'd enlisted in the Marines, determined to strike back, and had found his life skill, his calling. And if he ever wavered, if the fact that that calling was essentially to kill ever bothered him, he simply took the day he'd last seen them alive, cheerful and loving, and mentally juxtaposed it with the gruesome, smoking aftermath of the attack that had killed them and so many others.

He had no idea how long he'd been standing there lost in that haze when a second buzz from the phone snapped him out of the miasma that only trying to avoid thinking about Charlie could plunge him into. He looked down at the screen again.

That IS an order.

His gut tightened. Whatever was going on, Quinn didn't say that lightly. He sent back a single word.

Copy.

He did the tasks of putting away tools and supplies, securing them, then the plane, and at last the hangar itself as if by rote, the main part of his energy diverted into trying to control his racing imagination. This was not a problem he usually had, and again, only Charlie could bring it on.

It was only when he was back in the car and headed out of the airport that the other possibilities hit him. Was there some other reason she was here? Did she have some other bad news? Was she maybe…sick? Had she gotten some horrible health news?

He couldn't even process that one. The idea of Charlie, strong, smart, tough, fearless, and utterly gorgeous Charlie Foxworth brought low by some disease seemed as impossible to him as if the Mirage had blown up while just sitting there quietly.

The memory of the last time he'd seen her in person crashed, unwelcome, into his mind, as clear and vivid as if she were standing before him now as she had then. Her incredible dark hair tumbling down in thick waves, only slightly controlled by a sort of tiara thing that matched that sleek, silky blue dress, the same blue of the wedding decor, as she served as Hayley's maid of honor to his best man. A blue that made her already bright blue eyes glow in a way that had made his pulse kick up to ridiculous levels.

Only by focusing on his ceremonial task—and the pure love and joy glowing from both Quinn and Hayley—had he gotten through that day. Especially walking with her arm in arm down the aisle formed by the chairs laid out neatly in the meadow on that day, a day fate had gifted the bride and groom with what the locals called a severe clear winter day, bright, sunny, almost gilded. Only appropriate, he'd thought at the time, since no one deserved it more than those two. And after all, wasn't people getting what they deserved, good and bad, what Foxworth was all about?

"We set this aside today," she had said to him in the last moments before the ceremony had begun. Ironically, as she demanded peace she had sounded determined enough to fight him if necessary. It wasn't necessary, because he'd agreed completely.

"Yes. Today only Quinn and Hayley matter."

And they'd gotten through it. He knew how well when Hayley had whispered to him, just before they'd left for their honeymoon, "Thank you for the best gift of all."

He'd blinked at her. "What?"

"The truce."

He'd looked away then and repeated what he'd said to Charlie. And meant it. This was their day and they were the only ones who mattered.

Only after they'd gone and the guests had cleared out had he been left to deal with memories inspired by knowing instinctively what an amazing honeymoon these two would have. Because it would probably be as intense, as amazing, as incredibly hot as a certain three months of his own life had been. Months that had begun—

A rabbit darted across the road, and he barely managed not to hit it. It snapped him back to the present.

Focus, Crawford. If you were on a mission you'd probably be dead already.

The fact that he'd almost rather be dead than face Charlaine Foxworth again was something he tried to ignore.

Chapter 7

*D*amn it.

Charlie didn't swear often, but she couldn't help it this time. She also couldn't quite believe that even now he had that effect on her. Just watching him get out of the silver coupe down at the far end of the drive and start walking toward the headquarters building had her pulse in overdrive. It was the same effect he'd had on her since Quinn had brought him to her as a potential Foxworth operative.

The very first hire, in fact, after they'd decided they needed more than just her and Quinn to get everything they wanted to accomplish done.

After the tragedy that sent them to live with Uncle Paul, they'd lost track of the neighbor boy. They'd had enough to do to survive what had happened and adjust to their new, painful reality. She knew Quinn had missed his friend, but it had taken a back seat to simply surviving the hideous truth of their lives now. And the more time that passed, the more unreal that sweet, innocent life before had become.

That had made the shock when Quinn had come face-to-face with him more than a decade later even greater.

"It was Rafe," he'd told her, shock echoing in his voice over the phone on the overseas call.

"Rafe? Crawford? The boy from down the street?"

"Yes. He's the Marine sniper who saved us, on that mission that went haywire. He took out nearly every man in that nest we stumbled into, giving us time to get clear. And he did it from so far away they couldn't even begin to find him."

Inwardly she was still processing exactly who that expert sniper had been, but had managed a tone of mock horror when she'd said, "Is this my Army-to-the-core brother, admitting a Marine is good?"

The horror she felt at her beloved brother coming that close to death was anything but mock. She remembered the incident all too well, how the intelligence had failed them completely on where the terrorists were hiding, and they'd practically walked right into their hideout.

She knew how, after that harrowing incident, Quinn had pushed to meet the man who'd pulled off those deadly accurate shots that had saved them, the man who had volunteered to do it simply because he was in the area and was their best chance. Then only to discover it was the childhood friend he'd lost track of, the boy from down the block…

A boy who had never had much effect on her—then—at all. He'd just been a friend of Quinn's she found slightly less annoying than his other friends. Mainly because he was quieter, apparently by nature. And that nature was also apparently well suited to selective killing of the enemy, an idea she couldn't deny gave her a little chill.

"He's better than just good," Quinn had told her. "He's got his name on the highest level sniper trophy there is, twice. He got banged up on his last mission, almost lost a leg, and he's still working through that. But he's functional, and if I know him he'll stay that way, whatever it takes."

She'd felt the same pang she always did when she heard one of the country's warriors had paid such a price—which was why veteran's organizations were one of Foxworth's primary interests—but that this was someone she knew personally made it…well, more personal.

Then Quinn had delivered the decisive words. "Charlie…he enlisted because of what happened to Mom and Dad. He said they were always so nice and kind to him. He felt…it was a way to pay them back a little."

She'd had no words for how that made her feel. And a couple of years later, when Quinn was thankfully safely home and they were building the Foxworth Foundation into something their parents would approve of, he had come to her with the idea of hiring Rafe, who was also back home now. Back home, but not doing as well.

"We need more help, and he…" Her confident, fearless brother had hesitated then, and that was enough to make her zero in on his next words. "He needs this. We need him, especially if we're going to build out the way you want to, but he needs this, too. He could probably get a job with any private security firm in the world, with his record, but…he needs a cause he can believe in, before he goes completely off the rails. I can't explain it, but I know Foxworth is right for him."

She would have agreed to hiring him without the argument, simply because of what he'd done, saving her from losing the last of her family. And it was only later that Quinn had told her how he'd found Rafe after a long search, in an encampment of homeless vets under a bridge. Although Rafe himself hadn't fallen quite that far, having a small, rented room, it had only been a matter of time. Quinn had told her he barely recognized the man from that surprising reunion overseas, not with long, shaggy hair and a beard sporting a couple of spots of silver gray. But he'd recognized the haunted gray eyes and knew the look of a man who carried too many lingering memories.

But the Rafe he'd finally reintroduced to her had been a different man altogether—tall, rangy, clean-shaven, the only trace of civilian about him the couple of strands of dark, thick hair that tended to drop down over his forehead. That he'd once been the kid she remembered didn't even seem possible. Until she looked at his eyes. She had remembered those seemingly fathomless gray eyes, which even as a kid had seemed too old for his young face.

The possibility of putting his skills to use helping people who deserved it, people who had been wronged by another, or by the system itself, had clearly put new life into those eyes. Eyes that had an entirely different effect on the grown-up her. And the grown-up her had, as she never had with anyone before, reacted to him on three fronts—mentally, emotionally and, to her chagrin, physically—before he'd ever said a word. And when he did speak, that low, rumble of a voice had tipped her over the edge.

And for the first time in her life she had wanted, on a primal level.

And damn him, she still did. Even after what he'd done, the way he'd thrown them away as if what happened between them was no more than the fling he'd cuttingly called it. And when Quinn had headed here to the Northwest to set up this office, Rafe had gone with him. And stayed, demonstrating without saying a word that he wanted to be as far away from her as he could. He'd denied it, said he liked it here because it was about as far from desert as you could get. But she'd known that was only part of it. Known he hadn't wanted to be in St. Louis any longer because she was there, and as long as he was working for Foxworth, they would have to be in almost daily contact.

So she'd lost him first, and then Quinn had fallen in love with this cool, damp, forested place and decided to stay and she'd lost him, too.

As the thought formed and the emotions tried to well up yet again, she felt a nudge on her hand. She looked down and saw Cutter, looking up at her with an expression she could only describe as concerned, ridiculous as that was. Automatically she stroked the dark fur of his head. And couldn't deny the calming effect of it.

Calming enough for her to mutter to herself, *Well, aren't you just a puddle of self-pity?*

With an effort she buried all the tangled emotions. This was too important to let her stupid, apparently inescapable feelings get in the way. She gave Cutter another pat. "Thanks," she said, feeling a bit silly even as she said it. For all his undeniable cleverness, he was a dog, after all. But this must be why he'd succeeded at being a therapy dog.

And a matchmaker?

She nearly laughed out loud when that popped into her mind. She might have to admit the dog was smart, well-trained and had great instincts, but the matchmaker they talked of was a bridge too far. Or was it? Since she'd last been here, Hayley's brother Walker and her best friend, Amy, had married. Teague and Cutter's groomer, Laney, had married. Liam had married the schoolteacher he'd met on a case. Most shocking of all to her, after working closely with him before he, too, had decided to stay here permanently—what was it about this place?—even Gavin was engaged.

And that wasn't counting all the cases where people they'd helped had ended up with what Hayley called—without a trace of whimsy—their soul mate in the process.

The bemusement she felt at the idea helped her regain some modicum of equilibrium.

"Shall we give you two a few minutes alone?"

She didn't quite jump at Hayley's quiet question; she'd heard her coming down the stairs from the office/meeting room level, where she assumed Liam and Teague were still gathering information. Still, she hadn't expected the offer. She'd never admitted even to her brother what had happened between her and Rafe. But then, Hayley had an uncanny way of sensing what other people were thinking or reacting to. Almost as uncanny as her dog.

She turned to meet her sister-in-law's gaze. It was kind, understanding and gentle, as it always was when she knew someone was troubled. She had come to both love and respect this woman who had made her brother's life so much more simply by loving him.

"I think it would be better if you didn't," she said wryly, not denying or admitting anything. But Charlie suddenly and unexpectedly wished she'd confided in this warm, caring woman long ago. Perhaps she could tell her how to rid herself once and for all of this stupid, energy-wasting infatuation with a man who didn't want her.

It was not, as some would assume, an ego thing. She was more than used to men who were drawn by her looks, and she knew just how shallow a connection that could be. But she believed, with all her heart, that she'd found a connection so much deeper than that with Rafe. It had been as if her soul had been healed at last from the devastation her parents' tragic, horrible deaths had wrought.

And then he'd walked away. No, he'd run. To this far edge of the country, where he'd stayed except when a case demanded he return. And even then he went out of his way—sometimes far out of his way—to avoid having to be in the same room with her, and even farther out of his way to avoid being alone with her.

What would he do now? Try to dodge yet again? Or maybe just give her that cool stare that could turn a room to ice. The stare that always left her trying to convince herself it wouldn't be quite that cool unless he still felt…something.

She had no idea which way this would go, and she determinedly decided it didn't matter. Just as Quinn and Hayley's wedding had been, this was more important than their personal clash. And given he'd been one of the ones under fire thanks to Flood's machinations, he would likely see it the same way.

He'd better.

"All right, not alone, then," Hayley said. "But keep in mind Cutter doesn't like it when two of his family are at odds."

"Neither do I," she said, as close as she could come to admitting she was not now and had never been happy with the state of affairs.

And that she'd even thought the word *affair*, even in a totally different context, irritated her. But then, she'd never thought of what had happened between them as simply an affair. For her it had been much more, it had been dreams made reality, a happiness she'd never even dared hope to feel.

It had been Rafe who'd thrown it away so lightly.

Which makes you an idiot, for believing in some foolish, little girl fantasy of a happy ending.

She heard Quinn coming down the stairs from the office level. Resisted the urge to flee up to that third floor herself, right now. She felt Cutter's nose nudge her again. She petted him again, just to see if it would have the same effect. It did; she felt the calming, the soothing. It just wasn't enough to cancel out the boil that was beginning inside her.

It was enough to steady her, though, and that would have to do.

She murmured a thank-you to the animal, even as she felt a little silly doing it. Cutter swiped his tongue over her fingers, giving her the strangest feeling he understood both the thank-you and how she felt giving it.

Then, as if he'd sensed she was as composed as she was going to get, the dog trotted off to open the door.

Chapter 8

With all the years he'd spent expecting the unexpected, he would have thought the expected wouldn't have much effect.

He was fiercely, bloodily wrong. As he had ever been when it came to this one thing, this one person.

She wasn't as beautiful as ever. She was more beautiful. He'd seen her like this before, on the very rare occasions she emerged from the low profile she preferred. Those had been the worst, and after that brief, scorching three months with her he'd tried to avoid being around for those. Not simply because it hurt to look at her when she went all out and with glamorous makeup, her hair in impossibly glorious waves, and wearing some sleek, silky dress that reminded him of the body beneath it, but because he knew how well the outside masked the brilliance of the brain behind it.

She wasn't wearing the formal clothes now, but it didn't seem to make any difference at all. Even the simple black dress was beyond elegant on her, with the added distraction of baring a length of those long, fit legs.

The sight of those legs slammed him back into the past, to the day shortly after he'd started at Foxworth, when he'd encountered her in the local gym where he worked to keep his mangled leg functional. The injury had been much fresher then, and he hadn't yet learned to compensate for it as well as he eventually did. He'd walked by the training room—okay, limped—and heard her voice, asking a question of one of the personal coaches. He'd been unable to stop himself from looking through the open door. It had been quite a vision—a tall, willowy woman in snug black leggings and a red, abdomen-baring workout top that did little to disguise lovely curves. Her long, dark hair was pulled back and up into a practical tail, yet still hung past her shoulders.

She was utterly, totally absorbed with the hand weights she was using, under the coach's close direction. Focused, intent, determined. And the results showed in the body he couldn't help admiring; she was taut, fit and strong, yet as feminine as any woman he'd ever seen.

He reacted exactly as he had the first time he'd seen her, when Quinn had brought him into the Foxworth offices. Everything male in him had suddenly awakened after a long, long sleep.

That she was the long-ago girl from down the street had made him feel a little weird about the sudden kick.

That she was Quinn's sister made him feel almost appalled.

But that day at the gym, she'd looked toward the doorway, almost as if she'd sensed his presence. Their gazes had locked, and a small smile curved her mouth. That incredible mouth.

She'd looked at him as if she were happy to see him.

As if she were happy he was there.

As if she were as…interested as he was, in an eternal male/female way.

And all the time and effort he had put into quashing his own inappropriate response—she was as much his new boss as Quinn, after all—hadn't had much effect. No matter how hard he had tried to write it off as the oft-discussed back-home-at-last effect.

Then had come that night when, with Quinn out of town, he'd had to accompany her to some fancy function, even though he'd only been with Foxworth for a couple of months. He'd groaned inwardly when she'd come out wearing an amazing blue dress that clung to her slender but curved shape, and bared enough of her toned, sleek legs to make that groan even harder to suppress.

It was a private party, she'd explained, but it was for the head of the company that had been the most lucrative investment she'd ever made. This man's work had made the launch of the Foxworth Foundation possible.

There had been so much admiration in her voice when she spoke of the man, he'd wondered if there was more than business between them. But when he'd tried to tactfully—well, tactfully for him—ask if he should leave them alone, she'd answered, "Don't you dare!" and then laughed and said Mr. Trent was much more likely to be interested in him than her. Which, she'd added with a rather intent look, she could understand.

He did his best to forget that look. And to remind himself he was there as more of a bodyguard than anything else. He'd put on his most civilized demeanor, even though it was a bit rusty from lack of use, and pretended his way through most of the evening. And it had worked…until he'd come up behind her chatting with another woman, one he privately felt had overdone the glamming up a bit.

"Your escort this evening is quite something," the woman was saying.

"That he is." There had been an undertone in her voice he couldn't quite put a name to.

"He looks a bit...dangerous."

"Only when necessary," Charlie answered, and it felt strange to hear the words he'd often heard Quinn say coming from her. But then she had smiled and half turned to look at him, telling him without words that she'd known he was there. "And that's why I think the world of him," she'd said softly.

For a moment he couldn't breathe. Or had forgotten how.

"Not to mention he's sexy as hell," the other woman quipped, giving him a visual up and down that, oddly, had no effect whatsoever.

"That, too," Charlie had agreed softly.

That had nearly put him on his knees. And that night it had begun, the fiery, impossible three months that were burned into his memory so deeply that he knew he'd never be free of them.

And he wondered how twisted it was that sometimes, when the other memories, the horrible ones, rose up, it was the images from those months he used to hold them back.

The feel of Cutter's cold nose bumping his hand snapped him back to the present. He wondered how long he'd been standing there, staring at her, those images parading through his brain with vivid impact.

He summoned up a countering image, that of the smooth, polished former senator who, as far as Rafe could see, Gavin had been utterly right about.

He became a senator to build his power infrastructure. Now he figures he's got it in place, it's time to start pulling those behind-the-scenes strings.

And Rafe wondered what strings he was here in the Northwest to pull.

Or maybe he was just here to please the new lady in his life. Charlie.

He nearly laughed out loud at the thought, if only because he doubted the esteemed Senator Flood would use such an unsophisticated name. It was probably Charlaine all the way.

He gave Cutter a scratch behind the ears in thanks for the dog's returning him to the here and now. The reality he had tried so hard to avoid.

"Upstairs," Quinn said, a bit sharply. "This is all hands on deck, and—"

He stopped as Cutter let out one of his distinctive barks. Gavin's, Rafe recognized. Quinn really did mean all hands. He'd already seen both Teague's and Liam's cars parked outside. And a practical little sedan that looked like a rental, but hardly the kind of rental he'd expect the new girlfriend of someone on the level of Flood to be driving.

But exactly what Charlie would rent. Ever-practical Charlie.

And a bit belatedly he realized that this wasn't sounding like a social occasion at all. Charlie always did seem to slow down his thought process. But upstairs meant business, and Gavin meant serious business.

He watched as the lawyer, dynamic and commanding as ever, came in, Cutter escorting him happily. As if the dog knew that the gathering was now complete. Gavin greeted him with a nod, but Charlie got a hug. Rafe had gotten used to the high power attorney being here, and had almost forgotten he'd been in St. Louis with Charlie for longer.

"What's up?" Gavin asked.

"We're meeting upstairs," Hayley said. "Quinn will brief everyone there."

In the end, he and Charlie hadn't even spoken before they all headed up. He felt a jab of inwardly directed scorn as he resorted to using his leg to make sure he was the last one on the stairs; it wasn't bothering him much today at all. Which had him wondering not for the first time how much of the pain he usually felt was just from dwelling on it. Because it seemed if there was enough distraction around, he barely thought of it at all.

And there was no bigger distraction than Charlie Foxworth. Not for him, anyway.

It had been a while since the entire Foxworth staff—except for Ty, who never left St. Louis—had been gathered under one roof. If he included Charlie, it had been since Quinn and Hayley's wedding. And again he wondered if this case, whatever it was, had something to do with her, or if she was only here because she happened to be in the area with her new, high-profile boyfriend.

He kept his grimace turned inward. The idea of this woman who worked to avoid the limelight, at least the public kind, taking up with a man who craved it practically beyond all else, except maybe power, simply did not compute, as Liam would say.

Rafe could tell from the way that Quinn stayed edgily on his feet while the rest of them took the seats he indicated around the big meeting table that this was something big. And when they were all seated and looking at him expectantly, Quinn finally got to it.

"My sister brought us a present," he said.

Rafe's brow furrowed. He glanced around the room. Hayley, as he'd expected, showed no surprise. Obviously neither did Charlie. The rest of them all waited silently for Quinn to get to the crux of it. He did, in two words.

"The mole."

And in those two words, all his perspective abruptly shifted. The memory of that near escape flooded him.

The mole.

The one who had almost gotten them all killed, including then innocent bystanders Hayley and Cutter.

My sister brought us a present.

Flood? He was the mole? It fit. Oh, it fit. He was just the type.

And when he should be feeling jubilation that he'd finally been found, all Rafe could really feel was an overwhelming swell of relief that Charlie hadn't really fallen for a man like that.

And what that said about him would have to wait. Right now, there was a very large payment to extract. And he planned on being a central part of that.

Whether Charlaine Foxworth liked it or not.

Chapter 9

Charlie laid it out in her usual way, systematically, chronologically, although it was taking a bit more effort than it usually did for her. She told herself it had nothing to do with Rafe sitting across the table, not looking at her but tapping the table in that habit he had. It was simply that she was jet-lagged. She was her usual organized, focused self, just a little tired.

Another of those taunting memories arrowed through her mind. The day they'd talked about the differences between them.

I admit, I'm a bit of a control freak.

Probably comes from not having any control at all after your parents were killed.

She'd never thought of it quite like that before, and his quick—and probably accurate—assessment had startled her.

Do you always assess things and people, and so quickly? She'd given him a smile then. *And accurately?*

You want to control circumstances. I'm all about adapting to changing circumstances.

Because he'd had to be, she'd realized then. It was not only what made him the best sniper, it was what had made him able to adapt to the injury to his leg, most days ignoring it completely despite the fact that she knew it always ached a little and sometimes ached a lot.

She had to pull herself out of the memory and back to the present. Her explanation of why she hadn't told them anything before she could do it in person seemed a bit garbled to her, and she wondered if her thinking had been a bit garbled as well; Ty was the best, and if he said a system was secure, it was. But she realized she was, perhaps, getting a taste of what it felt like in the field when the adrenaline kicked in. Quinn had always told her one of the first things it affected was judgment, and she believed it now.

Adapting to changing circumstances...

"I probably overdid it on the secrecy thing," she admitted, "but I confess I also wanted to tell you in person, so you could see how sure I am. That said, I still think we shouldn't mention him by name in any communications."

"Agreed. Better safe than sorry," Quinn said. "The...subject has his fingers in pies all over the place." He glanced upward. "I assume you found a particularly interesting pie?"

Ty was on the big screen on the wall above the table now, ready with the explanation of how he'd found what had set her on this trail. He started with the money trail, as Quinn had taught him in the beginning. How that had led him to Flood, which had in turn, eventually, led him to the final pieces of the puzzle.

Quinn listened to the details of the discovery of the payoff. "So it was a ten-million-dollar transfer between two shell companies, one leading back to the cartel and the other to the subject, all about ten layers deep?"

"Yes, sir," Ty said. "And it was two days before the mission to move the witness." Taking his cue from Quinn, he carefully didn't mention Vicente Reynosa by name, either.

"And the subject—" Charlie used her brother's term "—announced his plan to retire at the end of his term as soon as the transfer cleared. But there's more. Ty, go on."

"Okay. We knew this wasn't really proof, the payment was buried so deep, we couldn't prove it had actually gone to the subject. Only to a company he's an owner of. Which is why my boss—" he flashed a grin at Charlie "—went for the personal contact when the opportunity came up."

He hesitated then, as if he thought Quinn was going to chew him—or her—out for making that move without consulting him first. But her brother only nodded. "While you did…?"

Ty gave his best nonchalant shrug. "I…er, hacked his calendar."

"Find an interesting appointment, did you?" Quinn asked, one brow raised.

"Actually, when I went way back, I found an evening with no appointments at all, something almost nonexistent for him. Just a blocked-out square at ten p.m. I thought that was strange, so I dug some more."

"Into?" Hayley asked, looking as if she could barely suppress a smile.

"Um," Ty began, then said, "Security cams. Since he was a senator, there were a bunch, near his office and home. And it seems like they keep the footage forever. Anyway, I found that night, and he left his DC townhouse at nine forty-five. On foot. Only his aide with him."

"At night in DC?" Quinn asked. "No security?"

Ty nodded. "That's what got me wondering. So I tracked him as best I could with other cameras, and…ended up with this."

The screen switched to a somewhat grainy black-and-white image that appeared to show a construction site of some sort. Ty's voice came through. "This was right down the street from Flood's place. Keep watching."

They did, and the two men they'd seen leaving the townhouse came into view. After a moment, a third figure emerged from the shadows of the construction site. The men were clearly expecting him and began a conversation. Charlie had watched this video repeatedly, so she spent the time when it was running watching her brother. She saw his jaw tighten in the moment Flood handed over something small enough to be hidden in his hand.

"We're guessing that's a flash drive," Charlie said.

"All right," Quinn said when Ty was back on screen. "Hit us with the rest."

"I did some facial recognition, and the closest match was this guy." An image of a face popped up beside Ty. Quinn immediately leaned toward it.

"The tatts." It was Rafe who said it.

"Yes," Quinn agreed.

The inked-in signature of the cartel Vicente Reynosa had lost his entire family to, and who had nearly cost her what remained of her own.

"He's the top US lieutenant in the cartel," Ty said. "And the clincher is this meeting also took place two days before the witness's scheduled transfer."

She heard a couple of muttered oaths. One she knew was Rafe, the other could have been either Teague or Liam.

"Two days," Quinn said. "Not much time to prepare."

"Lucky for us," Teague said.

Not having that tactical mindset, she hadn't really realized this, and it made her shiver a little now. If it had happened sooner, if the cartel had had more time to prepare their across-the-border operation...

Quinn looked thoughtful for a moment before asking Ty, "Any sign of an effort to repossess that payment?"

Ty grinned suddenly. "You mean after they failed miserably at taking you guys out and ended up going down?"

Quinn chuckled. Charlie wasn't sure his taking a bullet to the arm and Cutter getting clipped was failing miserably, but in the end she supposed it fit. The biggest drug cartel going up against a small, private team of four—plus the unexpected gift of support from Hayley and her dog—and losing had to have been a downer. The trial and hearings that had followed, with Reynosa's testimony, had blown things up completely.

But unfortunately not deep enough that it had reached Flood. Then again, Flood had protections the cartel could only dream of.

"That's what they get for taking out his family," Quinn said, his voice flat and uncompromising.

"Seems stupid," Ty said. "They destroyed their leverage against him by killing them all."

"I don't think that was the plan, from what the witness said," Quinn answered. "They just didn't know he'd gathered his family together to try and evacuate them when they blew up that house."

Ty's brow furrowed as it sometimes did when he, from the relative safety of his rather expansive tech lair, came face-to-face with a real-life tragedy. He snapped out of it quickly and returned to Quinn's original question.

"I had the same thought and looked, but no sign of even an attempt to take back the payoff. Do we think there's enough of their organization left to even try?"

"I suspect they've rebuilt a bit by now," Quinn said. "But maybe not enough to try that."

"Or maybe they decided having our subject in their stable, so to speak, is worth it," Liam said.

"They'd own a chunk of him, for sure," Teague agreed. "If word ever got out he was in their pocket—literally— he'd be done for."

Quinn's mouth quirked rather sourly. "Time was, I'd agree. But the cover-up apparatus is so powerful these days, it could go away completely."

"Then maybe he should go away completely," Charlie said, sounding just as sour as her brother had looked. That earned her a startled glance from the man in the room least likely to be startled by anything. And for the first time since they'd sat down here in the meeting room he actually looked at her. And stopped the quiet but incessant tapping of fingers on the table he'd been doing.

For a moment silence reigned in the meeting room. Then, holding her gaze with those steely gray eyes, he said quietly—too quietly, "Happy to oblige."

And that quickly she was back in the past again, in her office in St. Louis, in the final interview before she agreed to hire him. Even then there was something about him that had reached beneath the usually calm, composed exterior she'd built in the years since she'd had to become the responsible one in a futile effort to take on the job of parenting her brother.

Bottom line, he rattled her, she didn't like it, and so had pressed hard. And had been a little surprised, given it was an employment interview, when he'd struck back.

I'm concerned about you making the adjustment from shooting to kill to...not. Are you going to be able to do that, Rafer?

She'd used his full name intentionally, formally, to re- mind him this wasn't some reunion of childhood acquain- tances but a serious job interview. And she couldn't deny her tone had been a bit...snarky. His answer, on the other hand, had been cool and dismissive.

People like you, safe here in your little world, don't want to even admit people like me exist, let alone that there's a need for us.

She admitted to herself later she'd deserved that. But at the moment she'd struck back as if he'd slapped her. Something she never, ever did.

Get off your high horse, Crawford. I know perfectly well that you and men like you—and my brother—are the reason I'm able to have the life I have.

It hadn't been long before he'd proved himself quite capable of doing what was asked of him, and no more. On a case they'd been pulled sideways into a gang retribution murder in a back alley, he'd managed to shoot out every car window and mirror—including the one bare inches from the would-be killer's head—without actually hitting the guy, but terrifying him into giving up. And Quinn had told her it was done so rapidly it must have seemed like full-auto fire to the guy, when in fact it had been single shots.

He'd also explained that, in fact, it was harder to shoot not to kill, because it so limited your target zone. Something she'd never thought about, and that had made her even sorrier about the way she'd snapped at him that day.

She realized suddenly that the meeting had gone on while she'd been lost in the quagmire her mind made of the past. A past that she was apparently unable to keep where it belonged. And for her to admit that, she who had always prided herself on being in control—probably to make up for all the things she couldn't control—was both chastening and a tad humiliating.

"—how did you manage to connect with him?"

It was Hayley, and clearly directed at her. She gathered her scattered wits and answered as calmly as she could. "I saw he was going to be at a fundraising party in the city. So I wangled an invitation."

"Hence the new name, I presume?" Hayley asked.

"Yes. I couldn't chance that he wouldn't recognize the Foxworth name, after the witness and then the whole thing with the governor." Their name hadn't been widespread after they thwarted the effort kill the federal witness, although Flood likely had known it. And Quinn had managed to keep them pretty low profile in the case that had taken down former governor Ogilvie, but they had been mentioned here and there, and politicians tended to pay attention when one of their own went down. Especially for something like murder.

And especially if they're the same kind of slime themselves.

"So how did it go down at the party?" Quinn asked.

Back in control, she looked at her brother. Since they were sitting next to each other she was able to keep Rafe in her peripheral vision when she answered.

"Oh, that was the easy part. He made a pass at me."

The tapping on the table that had resumed stopped again. But he didn't look at her. He just sat there, staring at his own fingers on the table as if he'd suddenly grown an extra one. It was all the reaction she got, but it was enough. And she went on so smoothly she was almost proud of herself.

"That gave me the best opening I could ever get, and I knew I had to grab it. We'll never get a better chance at him."

"So you played into it, let him think you were receptive?" Hayley asked.

She looked at her sister-in-law, grimacing. "It wasn't easy, but yes."

"And he bought it?" Quinn asked.

Hayley grinned at her husband. "Look at her. Of course he did."

Charlie smiled with satisfaction. "He did. He thinks I'm

smitten with his looks, charm and power. So now I can use that to get what we need to take him down."

Quinn looked from her to his wife and back. "Sometimes," he said slowly, "you women scare the hell out of me."

"Keeps life interesting, don't it?" Liam drawled, grinning.

"Where is he now?" Teague asked.

She shifted her gaze to the other former Marine at the table and made sure her voice hadn't changed at all. "He has meetings scheduled for the rest of the week. He thinks I'm visiting friends in the area. His official fundraising meeting isn't until Saturday, but we're supposed to reconnect on Friday night for a big power cocktail party." She sniffed. "Early, because he wants to introduce me to some people."

"As what?"

Rafe's words weren't just chilly, they were icy. And even after all this time, he had the power to infuriate her with a single sentence. With two words.

She barely noticed that everyone else at the table had gone still. That Cutter's head had come up sharply. Quinn's head turned as he gave his operative—nice, distant word there, operative—a look she couldn't see from her angle.

Charlie had to work to keep her expression even. Which irritated her all over again. She should have been long over this by now. With one of the greater efforts of her life she kept her voice casual. She had to keep her gaze on her brother to do it, however.

"He knows me as Lita Marshall, an executive with an investment firm, which, if he checks, has existed for several years," she said, answering Rafe's question literally but avoiding what she knew had been the intent.

She didn't elaborate on the investment firm front, knowing they were all familiar with the company that existed only in the Foxworth computer system. "Ty has planted a full backstory for Lita," she went on. "Including some details and connections that should keep the subject intrigued for a while. He's already intrigued enough to accept my suggestion of the Puget View Hotel for a venue." She focused on Quinn. "I presume Mr. Linden will be willing to help?"

Quinn smiled quietly. William Linden and his missing family had been one of their first cases after opening Foxworth Northwest. The new branch of the Foxworth Foundation had then consisted of him and Rafe, but they'd pulled off a dramatic rescue of the two young children who had, terrifyingly, witnessed a murder and been taken by the street thugs who had done it. Thugs who had connections to a sex trafficking ring, which was where those two would have ended up. They'd had to move fast, strike hard, and they had, catching up to the crew just as they'd been meeting with the leader of the ring to hand the girls over.

And Mr. Linden happened to be the manager of the luxury Puget View Hotel.

"I'm sure he will," Quinn said. "In fact, I'm guessing we can even get Cutter in as a security or a service dog."

Charlie nodded and smiled at the dog before she went on; she was not one to argue with the success rate this dog had piled up.

"I'm sure I'll have to pass muster with those powerful friends of his Friday night first. It will be difficult—I do find him repugnantly smooth and inherently arrogant—but I can act that much."

"Because it's that important," Hayley said quietly.

Charlie looked at the other woman and saw total understanding in her steady gaze. Quinn had gotten very, very lucky.

Luckier than you will ever be.

Chapter 10

"So what's the plan?"

Rafe grimaced inwardly. Sometimes Liam's bright energy was annoying. And since he'd gotten married a couple of months ago, it had downright exploded. Enough to get on his nerves.

Nerves that were already a bit raw.

A bit? Keep telling yourself that, Crawford.

He'd made himself stop tapping on the table when he'd realized Charlie had noticed. So now that hand was massaging his leg, pressing hard into the spot that usually caused the most pain. It hadn't been too bad today, but he was going to aggravate it just sitting here if he didn't ease up a little.

"We need to go slowly," Charlie said. "Can't do anything to make him suspicious. Ty will keep digging for more, something more out in the open than what we have, but we can't be sure he'll find anything."

"Agreed. The subject is too careful. Nor is he stupid," Quinn said.

"Also you need to be aware he has a personal bodyguard. A man named Cort Ducane. He's always armed, and more than capable." She held Quinn's gaze for a second, then Teague's. Him she barely gave a glance. "He reminds me of you guys. I have no doubt that he can be lethal if required."

"Would he consider it required if the subject simply ordered it?" Quinn asked.

Charlie let out a long breath, obviously considering. "I don't know."

"What else do you know about him?" Hayley asked.

Charlie was silent for a moment, probably to mentally organize her thoughts, then laid it all out. "He wears a wedding ring and is constantly fiddling with it. That might mean trouble on the home front. But he has been nothing but scrupulously polite to me, the few times we've spoken. I once saw him when no one else was around, and he looked…weighed down. But it vanished the moment he realized I was there. I asked him if he liked his work, hoping to get him to say something about his employer, but he only said it was what he does."

"Sounds like a guy who's not ecstatic about his job," Liam said.

"Or like a guy who doesn't blab to strangers, even ones that look like her."

Rafe hadn't really meant to say that, or at least not that sharply, but Liam's overflow of happy was starting to get to him. And yet again everyone at the table went still for a moment. He could feel Quinn's gaze fastened on him, and knew he'd been out of line and was going to hear about it.

He'd have been better off just maintaining the silence he'd always been known for. It was just that everything seemed to blow up when he was around Charlie. He lost his reticence, he lost his judgment and above all he lost his cool. And he couldn't seem to do a damned thing about it.

Fortunately, Ty jumped back in as an image popped up on the screen, of a serious-looking young man in uniform. "I ran a check on the name. That him?"

"It is," Charlie said with a nod. "Longer hair now. And his eyes are much more strikingly green than in that picture."

Strikingly green? Rafe felt a sudden jolt, and it was all he could do not to look at her.

I love how your eyes shift color, get stormy dark when you—

He chopped off that memory with the biggest mental axe he could summon as Ty went on.

"Marines, as you can see, so maybe Rafe or Teague can ask around."

It was only a headshot so Rafe couldn't tell how tall he was, but he looked solid, fit and…determined. He wasn't sure how that last made him feel, given the circumstances, but there it was. Cort Ducane looked like a man who would get the job done. Striking green eyes or not.

He wondered if the guy knew the truth about his boss. If he knew he'd set up three other vets for destruction, two of them fellow Marines.

"What I found," Ty continued, "showed a pretty clean record. Two tours overseas, a couple of combat ribbons, left as a first sergeant eighteen months ago. One minor disciplinary ding."

"For what?" Quinn asked.

"Punching an officer."

Quinn blinked. Teague looked up at the screen at the same time he himself did. "Punching a superior officer is a minor ding?" Teague asked.

Ty grinned, as if he'd known that was coming. "In this case, yeah. The officer in question gave a statement for the defense, as it were. Said he had it coming, he'd been out of line in something he'd said."

Quinn leaned back in his chair. "Well, isn't that interesting."

It was. Rafe found himself more curious about that officer than the man they were discussing. That is, until he reminded himself the man was Flood's bodyguard, and if Charlie was going to continue this farce she'd begun, she was going to be too often within reach of the guy. And she thought his eyes were striking.

He gave himself a mental shake, made himself focus. She was obviously pretty determined to continue. And nobody knew better than he did that getting Charlie Foxworth to change course when she was convinced she was right was a futile exercise. That didn't make the idea of her spending time with a slime like Flood any more palatable. Especially up close and personal time.

How personal, he didn't want to even speculate. Didn't want to, but as was usual for him around her, he couldn't seem to control his imagination. Him, a guy who dealt in what was, not what he wanted it to be, not some fantasy that would never be real, couldn't be real. That couldn't be, because the bottom line never changed.

He was who and what he was, and no match for the likes of Charlaine Foxworth.

"She really gets to you, doesn't she?"

Rafe slowly turned his head to stare at Liam. "Sometimes," he said slowly, "I fear for your life, Burnett."

Liam only grinned at him. "And when you give me that death's head stare, I know I'm over the target."

He went back to staring out the window, focusing on the bald eagle pair that had taken up their frequent spot in the big maple on the far side of the meadow. The same pair that had seemed to give a soaring salute to the marriage of Hayley and Quinn by an uncannily timed flight over the ceremony just as the minister made the pronouncement they were husband and wife. Rafe knew he would never forget the way they swooped into view, circled overhead, dived, rolled, soared again and then vanished into the trees.

The memory made his throat tighten, as it had then. He'd known they had it, that something that practically shouted they were meant to be, but that eagle flight had pounded it home to him in a way nothing else could have.

And then he'd glanced at the woman opposite him, impossibly beautiful in that royal blue dress that made her look like the royalty the color was named after, had seen the sheen in those eyes that matched the dress. And it had nearly broken him. Because the last time he'd seen tears in those eyes, he had been the cause. He'd hurt her, badly.

But he'd saved her from worse.

And that was the one thing that enabled him to keep going, keep functioning. He'd hurt her, but he'd saved her from even worse pain.

Don't worry about it, Crawford. You made me what I am, utterly focused and committed to Foxworth. In a way, you're why it is what it is today.

She'd said it to him the day of the wedding rehearsal, said it in a cool, unruffled way that rattled him even more. She'd said it as if she'd really meant it, as if he were, in a twisted sort of way, partly responsible for why Foxworth was what it was. Because he'd hurt her so badly she'd done nothing else but make building Foxworth her focus. Her obsession.

"—don't like it."

Quinn's voice snapped him out of this morass, the latest in the string of useless reveries.

"It's the only way," Charlie insisted. "I'm in, and he doesn't suspect a thing. It would be foolish for me to walk away now, when we don't have enough yet to take him down."

"I know," Quinn said, but he clearly wasn't happy.

"Don't trust me, bro? Think I'll mess it up?"

"I think for all your genius, this isn't your bailiwick," he said flatly.

"Oh, believe me, I know that. And normally I'd leave all this undercover, secretive stuff to you. But three years of trying that got us nowhere."

"And you," Hayley said cheerfully, her tone breaking the tension with an almost audible snap, "grabbed a chance and put us where it could have taken three years longer to get the old way."

"Exactly," Charlie said, smiling back at Hayley.

"Now," Hayley said, briskly this time as she looked at her husband, "I'll call Ty and have him put that fake ID machine to work again for us, while you make some calls and get us into that soiree Friday night. And since you've got the hotel contact, get Rafe on the security team. And Cutter, if Mr. Linden is willing. Teague, Liam, you'll look great in formal staff attire."

The two men looked at each other with very visible eye rolls. But they were smiling.

Rafe had to look away again. Those two women... They were incredible. Impossible.

Quinn might be the spine, he, Teague and Liam the ribs maybe, but those two...

They were the brain, heart and soul of Foxworth.

Chapter 11

"I used to wonder if you left the main office because of me," Charlie said, looking at her brother over the rim of her wineglass. "If I was just too hard to work with."

Quinn lifted a brow at her. "I left for the exact reasons I told you then. Not," he added with an upward quirk of one side of his mouth, "that you're not a pain in the butt to work with."

"Thanks," she said, lifting her glass in a mock toast just as Cutter came through the dog door and joined them. He'd been out, Hayley had explained, making his rounds to check on the neighborhood. And the neighbors loved it, said they felt safer knowing he was keeping an eye and nose on things.

They'd come back to Quinn and Hayley's home after an exhausting day hammering out a plan. A plan that, Quinn had warned her, would no doubt have to change on the fly since in the field a plan was a great thing until reality kicked it in the teeth.

"Reality?" she'd asked.

Unexpectedly Rafe had answered, in that wryly amused tone she hadn't heard in so long. That she had missed so much. "The fact that the other side doesn't know or follow the plan."

She glanced at him, but looked back at Quinn before she'd said, an edge in her voice, "I think I'm capable of at least a little thinking on my feet."

"I'm sure you are capable," Quinn had said. "After all, you already do what Rafe does."

That had startled her into gaping at him. "What?"

Quinn shrugged. "You both plan and figure trajectories with what data you have. For you it's financial things, stocks, bonds, whatever. For him it's weapons and bullets."

At that she'd had to glance back at Rafe. The man was staring at Quinn as if he felt the same way she did about the analogy. A little stunned at how much sense it made.

She'd been more than relieved to come to this quiet refuge her brother and Hayley had made here, the charming, lovely but understated home amid tall trees and assorted other greenery. For someone used to all the trees turning autumn colors by now, the green was…refreshing. Somehow the spots of color that were here, on various maple and oak trees, stood out even more against the green.

"I have to admit," she said now, "there is something quite appealing about this place. I didn't realize what a difference always having green trees around could make."

"And not a tornado in sight," Quinn said cheerfully.

"You get them," she protested.

"Sure. Once a year, maybe, just to remind us what they are."

Hayley laughed at them both. "We prefer natural disasters of the earthquake or volcanic variety."

Charlie laughed right along with her sister-in-law, and

as some of the pressure inside eased, said to Quinn, "You do know, brother mine, how lucky you are?"

"Oh, I've gone way beyond luck," Quinn said, turning his head to look at his wife. "And ended up in paradise."

Hayley actually blushed slightly, and that she still could at a compliment from her husband Charlie took as simply further proof that these two were just as perfect together as she'd thought from the moment she'd met her sister-in-law for the first time.

Later, after a wonderful dinner and a second glass of wine, Hayley excused herself to go do something Charlie suspected was merely a way to leave her and Quinn alone together. Well, alone except for Cutter, who showed no inclination to leave. As if the three of them had planned it this way.

She knew her brother well enough to see that he wanted to say something, but was having to work up to it. And that in itself was rare enough that she knew it had to be something personal; if it was strategic or tactical, he'd never have hesitated.

"Out with it, little brother."

Quinn's mouth twisted upward at one corner, as it did every time she used the appellation. "Yeah, yeah," he muttered. Then he took a visible breath and met her gaze. "Are you ever going to tell me?"

"Tell you what?"

She was glad it came out evenly, with just the right amount of normal curiosity. But just as he couldn't fool her, she couldn't fool him anymore, either. Not like she'd been able to when he'd been a kid, when she'd tell him everything would be okay when she herself had no idea if they'd ever come out of that long, dark tunnel.

"No games, please. You know what I mean. You and Rafe."

"There is no me and Rafe."

"But there was."

"*Was* being the operative word."

She saw that register. Understood why. Because she'd never really admitted to him before that there had been something more than a working-for-Foxworth connection between her and Rafe.

After a moment of wearing his processing-new-information expression he asked, "What happened?"

She drew herself up straight on the couch. Her instant reaction was a fierce resistance. She shouldn't have done it, shouldn't have admitted even as much as she had. Shouldn't have—

Her runaway train of thought cut off as Cutter, who had been sprawled on his bed near the fireplace, came quickly to sit beside her. He plopped his chin on her knee. With those dark eyes looking up at her, she couldn't deny what he was obviously asking for, so stroked his head.

And there it was again, that sense of comfort. Looking down into those eyes, she found herself soothed enough that her anger at her brother for asking—and at herself for answering—faded. Enough for her to meet his gaze and answer in a much different manner than her initial jolt of irritation would have dictated.

"I loved him. He didn't love me."

Quinn looked as close to gaping as her cool-headed brother ever did. "What?"

"How else should I interpret him saying, 'This isn't for me,' and then walking out of my life for good?"

"He…said that?"

"He did say that. And nothing else about it, ever. Not a word. But I obviously wasn't enough for him." And that was not something she was used to thinking, she who had fought hard every minute after their parents had been killed to be enough. Enough to fill the void they'd left behind.

Quinn sat, wine forgotten, staring at her. But she could tell by the look in his eyes that he wasn't really seeing her, that his brain was working, assessing, considering options, as he always did.

Finally he asked, "Then how do you explain the way he reacts around you? The way he reacts to just seeing you on a video call? Hell, the way he reacts when he just hears your name? That's not somebody who doesn't care."

"Someone who feels guilty for ending it like an ass?" she suggested sweetly.

Again he went quiet. And in this conversation that did not bode well for her, she found herself tensing, as if she were waiting for the timer on a bomb to reach zero. Cutter, who had settled at her feet, was suddenly up again, nudging her hand, practically demanding she pet him. As if he'd sensed the rising pressure within her somehow. And when she did stroke the dark fur of his head, she felt it again, that soothing calm.

She'd read the reports, knew what Quinn and Hayley had told her about the dog's aptitude for just about any job they gave him, but this aspect was the one that surprised her most. She never would have expected a dog that could be as fierce as any trained military or police dog, or as playfully funny as any household pet, could also have this knack for comfort. He was taking jack-of-all-trades to new heights.

And she knew she was dwelling on that to avoid thinking about the way she'd just poured her guts out to her brother. The brother whose mind she could practically hear working.

"Did you never think," Quinn finally said, speaking carefully, "that maybe he thought he wasn't enough for you?"

She stared back at him. For a long moment she was at a loss for words, hardly a frequent situation for her.

"How," she finally said, just as carefully, "could he possibly think that? He's not only integral to Foxworth and works as hard at keeping things running—and I don't mean just machinery—as anyone, but he's a freaking war hero."

"Right on all points. And no one knows that better than me. After all, he saved my life and the lives of my entire platoon. And I'm the one who has to practically force him to take time off—which for him means working on machines instead of a case—now and then."

"Then—"

She stopped when Quinn held up a hand. "If I've learned nothing else from my lovely wife, it's to realize that we all have emotions. Even those of us who have them buried so deep they rarely ever surface. And that, being emotions, they don't always have a basis in truth."

"What are you saying?"

"That the people who bury them the deepest—like Rafe—do it for a reason. Maybe he does it because he feels he's not any of the things you just said."

It sounded so impossible to her she nearly rolled her eyes. "So they just put his name on the Hathcock Trophy twice on a whim?"

"Oh, he knows he's good at that. If he didn't, if he wasn't, we would have lost him long ago."

"I did lose him long ago."

She rarely ever acknowledged loss aloud, hadn't since they'd lost their parents so young. As if hiding it, not acknowledging it could somehow make it not real. She'd known even at fourteen it didn't change anything, but she'd gotten into the habit and had never quite been able to break it.

She knew that, and knew he knew it, too, so she wasn't surprised when her brother went very still.

"And," he began, so quietly she knew that, Quinn-like,

a bombshell was coming, "you're doing exactly what he's done. You bury yourself in your work, devote every waking hour—which is far too many I'm guessing—to Foxworth, and above all you don't let anyone in past a certain point."

"And just when did you become a shrink?" she retorted, stung. Probably because he was right.

"I haven't. I just recognized it, once it was pointed out to me. About me, I might add." He gave her a wry smile then. "That's why I recognize it in you."

She studied him in turn for a moment. "Hayley," she guessed.

"Exactly. So take it seriously, because she's almost always right about things like this."

"I know." It was nothing less than the truth. Her sister-in-law had the most uncanny knack for understanding people that she'd ever seen. She let out a long breath. "You truly have landed in paradise, little brother."

"Don't I know it," he agreed.

"I'm glad." She meant it. She loved him deeply and was more than glad for him. He deserved every bit of the happy he'd found with Hayley.

She just knew it wasn't in the cards for her.

And later, when she lay sleeplessly in the cozy, comfortable guest room of her brother's home—with Cutter, surprisingly, snuggled beside her as if he realized she needed the kind of comfort he could provide—what Quinn had said played back in her mind in a seemingly endless loop.

Did you never think that maybe he thought he wasn't enough for you?

It still seemed impossible to her. How could a man like Rafer Crawford possibly think he wasn't good enough for…anyone?

Difficult, yes, with his reticence and the fact that you

practically had to pry what he was thinking out of him. But she'd always assumed it was simply because he had so many awful memories in his head. She knew all about those; although as bad as hers were, she guessed they were nothing compared to his, by sheer volume if nothing else. And eventually he had actually begun to open up with her.

Yes. Right before he walked out on you.

And that night had been the capper on her collection of awful memories. Him breaking what had been the most powerful kiss of her life, saying those blunt words, then turning and walking away, out her front door and out of her life.

She'd been foolish enough to believe something else must be wrong. Something he was keeping secret.

Then she'd resorted to thinking he'd just been in pain, because his limp had been a little worse that night.

Then she'd told herself there had to be some outside reason he'd ended them. Something she could fix, some way she could make it right. She only had to find out what it was, and she could fix it, then he'd come back.

It had taken a while for her to realize it was none of those things. And a while more for her to admit it wasn't anything she could fix.

She then had spent a long time waiting for him to wake up, to realize it had been a mistake.

That had morphed into just…waiting.

But the longest time of all was how long it took her to understand he was gone forever.

Chapter 12

Rafe checked his gear bag for a third time, because he didn't trust himself at the moment. Not when he hadn't slept more than a couple of hours at a time since he'd overheard that conversation between Quinn and Hayley. Not with his brain careening around in all directions, only to keep coming back to the thing he least wanted to think about.

The truth of that brief idyll years ago.

She had to have known he'd been right to walk away. She was too smart not to have known. It had been a mistake from the beginning, she had to have seen that. And if she hadn't seen it then, surely she had by now.

And the fact that she still dug at him every time they faced each other in person or otherwise? That he didn't understand. Reactions like that usually meant the person felt…something. Cared enough, even if in a negative way, to not just move on. She should treat him as she did any other member of the Foxworth team, and yet she still, after all this time, acted as if he in particular needed to be the recipient of her barbed wit.

Maybe it was as simple as she was giving him what he deserved. What she knew he deserved, probably better than anyone.

Except himself.

Quinn had to have told her. Rafe knew Quinn knew he'd been teetering on a crumbling edge. His long, shaggy, neglected hair, his rough, untrimmed beard, and the fact that he probably weighed twenty pounds less than he had back when Quinn had hunted him down to thank him for taking out that terrorist nest, had been sign enough. The guy Quinn had found under the bridge that day was not the kind of guy who deserved a woman like Charlie Foxworth. And she was too smart not to know it. He'd spent their last month together expecting to hear her say the inevitable.

Except she hadn't. So in the end he'd had to do it.

The right thing. You had to do the right thing.

The refrain wasn't helping any more now than it had then. Even knowing the truth of it didn't help.

He zipped up the bag and slung it over his shoulder, ready to take it out to his car. The plan was that he would get himself and Cutter to the other side and report to the head of hotel security. Liam and Teague would report to the head of the hotel staff. Quinn and Hayley would check in to the suite they'd reserved, then pick up their invitations to the gala, secured through the event coordinator upon the order of the manager, who had given them carte blanche after they'd saved his family.

That had, in fact, been Rafe's first case out of this office. The first one after he'd left the St. Louis headquarters. Left Charlie. Left her to continue to make it possible for them to expand, to help more people. Left her to work sixteen-hour days, including weekends, the schedule Quinn had been worried about but got only "I'll take a break when we're solid" in response.

Well, they were more than solid now. Much more. They were well funded, and all five branches were set up, staffed and working well. And it was all because of Charlie, because of those long hours and her brilliance with finance and investments.

In a way, you're why it is what it is today.

The words she'd said the day of Quinn and Hayley's wedding, right here in the meadow, rang in his head now. Among the many things he didn't want credit for, that probably topped the list.

His Foxworth phone sounded a message. The screen read merely, Final meeting in fifteen.

Time to get your brain in gear, Crawford.

He took the gear bag out, stowed it in the locker in the trunk of his car, secured it, then closed the trunk and locked it as well. He heard the sound of the front door opening, and a moment later saw Cutter racing toward him. The dog greeted him with a sniff and a soft *whuff*, but then promptly circled behind him and nudged.

"In a hurry, dog?" Another nudge. "Everybody pouring themselves some of Hayley's great coffee, huh?" He wasn't sure what she did to it, but she'd gotten even his need-the-spoon-melting-stuff taste buds to like the richer flavor.

Cutter trotted ahead, head up in that mission-accomplished way he had. The dog had trained them all, at least in his ways. And given how often he'd been the crucial factor in making a plan come together, none of them would really complain about him trying to run everything else in their life. Although he did wish the dog would stop putting on that damned matchmaker hat of his whenever Charlie was around. Which thankfully wasn't very often.

But she's here now. And will be for a while.

He watched Cutter trot ahead and bat the pad beside the door to open it. He wasn't looking forward to this. But he had no choice. And this was the most important cold case on his list. He'd just have to focus on that and ignore the rest.

Right. Like Charlie Foxworth is ignorable in any way.

Or Cutter, for that matter. Not when every time he and Charlie were in the same vicinity, the dog started his routine of trying to get and keep them together.

When Charlie was safely tucked away in St. Louis he didn't think about it. He'd convinced himself the dog knew better than to try his tricks with him. But now he was the one who knew better. Cutter had just been waiting, biding his time. He'd no more lost sight of the goal then Rafe had been able to stop reacting to Charlie like a starving wolf.

He stepped inside just as the door started to swing shut. Cutter was already into the seating area in front of the fireplace. And then he heard a voice, speaking softly. A voice he knew all too well. The others might be already upstairs, but Charlie was down here, standing in front of the at the moment inactive fireplace. No, pacing in front of it, as she spoke into her phone. Not the Foxworth phone, but the personal one she'd said was a burner Ty had set up under her fictitious name.

"—of course I will," she was saying, in a light, cheerful tone he'd never heard directed at him. A pause, then a light laugh that seemed the tiniest bit forced to him. But to someone who didn't know her well, it probably sounded fine. "Max, dear, you worry too much. I'll be there in plenty of time." And that wasn't forced at all. Which made his nerves start to hum. Another pause, another laugh. "I miss you, too. Can't wait until tonight. See you soon!"

She ended it gaily. Stood there holding the phone for a moment, obviously unaware of his presence. While his nerves went from humming to buzzing. Loudly. As if he could actually hear it in his ears.

"Can't wait until tonight, huh?" The words broke from him before he could stop them. She spun around, clearly startled. "You sure you want us to take 'Max, dear' down?"

"What?"

"Maybe you'd prefer we stay out of your…budding romance? Or are you already past the budding stage?"

He didn't know what was driving him, other than the image his brain insisted on forming of her sleeping with the traitor. But the look that came over her face then told him just how far over the line he'd gone. Her eyes were even icier than her expression.

"Were it not for the fact that I'd have to explain the blood, I would punch that insulting mouth of yours right now." She held up the phone she'd been using. "This soul sucker aside, what I do, when and with who is not your business. You threw away that right long ago, *Mister* Crawford."

She dropped the phone onto the coffee table. It hit with a crack. She ignored it, turned on her heel and headed for the stairway.

It stung, but he knew he'd had it coming. Charlie would no more get genuinely involved with the mole who had set them up than she would disown her beloved brother. It had been stupid to even suggest it, no matter how his gut had reacted to that cheerful, excited tone she'd used on the phone. He'd insulted her on a primal level, and if she had punched him, he would have deserved it.

And she was right. He had thrown it away. He'd thrown them away. And that it had had to be, that it was the only possible outcome, didn't ease the pain of that even now, years later.

Snipers were supposedly capable of utter and complete concentration, shutting out anything that didn't affect their potential shot. Yet when she was around he felt constantly distracted. Snipers were also touted to be among the most patient people in the world. And he was...except with her. She rattled him like nothing else could. Got to him like nothing else could.

And he hated that she still could, after all this time.

Chapter 13

Charlie wished that she had punched him. Even now, as she stood upstairs looking out the window, her right hand curled into a fist. But if she'd punched him as hard as she'd wanted to, she'd probably have broken a finger. And it wasn't worth that. There had been a time when she would have sacrificed a lot more than a finger for him, but not anymore.

On a case he'd get her all, as any Foxworth operative would. Personally, he'd get from her exactly what he'd given her. That chilly remoteness and…she would have said heartache, except she wasn't sure his was capable of pain anymore.

She smothered a sigh. She remembered again when Quinn had first proposed hiring Rafe. He'd warned her that Rafe was closed off, withdrawn. He'd told her they would get his best work but not to expect him to open up and be a friend, not like the friend he'd been back when they were kids in the neighborhood. That he'd seen too much, had to do things that scarred a person.

"So have you," she'd protested then.

"It's different," he'd insisted. "Snipers are different. Set apart. In some quarters they aren't even allowed to call them that, they just say they have overwatch. Or in his case, long-range overwatch. They're essential, but scary. And they work alone, unless they're with a spotter."

"Is that why he's so closed off, as you say? He wasn't that way as a kid."

"Probably partly."

She'd thought then about the skinny kid who had hung around their house a lot, because apparently his wasn't the most pleasant place to be. She'd found out later why. But then she'd only asked her brother, "You're okay with asking him to do more of it?"

"I'm okay with asking him to be our backup, our last resort. And to act defensively, not offensively." He'd given an admiring shake of his head. "Rafe is quite simply the best. Talk about cool under fire, he's the personification of it."

"You mean like that joke that was going around about a reporter asking a sniper what he felt when killing a terrorist, and he shrugged and said, 'Recoil'?"

"Not sure it was a joke."

"And we...need this?"

"If we're certain of our mission." He'd given her that very Quinn look then, that steady, determined look. Then he'd said quietly, "If you're going to fight the good fight, you need warriors."

A glimpse of movement near the trees across the meadow snapped her out of the recollection. She focused on it just in time to see an eagle flare its wings to land on a sturdy branch. A branch where a second eagle was already perched. The same pair that had made that dramatic flight at Quinn and Hayley's wedding? She'd read somewhere that they mated for life.

I guess you're better at it than we humans are.

But now, when Quinn called them all to the table, and Hayley took her seat beside him, she knew she had to amend that thought. Because there was no doubt in her mind her brother had found his life's mate.

"All right," Quinn said, "we all know this is mainly a research and observation mission. We're nearly positive this is our mole, but we don't have enough evidence to prove that to anyone outside. So we're all clear on that, right? That we're looking to find evidence, not take action?"

The people around the table nodded, although Liam said, "Can we add a 'yet' to that?"

Quinn smiled at the question. "We can," he affirmed.

"Good," Teague agreed.

Hayley smiled as widely as Quinn had. Charlie thought she even saw Rafe's mouth twitch slightly. But all humor vanished when Quinn went on.

"If we're right that this is the guy, he's gotten others killed. Those three feds who were hunting for where they had Reynosa stashed walked into an ambush. Because somebody knew they were coming." He zeroed in on Charlie. "We all need to remember that."

"Oh, I do," she said. "And I won't be in the least surprised if, when all's said and done, it turns out he's got a lot more to answer for. His tentacles are far reaching and widespread."

She'd kept Rafe in her peripheral vision when she'd answered her brother, but he didn't react. Not even a blink. So the armor was back up. Ironic, given he was the one who'd insulted her with the suggestion she was sleeping with Flood. Just the idea of being intimate with that man nauseated her.

Of course, that thought only brought on a string of memories of the only man who had ever made her feel that mating for life was possible for her.

"All right," Quinn said briskly, "let's get into the details. Hayley and I will be hitting the cocktail party rather than the fundraiser for a couple of reasons."

"For me," Hayley said dryly, "it's because I don't want to be among those who'd actually donate to the guy."

Quinn grinned at her. "That, too. But the main one is that there will be people at the fundraiser we know might recognize us. But also because it's Flood's job to schmooze everyone at the party so donors will give more at the fundraiser. I want to see who he thinks will be receptive. And any other connections he might make in a more informal setting."

"Does he drink?" Liam asked, looking at Charlie.

"Not when he needs not to, from what I've seen. And Alec Brown, his personal aide, once said he can nurse a glass for an entire function. He's many things, including probably evil, but he's not careless."

"Noted," Quinn said. "Now, Hayley and I have a suite reserved. That'll be our on-site fallback position if necessary."

"You'll all get key cards once we're there," Hayley added. "Liam, Teague, you're set?"

"Ready," Liam said. "Comms gear will be masked until we're inside, just in case. I'll get you all the earpieces."

"I don't know if his paranoia has reached this level yet," Charlie said, "or whether he could even demand scans and security checks of every guest, given he's not really the host."

"We're prepared anyway," Quinn said. "We don't want to blow it at this early stage. Better safe."

Of course. She should have realized. She should also, she told herself, leave this to the experts. While she'd had some training in self-defense—at Quinn's insistence—she was nowhere near as proficient as her brother on this front.

She knew all the ins and outs of her world, but Quinn was the expert at fieldwork, and she would bow to that expertise. And be glad it was her brother she was acceding to, and not...someone else.

"Everybody have the Flood crew fixed in your mind?" Hayley asked. Charlie had shown them the photo of Alec Brown, who was always at his side. And of course Ducane, whom she'd labeled as security and added a note reading "don't take him lightly."

"That the guest list?" Teague asked, nodding toward a printout on the table in front of Quinn.

Quinn nodded. "Ty got it last night. Didn't want to push Linden too far and get him in trouble. We went over it this morning. You should have photos to go with the names shortly. No one unexpected, although a couple of unknowns that could be aliases. Or not."

Charlie started to speak, then stopped herself, remembering what she'd just lectured herself about.

"Open floor, go for it," Quinn said. "You've had the personal contact with the subject."

"This is just a feeling I've gotten about him," she began, more carefully than she usually would, now that she'd acknowledged and accepted she was out of her depth here. "That he's careful to keep anything that might be subject to scrutiny private. Very private. He might meet someone with questionable connections in a back room, but he won't be seen with them at such a public gathering. He's too conscious of his public image and the benefits that brings."

"And too shrewd about his future plans?" Hayley asked.

"Exactly," Charlie answered.

"Noted," Quinn said with a nod. "So aware, but not the top focus. Okay, transceivers are ready."

He slid a small box across the table, and a smaller one to her. Liam had cleverly hidden her earpiece in a pretty set of earrings she wouldn't have minded wearing anyway. They had a curve that rested against her skull above her ear, and that was where the sound conduction device was. She would hear communications in her ear, but nothing would actually be in her ear. These days, earbuds were the rule rather than the exception it sometimes seemed, but Flood was very observant. Her hair would have covered her ears, anyway, but as Quinn had said, better safe.

"Charlie," Hayley said, "want to give us the details of your cover ID, in case we overhear anybody talking about you?"

"You mean gossiping about the esteemed Maximilian Flood's new lady friend?" she asked dryly.

"Pretty much," Hayley agreed with a grin.

She really did like her sister-in-law. And she was sure Rafe hadn't reacted at all; he'd been staring at the table since he'd answered Quinn. And the finger tapping, well that was just Rafe.

"Lita Marshall, granddaughter of immigrants who made good, and daughter of parents who lean his way politically. Ty even planted a donation to his first senate campaign from them."

"Nice touch," Quinn said.

"We thought so. She's also a widow."

"Oh, even nicer touch," Hayley said.

Charlie nodded. She'd been certain Hayley, with her keen sense about people and the way they reacted and responded to things, would get it. "Her fictional husband died four years ago."

"The same time his wife was killed," Hayley said. "So you not only play the sympathy card, you also get people—including him—thinking how much in common you two have."

"Exactly. I thought it would feed the publicity, once

Flood and Ms. Marshall were seen together." Her mouth twisted in the manner of someone who had a distasteful task ahead, as she indeed did. "And we were, at the airport in St. Louis. He seemed quite pleased with the speculation that's already begun."

"Saw that early this morning," Liam said. "Or rather Ria did. She doesn't know what our case is, of course, but she saw the blurb online about the former senator and his new lady." He grinned his slightly crooked grin. "First thing she said was, 'Someone should warn her.'"

"I already like her," Charlie said with a smile at the young Texan.

They went over all the details, in detail. Charlie mostly listened. She knew each Foxworth team had their own way of working, the tone set by the team leader. Since here it was Quinn, she was more familiar, but she was still well aware she was the outsider. And it was obvious they were in essence the proverbial well-oiled machine. In fact, sometimes the verbal shorthand they clearly all understood took her a moment to translate.

Finally Quinn wound it down, saying, "I'm hoping we can wrap this up for good while he's here, but if we can't, I at least will be following them when they leave."

All the others talked over themselves, volunteering. Except, she noticed, Rafe. Would he just quietly wait for Quinn's orders? Or was he assuming he'd be one who went along, because of his…unique skills?

When they had covered everything, a glance at the time told Charlie she needed to go, and she stood up. "I have to get back in time for my appointment with the hair stylist and manicurist at the hotel beauty salon," she said with distaste in both her tone and her expression. And she carefully avoided looking in Rafe's direction when she added, "Dear Max wants me to look especially impressive tonight."

"Your debut as an official couple?" Hayley asked.

She truly did get everything, Charlie thought. "I think so, although he hasn't bothered to tell me so."

"You're supposed to be so delighted you won't care," Hayley said dryly.

Charlie couldn't hold back a snort of laughter. Yes, she did so like this woman.

Cutter walked with her to the top of the stairs, then glanced back toward the others, who had also gotten to their feet. He seemed to be looking at Rafe rather expectantly.

Don't even try with us, furry one. It's over and done, blown to bits, shattered, or whatever other cliché you want to use.

Finally the dog's seeming sense of propriety won out, and he escorted her politely downstairs and to the front door, opened it, then went with her out to her rental car.

And on her way to the ferry to make her way back to the city, she confirmed her earlier thought. She needed to spend more time with her sister-in-law. She didn't have a lot of female friends—she got bored and thus ran out of patience too easily—but she had a feeling Hayley would keep her on her toes. Hayley had known tragedy as she and Quinn had, and Charlie had a suspicion she had as little patience with people obsessed with mundane, insignificant things as she herself did.

Yes, she definitely needed to spend more time here with Hayley. Or maybe this cool, green, admittedly beautiful place was simply growing on her. She found even the thought hard to accept. She'd been inclined to hate the area because it had taken her brother away. And had cost her any hope of mending things with Rafe.

But now she was beginning to wonder if there was something…elemental about it that simply drew people of a certain nature. Which she had assumed she was not.

She almost laughed at herself then, imagining how her relocating here would be interpreted. As if Charlaine Foxworth, known throughout Foxworth as tough and no-nonsense, had succumbed to pure emotion.

Not going to happen.

That vow made, she began to brace herself for the task ahead.

Chapter 14

"You look utterly striking."

Rafe rolled his eyes at Hayley's compliment as he stood in what the hotel rather grandiosely called the parlor of their suite, while she adjusted his bow tie. He'd never been much good at tying the, for him, unusual kind of neckwear, but Hayley had a knack. As she had with so many things.

She suddenly stopped, a quiet sort of smile curving her mouth. "I remember the last time I did this."

"So do I," he said softly.

It had been the day of her and Quinn's wedding, and the first time he'd been in a tux. She'd looked up at him then, and the sheer happiness in her eyes seemed to spill over, even into him a little. It made him ache a little inside just to look at her now, and think about what she'd brought to Quinn's life.

"You're the best thing that could ever have happened to him." Even he could hear the slightly husky note that had crept into his voice.

"I'm happier than I've ever been," she said, still looking up at him. Then she reached up and patted the now properly knotted tie. "So happy that I want everyone around me happy."

He went very still, his brain scrambling for a way to tell her to back off without being curt or rude.

"I'm not asking you to kiss and make up, Rafe. Just to clear the air so it doesn't feel like we're going to have a bomb go off every time you're in the same room."

Kiss and make up.

Just the thought nearly made him turn on his heel and walk away. Only the fact that it was Hayley stopped him. He didn't know if it had just been a figure of speech or if she knew. Maybe she had figured it out with that sometimes impossible-seeming instinct of hers. Or maybe Quinn had figured it out and told her; there were few, if any secrets between the couple.

Maybe Charlie really had told her brother. Told him about the iceman, as she had once called him. And he wondered, as he had occasionally, if Quinn was the only reason he hadn't been kicked out of Foxworth back then. If she'd wanted him out. He wouldn't blame her. Maybe it would have been better if Quinn had. Sometimes he thought it would have been better for everyone if he'd been one of those who'd never come home, if he—

"Stop it!" Hayley's sharp, snapped command startled him out of a morass he hadn't revisited in a while. But he was even more startled when she hugged him fiercely. Her voice was quieter but no less urgent when she said, "I hate it when you get that look in your eyes. You're crucial to Foxworth, and you're even more crucial to us, Rafer Crawford, and don't you ever forget that."

He couldn't speak, couldn't find any words to say what he wanted to express. So instead he hugged her back, and after a moment murmured, "I'm fine. It was just a...flash." And when she pulled back far enough to look up at him, he said simply, "Thank you."

After a moment she nodded and stepped back. "I'd better finish getting ready for tonight, and you need to meet with the head of security shortly, right?"

He nodded. It was mainly to introduce him—and Cutter, who would be playing security dog—to the regular hotel team who'd be working the event, so they'd recognize him if anything happened. Mr. Linden, the hotel manager, had presented the idea of the dog to Flood, and had done it hitting Charlie's suggested points about precautions, protection, and rich people wanting to feel safe, and it had worked perfectly. Given the state of the city these days, he would have been surprised if it hadn't.

"Cutter's going to draw attention," Rafe said, thinking that if Flood's security was anywhere near competent, they'd recognize the lethal capabilities of the dog.

"Yes. Which means they'll be paying less attention to us and more to him," Hayley said. "Besides, try changing that dog's mind once it's made up."

"No, thanks." *I know all too well what he's like when he's set on something.*

"Oh, and something else you should probably know."

Uh-oh. He recognized that tone, that Hayley's-about-to-nuke-you tone. "What?" he asked warily.

"We've made it official. If anything should happen to Quinn and I, Cutter goes to you."

He felt as if she'd punched him in the gut. Yet all Hayley did after that shock of an announcement was smile widely as she left to finish her own preparations for the evening.

Him, take Cutter? Of all the people... Teague and Laney would be better, surely? Laney was the dog's groomer after all. Sure, when not with Quinn and Hayley, Cutter probably spent more time here at headquarters with him than anyone else, but…

At the same time he couldn't deny he didn't mind the thought. Of course it would be a big responsibility, taking care of a dog this smart, this capable of getting into and downright causing trouble. He'd have to—

He'd have to be around to do it.

His mouth quirked. She was nothing if not clever, was Hayley Foxworth. What better way to ensure he didn't go off some deep end if something indeed happened to them than to saddle him with the dog who had brought them together?

A glance at his watch told him he'd better leave now to meet the head of security. He started toward the door, and as he turned he caught a glimpse of himself in a mirror on the far wall. He never looked at mirrors unless he was shaving, so it caught him a little off guard. Especially in the formal wear. He'd never worn a tuxedo in his life before he'd come to Foxworth, and then it was only the one time.

You look utterly striking.

Hayley was too nice. He looked…different, now that he'd buy. Barely recognizable even. But he had to hope she was wrong, because striking implied attention getting, and that was the last thing he wanted. Ever, but especially while working. It was not in a sniper's nature to be out in the open, attracting attention.

Of course, if this devolved into something where his shooting skills were needed, it wasn't really going to matter.

"You just take your time, honey. I know you want to impress."

The guests? Or you?

She knew which one she'd put her money on. She was positive he thought he was the one she wanted to impress.

The rest of this rich donor crowd tonight was just a side benefit.

He leaned in to give her a kiss. She turned her head at the right moment to make sure it landed on her cheek. It didn't rattle him. She had the feeling it played right into his plan. She'd even overheard him discussing with Alec how to play it up, that they were two bereaved people who were taking it very slow and carefully.

"Great idea, sir. People will eat it up."

No wonder the guy gave her the creeps.

Flood thankfully then went to ready himself. If it wasn't for the circumstances, it might be funny that he usually took longer than she did. Creams for his skin, to keep that youthful look of energetic leader, and that thick sweep of hair he was so proud of and combed straight back, probably to show off the fact that he still had a full head of it, unlike many of his contemporaries who were already losing theirs.

Or pulling it out after having to deal with the likes of him.

She cut off the thought. She had to stop letting those ideas form because it was too hard to hide them. And hide them she must. Even if it did make her cringe inwardly when she tried to believably coo over that famous head of hair.

True, the reason her prep had taken longer today was also the hair. She'd wanted the full effect of the curved, shiny waves of hair that had attracted him in the first place, the cause of the first compliment he'd given her when he'd approached her at that party back home. Normally she preferred to let her hair just fall in its usual way, smooth and straight down well past her shoulders. But he'd fallen for the full mass of waves, which were far more trouble than they were worth to her on any normal day.

But today wasn't a normal day. And there wouldn't be a normal day until they had their mole put down.

She tugged, pulled and sprayed until she was happy with the mane she sometimes hated. Then she slipped on the dress she'd chosen. With dear Max's input, of course.

If this was real, if we were real, I'd ask him to zip it up for me.

The thought caused a near painful clash in her mind, repugnance at the thought of Flood doing that, and the pure, overflowing delight she'd felt back then, when Rafe had done the same. More so when he'd been unzipping her. When his fingertips had brushed the bare skin of her back, all it took to send a fierce shiver through her.

Be honest, at least with yourself. He's the real reason you're going to all this trouble. You know he'll be there, in the room, and you want to show him what he threw away.

Not even to herself could she deny the truth of that. It made her a tiny bit unsteady just realizing he was here in the same hotel, let alone that he'd be there tonight, camouflaged as part of the hotel's security staff.

She took a last look in the mirror and had to admit the dress, with its figure-skimming cut and gold fabric with just a slight sheen, was flattering. She wasn't comfortable with the diamond necklace—it erred just slightly on the side of flashy to her mind—but Flood had given it to her to wear tonight, saying it had been his mother's.

She'd done her homework before making first contact, and knew there were photographs out there of the rather imperious woman wearing it. And she was sure some internet sleuth would find them and point this out after this event. She wouldn't put it past Flood to have asked her to wear it for precisely that reason. All a carefully constructed and timed progression of events to keep his name out there, for whatever his next grandiose plan was.

Lastly she put on the simple—thankfully, given the necklace—gold earrings. Liam had managed to make them match, even though only one functioned as a transceiver, putting an extra bit of gold metal on each that curved over her ear and touched her head behind it, conducting the incoming sound on the activated side. And he'd sworn they would pick up her voice fine, even if she had to whisper.

She glanced at the time. They were due to go live in less than a minute. She spent those last seconds sliding her feet into the heels she'd picked out not only because they matched the dress, but because the heel wasn't so high that she'd be taller than Flood. He didn't like it when men were taller than he, but he really didn't like it when women were.

She heard a familiar voice in her ear just as she got the second shoe on. Liam's Texas drawl was barely discernable but his voice as crystal clear as he'd promised. "Check-ins, please,"

They'd worked it all out and decided going by number would be the simplest, since there were going to be six of them on the channel, plus Ty when necessary, who with a laugh had insisted on being called Data.

"Data, you there?"

"Here. I'll be monitoring and recording only, unless otherwise indicated."

She, however, was designated Focus. She'd picked it both for being the person closest to the subject, and because it was something she could say to indicate whoever she was with was of interest, and if overheard, pretend she was merely telling herself to focus despite the noise of the gathering.

She said it now. "Loud and clear," Liam responded.

"One." Her brother's voice was also clear and strong. Each of them came through. Hayley, Teague, Liam himself and lastly the low, rough-edged voice she'd been edgily waiting for.

"Five."

Even as he said it she remembered the exchange he'd had with Liam that she'd overheard.

How'd you end up last? I've got the least time here, so it should be me, shouldn't it?

I'm last because I'm the last resort.

His voice had been flat. Accepting. A bit weary. And she'd felt an unwelcome tug of concern.

"We're live," Liam pronounced now. Then added, in a lighter tone, "Just remember we're on voice activated now. We can all hear everything going both ways, so anything you say can and will be used against you at the earliest opportunity."

She could picture everyone smiling at that. Well, almost everyone. She may not have worked with a team like this often, but she could already see what a valuable asset each was in their own way. Including Liam's humor lightening the stress.

When she came out of her bedroom in the luxurious suite, she found the one exception to that no-taller-than-Flood rule waiting in one of the side chairs. When it came to his security, Flood thought the bigger the better, and Ducane was a tall, broad-shouldered man. He immediately stood and greeted her with a respectful nod. She didn't miss that he'd looked her up and down first, and decided to try and pry a bit more out of him. After all, she had some experience with laconic, reticent males. And this one reminded her of the one she was trying to stop thinking about.

But it was her job to talk to everyone, so the group could hear the voices and connect them to names. She was going to have to be careful, because thanks to the voluminous

Foxworth research, she already knew a great deal about all of them, and she could all too easily get herself in trouble by betraying that.

So she took a deep breath and smiled at the man before her now.

"Hello, Cort," she said, labeling him for the listeners. "Will I pass muster, do you think?"

"Only with living, breathing people."

She didn't know which surprised her more, that he'd said more than three words, or that they were undeniably a compliment. And she couldn't deny either that the knowledge that Rafe had heard it gave her a little kick of satisfaction.

"Thank you," she said, and he looked away as if he regretted saying it. *Oh, I do know another like you, Mr. Ducane. Which has me wondering exactly who and what you used to be.*

Charlie quickly decided giving him options would be more likely to get him talking than a straight-out question. So even though she already knew the answer, she asked, "Is your background police, or military?"

She thought he looked surprised, she guessed because she'd asked at all as much as anything. And it worked, because he did make the choice.

"Military. Marines."

Charlie didn't think she'd mistaken the tiny note of pride that had crept into his voice. She'd hoped for it. Even Rafe had never lost that. And that small sign made her go on.

"Are you one who would prefer not to be thanked for their service?"

Now she was sure about the surprise. And she guessed this wasn't a man who surprised easily. Kind of like someone else she knew. "Uh…it's not necessary, but no."

She smiled at him then, meaning it as she did for any veteran. "Then thank you."

For just a moment, he smiled back. Then Flood was there and he was back to all business.

"You look lovely, dear Lita," Flood said, smiling.

"And you look like a man to remember," she said, choosing her words carefully as she always did with him. Then, for the listeners, she added, "I like the gold bow tie. A nice, subtle way to stand out."

He seemed pleased—almost puffed up—that she had noticed, although she was sure he'd done it to match her dress. He offered her his arm and she took it, ignoring the distaste that rippled through her. She'd done things that made her stomach churn before.

But never one more important than this.

She knew he had timed their entrance after everyone else had arrived, for maximum impact. Wondered briefly what it must be like, to spend every waking moment calculating such things, always looking for the best way to impress, to be memorable, to inspire people to trust you no matter how little you deserve it.

And she couldn't help but feel a little disappointed that it seemed to work so well. But then perhaps it was just that like attracted like, and the kind of person who would react that way was the kind of person he attracted.

Nothing like hanging around a politician to make you lose faith in humanity.

And he drew that humanity like flies to something rotting. He introduced her to each person, sometimes merely politely, sometimes more effusively, and on a couple of occasions with some over-the-top fervor. Tailored, she supposed, by what each person was worth to him. She carefully repeated each name as she acknowledged their greetings, so that the team clearly had them all.

She knew they'd register the difference in tone and approach, and Ty was probably already searching out connections, data on why one person was more important to Flood than another. Money or influence were the obvious ones, but with this guy there was no limit to what he might search out.

As Flood was talking to one guest he deemed worthy of more attention, Charlie scanned the big ballroom. It was glitzy, as expected, and the wait staff was quick, efficient and unobtrusive. She spotted Teague, with the typical towel draped over his arm, serving a tray of appetizers. Liam was apparently assisting the bartender, although she suspected his location was mainly to enable him to monitor the electronics allowing them to communicate. And on the floor beside the entrance doorway, mostly hidden by a purposely long tablecloth on the table holding the guest register, Cutter was in what Hayley called his sphinx pose, upright and alert, and although she couldn't see anything but his front paws, she guessed his ears and nose were twitching as he took everything in.

And then her scanning came to an abrupt, almost slamming halt as her gaze snagged on the man just a few feet from the dog, scanning just as she had been. He wasn't looking her way, so for a moment she simply stared. Tall, lean, dark haired and looking impossibly elegant in that perfectly tailored tuxedo, if she hadn't known she would have pegged him for someone who fit into this wealthy crowd of highfliers perfectly.

Charlie remembered her earlier thought, about him being here.

...camouflaged as part of the hotel's security staff.

Camouflaged?

Not looking like that he wasn't.

It was going to be a very long night.

Chapter 15

It was strange how, after all this time, he still knew the instant she had walked into even this huge room. It was as if the entire atmosphere shifted. It was like a low-grade hum, and it happened no matter how hard he tried to shove her out of his mind. His heart. His soul.

If he still had one.

In that gold dress she looked like some gorgeous trophy an ordinary guy could never hope to even get close to. Wondered if that was the not-so-subtle message Flood was trying to convey, that she was a prize he'd won. She certainly looked the part.

He forced himself to look away, telling himself he was on a job and needed to do it. That it wasn't because he couldn't stomach the way she smiled and greeted everyone Flood introduced her to as if she were honored, when in fact it should be the other way around.

He scanned the room methodically, noting and assessing anyone he recognized from the guest list, coordinating with the rest of the team who were doing the same. Some present were the known quantities they had researched, some were familiars from the city, many of the rest unknowns. He also watched Cutter for his reaction; the dog's sense about people was uncanny. The dog was acting as if he liked none of them, but neither did he give any signal that he'd sensed an enemy.

Except for Flood, but they already knew that. But Cutter had never met the man before, so it had to be that instinct again that had his lip curling at the guy. Rafe wondered what the dog would have done if Charlie hadn't been with him. Cutter gave the aide the lip curl as well. Or maybe he was just too close to Flood. It was hard to tell.

He went back to scanning before his thoughts could stray again. Some people stood out more than others, whether by their own effort to do just that, or simply by way of their own sort of presence. He quickly spotted Quinn and Hayley, looking as if they fit here, elegant and putting out that classy air they did so well.

Because they are. Pure class. The real kind, not the kind too many of these people here just paint on.

Teague was doing a fine job, whenever one of them spotted someone from the list that they'd wanted a closer look at, of approaching them with his tray and doing the best assessment possible in that limited interaction. If he thought it was worth more, he relayed it to One and Two, and Quinn and Hayley made sure to approach and make contact.

So far, nothing unexpected had turned up. Just the expected self-important types. Or more generic types who hung out at this kind of thing. Like the already drunk man who had just careened into him. That was what he got for stepping too far into the muck—what he was mentally calling this gathering of what they themselves called movers and shakers. He should have stayed on the perimeter.

Rafe stepped back. The guy tried to salute him with his glass, but only made the contents—Scotch, if he had to guess by the aroma—slop over the rim.

"Oops."

Even the muttered apology was slurred. Rafe kept his eyes on the room, the drunk only in his peripheral vision, knowing too well that this could be a distraction technique. But nothing else out of the ordinary—at least, ordinary for this kind of gathering—seemed to be happening, at least not here in the main room. A verbal check with the team confirmed it.

"Five, that's a known quantity to my colleague here," Liam's voice murmured in his ear, indicating that the bartender said the drunk was just that.

"Copy," Rafe acknowledged, shifting his gaze back to the drunk.

The man stopped moving, although still swaying a bit. He seemed to almost focus for a moment as he met Rafe's eyes. He hadn't said a word and yet the drunk stumbled back a couple of steps, then darted away as fast as his unsteady gait could manage. It was almost amusing, if Rafe had been in any mood to be amused.

It's some deep down human instinct. People recognize when they're looking at lethal force personified.

Teague's words, spoken long ago—on the case where he'd first connected with his now-wife, Laney—popped into his mind. He didn't know why it happened, but Teague was one of the smartest guys he knew, and a former Marine to boot, so he believed him. So perhaps, drunk as he was, the guy had still recognized that Rafe was not a man to cross.

Especially now, when I'm stuck here in this swamp.

He moved to his right, out of the crowd, and went back to scrutinizing the room's occupants. It was definitely a crowd now; they were nearly at capacity, which made their job that much more difficult. Especially difficult for him, because he loathed being in a swarm of people. He'd always said it didn't take trees to make a jungle, and nothing proved it to him more than a group like this.

He wondered how long he had before the ibuprofen he'd taken would wear off. He rarely resorted to that, but he'd be on his feet for a long time tonight, and he didn't want his leg putting up a major protest at some critical moment. If he was moving, it was fine, but just standing around like this really got to him.

He became aware of another man approaching from the left a split second before Teague's voice came through, saying, "Five, on your port."

"Got him," he acknowledged quietly.

This man most definitely was not drunk. When he turned his head to focus on him, a pair of steady, green eyes met and held his gaze. He immediately recognized the bodyguard. The man Charlie had said barely spoke, yet who had been so blown away by her appearance tonight that he'd admitted it.

Not that he could blame the guy. Not when, if he didn't know better, he himself would swear that damn gold dress was glowing, the way it stood out in this throng. Or she did.

Cutter's head turned slightly, and Rafe knew the animal had sensed the approach. He didn't react as if it were a threat, but more like he somehow knew this was a man to pay attention to.

As Flood's bodyguard got closer, Rafe recognized the expression of a man who was trying to figure something out. That did not bode well. Nor did the first words out of his mouth.

"I know you."

"Don't think so," Rafe said, rapidly assessing.

He assumed the man was armed, although his formal wear was well tailored enough to hide a sidearm. There was no sign of a comms device, not even one as subtle as Foxworth's, so apparently he worked alone.

His assessment was interrupted when the man's eyes widened just slightly. "Crawford. You're Rafer Crawford."

Well, that was unexpected. Rafe wasn't sure what to say, so said nothing, merely waited for the man to say more, so he could assess how much trouble this was going to be.

"I saw you shoot, in the competition at Fort Gordon. Watched you blow away the Army, even the Rangers, the National Guard, all of them."

"Did you," Rafe said neutrally.

"And you brought those clowns down a peg at the USASOC competition. Upheld the pride of the Corps." Ducane's mouth twisted wryly. "Then you left and we lost to the freaking Coast Guard."

He well remembered that last time at the United States Army Special Operations Command's international sniper competition. But he'd gone downhill a bit sharply and in a hurry after he'd left the Marines, and only much later heard about the victory of the Coast Guard team. He'd dealt a bit with the Coast Guard since he'd come to Foxworth Northwest, and had to admit his opinion of them had moved up several notches, so it didn't sting the way it once might have.

"Good is good, whatever the uniform." He gave the man a steady look. "Or without."

The Marine-to-Marine acknowledgment done, Ducane asked, "So is it true, that old rhyme about snipers? The 'One shot, one kill, not luck, all skill' thing?"

He'd heard it a hundred times but managed not to roll his eyes. "Only part that matters is the end."

"'Kill first, die last'?"

"Exactly."

The man grinned then. "Cort Ducane. An honor to meet you." Rafe shook the offered hand, but quickly. "What are you doing here?" the guy asked.

Rafe half expected Quinn to pop up with a suggested answer, but apparently he trusted him to come up with something. *Great.*

"I suspect sort of the same thing you are," he finally said.

Ducane grimaced. "Kind of what's left to us."

Rafe nodded. "Only choice is who you do it for, the good guys or...the not-so."

"Mmm."

He registered the noncommittal answer, and after a moment of silence said, "You look like a guy who's not sure he chose the right one."

"But you did?"

There was something in the man's gaze that made him dig deep for an answer. "I'm prouder of what I do now than anything I did in uniform."

Although it was much more Hayley's skill, he didn't think he was wrong in seeing regret with a touch of envy in the other man's eyes.

"Well, it's an honor to meet you."

Rafe only nodded. He was never sure what to say at times like this.

"Thanks for that, Five," Quinn said in his ear as Ducane walked away.

"Beautifully done." Hayley's voice held a note of pride that almost embarrassed him.

"Indeed." Charlie. Funny how the compliment from her felt...different. "That's the most I've heard that man say since I met him."

Again he remembered Ducane's reaction to her and hastened to blot it out. "I don't think he's happy with Flood."

"Who could be?" Charlie clearly must be far enough away from the subject to speak freely at the moment.

"Turnable?" Quinn asked, getting back to business.

"Maybe."

"Might be worth pursuing, if you get a chance."

"The thought occurred," he agreed. And meant it. He'd recognized that look in the other man's eyes.

It was the same as he'd seen in the mirror, in the days before Quinn had found him and offered him the lifeline of Foxworth.

Chapter 16

"Have I told you that you look lovely this evening? You're making quite an impression, Lita dear."

Charlie managed, barely, not to pull away when Flood came up behind her and put his hands on her shoulders, leaning in to speak softly into her ear. She thought if she heard him talk about making and giving impressions one more time she might blow it all and slug him. She knew it was supposed to be a compliment, and that in his world it likely was.

But not in hers. No, in the Foxworth world, reality mattered, not impressions. What people did, not what they said. What they were really like, not what they looked or acted like.

Now, if he'd told her people were impressed with her brain power, that might be different.

She inwardly laughed that thought off as soon as it occurred. Nothing could change her opinion of this man and the world he moved in. Or swam in, with all the other sharks.

Might be an insult to sharks. At least they don't generally try to hide what they are. Especially the teeth.

She used the internal laughing at her own thoughts to make her voice light. It was a little harder to inject a certain tone of appreciation, but she managed it. "Thank you, Max. I'm glad. This is quite a gathering."

"Yes. A couple of very promising new potential donors."

"I'm sure you'll nudge them out of that potential category," she said, trying to make it sound as if that was something she appreciated. Inwardly, she made a mental note to take a look at that donor list when she got home, to compare against the Foxworth investment portfolio. She didn't want to have any financial dealings with people dimwitted enough to believe in this man.

She had to suppress a wave of disgust. The longer she spent in this swamp he lived in, the more she hated it. And if she wasn't careful, eventually it was going to show. This was the man who had been on an investigative committee privy to information. Information on Foxworth moving star witness Vicente Reynosa, which he had then sold to the cartel.

But that part of that memory always made her smile. Never had a case of the wrong place, wrong time turned into such a case of a perfect match. She had only to look at her brother and his wife to see that.

Flood took her smile as approval and murmured a suggestion of what they might do later on tonight.

Charlie felt her cheeks heat, and Flood gave a low chuckle. "Not ready yet, I see. That's fine, honey. I find it charming that you're capable of being embarrassed by that. And that blush will charm others as well. You're indeed a prize, Lita."

Fortunately for her, someone approached him then, and

he straightened up to turn and shake hands. She doubted very much he would be as pleased if he knew the real reason for her embarrassment was that the entire Foxworth team had heard his suggestion.

Including Rafe.

By now it was clear what people were assuming, that she and Flood were definitely a couple. Some were congratulatory to him, saying they were glad to see him coming out of his grief, and they sounded almost sincere. Others were merely assessing, as if trying to gauge how much influence she might have with him, to decide if it was worth spending any time and effort on her.

Frankly, she preferred the latter, because it meant she didn't have to try and gauge in turn how sincere anyone was; she knew up front they were cut from the same cloth as Flood. The kind who would do as he had, if they had the chance. Selling out justice for the payment that had insured his newly started political action committee began with enough money to buy the people they needed would be seen as smart and admirable in some quarters.

The fact that only the cartel's soldiers had died was down to luck, and the pure skill of her brother and his team. Just thinking about how close they'd come to disaster that day three years ago burned away all the irritation and purified her cluttered mind, making the goal here once again paramount.

She purposely but subtly nudged Flood toward a knot of people near the entrance to the ballroom, not because she knew any of them or wanted to meet them, but because she wanted to see Cutter's reaction again. There was no way he could have known Flood was their target, and yet...he had.

The guests moved farther into the room. The dog stayed in his hiding place, unnoticed except by the most alert.

Because they're all staring at Rafe in that tux...

If only they knew how...lethal he was. To her, it radiated from him. But was that only because she knew him?

You don't know him. Not really. If you did, you'd understand why he left. You wouldn't still be wondering, after all this time. Wondering what you'd done wrong, what sign you missed, why he wouldn't even give you a chance to fix whatever it was that had driven him away.

She only heard Cutter's low growl because she was listening for it; to anyone else it would have been buried in the ambient noise of the party. But beyond the edge of the tablecloth she saw his ears and his nose, both aimed at Flood, so she knew that was who he was reacting to.

The dog was as smart as her brother said he was.

Rafe didn't even look at her. He just kept scanning the crowd.

"Their security team is impressive," Flood whispered to her, "but I have to admit the dog makes me nervous."

If you knew what he probably wants to do, you'd be beyond nervous. I wish he was free to do it.

But Cutter was also incredibly well trained, so his reaction never went beyond that low sound of warning. The sound that one predator might make to another, warning them off.

She spent another ninety minutes or so being introduced to even more people—and trying not to notice how closely Rafe was watching her. After what Flood had said, or just doing his job? She couldn't tell, and couldn't dwell on it and lose her focus on what was happening.

At last, Flood said he wanted to make a final circuit of the room. Relieved at that word *final*, she pleaded needing to get off her feet for a bit to avoid going with him. He'd allowed it, indulgently, and walked her over to a chair.

Thank you so much, your highness.

She grimaced, covering it by rubbing at a foot that indeed wasn't happy at being this long in heels, even non-towering ones. She watched as he started on his tour, indeed acting as if he were royalty and should be treated as such. And for the most part, the guests complied. Which made her feel even more out of place here. Along with not liking to think that there were truly this many people who believed in this man and his policies.

There were a few, though…

"Focus," she identified herself softly. "Are we tracking those who look…less than impressed?" That word again.

"One, yes," Quinn came back. "They've been noted."

That, she suddenly realized, explained the times she'd heard someone say "Note" followed by a name. Had they explained this earlier and she'd missed it? Had she been so distracted?

"And Four's making a list to be followed up on," Hayley added.

Charlie wondered what kind of clever method the Texan had come up with to do all these things at once. He and Ty had a friendly competition ongoing over which one could out-tech the other, and as frighteningly good as Tyler Hewitt was, she wasn't always sure Liam Burnett couldn't beat him. At least at some things, like this live, ongoing interaction.

As if the mention of his call name had triggered it, Liam spoke. "The subject's a big tipper, by the way. He dumped a hundred in the tip jar here at the bar."

"Shows where his priority is," Quinn said. "People do things drunk they'd never do normally."

Finally Rafe spoke, in that wry, ironic tone that seemed to say life and most of the people in it were just a big joke. She wasn't sure he was wrong. "Like commit to donations?"

"Exactly." She could agree with him, when he was right.

"Three, I can confirm on the tipping," added Teague. "He just dropped a twenty on my tray, along with some others. Times all the staff, that's a chunk of cash."

"Plus he wants good word of mouth among the peons," Charlie said. "Of course, then he'll turn right around and undermine them with his political policies, but in his view they're too dumb or blind to notice."

"Easy, Focus. Your animosity is showing." Her brother sounded more teasing than serious, and the sound of that tone so well remembered from throughout her entire life did a lot to help keep her temper in check.

As Flood continued to work the room one last time, she wondered how on earth she was going to get through that fundraiser tomorrow. She'd hoped he wouldn't expect her to be there, since he was the one people came to see and listen to, but he'd informed her that her presence was required. She gathered her function was to sit among the donors and listen raptly to his speech, and make appropriate comments to the person sitting next to her, who of course would be one of the biggest fish Flood wanted to reel in. He'd made sure of that.

"Just pour on your usual charm, Lita," he'd said. "You're such a help."

She had only smiled, but had wondered what he'd do if she'd sighed and said, "My only goal in life is to help you," while fluttering her eyelashes at him. Because it felt like that to her, as if she were acting as much as some on-screen performer. Probably felt like it more, because they likely didn't hate everything about what they were doing.

I'm prouder of what I do now than anything I did in uniform.

Rafe's words had taken her breath away for a moment. And she'd felt a burst of pride herself, pride in what she'd helped build. It was leavened with satisfaction in the simple fact that they helped people, both clients and their own people, by giving them work they could say that about.

Cort Ducane appeared before her, once more reminding her of Rafe in the quiet, almost stealthy way he moved. And she reminded herself yet again these mental plunges into the past had to stop.

"Are you ready to leave, Ms. Marshall?"

"More than." She let the pure truth of that creep into her voice. And she thought she caught the corners of his mouth twitch, as if he were stifling a smile. "Is he finally done?"

The smile threatened again, she was sure this time. "He will be ready to leave momentarily."

"And he needs me for the grand exit," she said.

"Easy there, Focus," Quinn cautioned in her ear. "We're not sure he's not tasked to report everything you say to him back to his boss."

She hadn't really thought of that, although she should have. But ever since his exchange with Rafe, she'd been looking at Cort a little differently. And in this case she had to agree, because he looked as if he wasn't quite happy with his current position.

As if he were perhaps not completely Flood's man.

"Sorry," she said, putting on the most pained expression she could manage. "I'm a bit cranky. My feet don't care for these shoes."

"Understandable," he said, rather gruffly but kindly. "I'll escort you back to Mr. Flood."

So Flood had sent him to be essentially an errand boy. As if anyone who worked for him was expected to do anything he asked. She wondered how he felt about that.

"Thank you, Cort."

She always used his first name, despite him always calling her Ms. Marshall even though she'd told him to call her Lita. She guessed that was a case of Flood's orders far superseding her own preference.

They walked toward a knot of people near the double doors at the far end of the room. She knew that Flood would be at the center of that knot, because that's where he preferred to be. Making his last, charming bid for their trust and probably inviting a few more to the fundraiser tomorrow.

She felt an odd sort of tickle at the back of her neck. And she knew if she turned her head she would find Rafe staring at them as they crossed the room.

She didn't do it.

Chapter 17

The only thing better about this fundraiser than that glittery function last night, Rafe thought as he settled the earpiece and took up a position inside the ballroom door again, was that he didn't have to wear the tux. This suit was bad enough. But he had to look the part, so he wore the ridiculously expensive thing Hayley had insisted they all have, just for assignments like this.

"You're lucky, dog," he muttered to Cutter, who had taken up the same station as he had last night. "You get to wear the same thing every day."

Cutter let out a low woof, as if he somehow knew he shouldn't draw attention.

"Got this undercover thing down, don't you?" Rafe said, smiling despite himself as he went back to once again scanning the room and its occupants. Both looked completely different. Gone were the sparkling lights, and the equally sparkling cuff links and jewelry.

And glowing golden gowns.

He knew it was bad when he sunk into alliteration.

This afternoon—they'd had to give people a chance to get over their hangovers, he supposed—the room was much more businesslike. Rows of chairs faced a slightly raised stage with a lectern adorned with a microphone and the logo of Flood's new PAC.

This was clearly going to be a speechifying event, and he hoped he could stay awake after a fairly sleepless night. They had slept—or in his case tried to—in shifts in the suite, with someone always awake and monitoring things just in case. He knew Quinn was taking extra care, with his sister being on the front line, and he certainly wasn't going to argue with that.

But when his turn came to hit the rack, all he could think about was that barely audible suggestion Flood had made, about "Lita" sleeping in his bed that night.

He knew he'd been both over the line and very wrong when he'd made that nasty accusation about her relationship with Flood. He'd seen too clearly now how much she detested the man. Others wouldn't, but he knew her. Probably better than anyone except her brother. And he knew she detested the man for more than just what he'd done to Foxworth, selling them out for that big chunk of cartel cash.

There had been no reason at all to think she would ever even consider sleeping with the dirtbag.

Which left him with only one explanation for his reaction, and it was one he didn't want to face. He never had wanted to face it. The simple fact that he'd never, ever gotten over having to throw away the best, the only real relationship of his life was something he'd acknowledged but never really dealt with. When it surfaced he shoved it back down again, into the mental box labeled No Choice.

He hadn't had to do that this much since…the last time

Charlie had been in town, Quinn's wedding. Thankfully, for him, she'd been unable to attend either Teague or Liam's weddings, although she'd arranged their honeymoons and sent strikingly appropriate gifts. But he knew she wouldn't miss Gavin's, not after they'd worked so closely together at the St. Louis headquarters. So she'd be back soon regardless. Gavin had even joked about having her as his best man. And if that came to be, she would pull it off, and with flair. Because she always did.

Unlike himself.

When there was half a continent between them, it was a lot easier to keep her out of his mind. But when she was here, in the same room, he wondered if he'd made any progress at all. Hell, if she was even in the state he was fairly sure he would be a mess. And for a guy whose life had so often depended on total concentration, he seemed incapable of it when she was around. And no amount of shoving thoughts aside, of focusing on something else, of reminding himself he hadn't just burned that bridge, he'd vaporized it, seemed to help.

"Status, everyone?" Quinn's query brought him out of his useless haze.

"Focus, en route in a couple." Charlie's voice was barely a whisper, indicating she wasn't alone, but whoever else she was with—he didn't doubt who—wasn't so close she couldn't respond at all.

"Three, on duty." Rafe knew that Teague and Liam were playing ushers today, escorting attendees to their seats along with a couple of regular hotel employees.

"And Four," came Liam's response.

"Five plus—" the plus to acknowledge Cutter "—in position," he said. And smiled wryly at the fact that, in essence, he was a door monitor. Ticket taker.

You've done worse. Much worse.

Most of the seats were full when the speeches started. He knew he didn't dare actually pay attention to what was being said, or the occasional bursts of applause at some of the ideas that were being promoted would make him want to walk away. Especially when he thought about the huge amounts of money that would likely end up in the coffers of this PAC, to promote those ideas and causes. To buy politicians who could get it done.

And line the pockets of the administrators, of course.

He cleared one latecomer, a woman who looked for all the world like somebody's doddering grandmother, but who had scanned him up and down and rather sassily said that the decor had definitely improved around here.

Then he set his brain to tune out the drone and focus on any unexpected sounds. One person came toward the room from the lobby, looked around and apparently realized he was in the wrong place and went back the way he'd come. A couple of people in hotel uniforms went past, barely giving him a glance. He was watching to be sure they kept going when he realized that hum in his head had started again. He knew before he looked down the wide hallway what he was going to see. Braced himself.

And there they were, Flood with his best game face—that too wide, too disingenuous, too practiced smile, baring too white, too perfect teeth—and on his arm, looking up at him with a fatuous expression he'd never seen on her face in all the years he'd known her, was Charlie. Flood couldn't see through that? Couldn't see it was a facade? Was he blind, or just utterly convinced of his own appeal?

Maybe Ms. Foxworth is just that good at it.

He yanked his mind back to the job at hand. There were two others with them. Brown, Flood's personal aide who seemed glued to his side even more than "Lita," and of course Ducane, at the moment scanning their surroundings in a way Rafe recognized. It was instinctive for him to assess the biggest threat, and there was no doubt that in this group it was Flood's bodyguard.

As long as you don't count the biggest threat to you, personally.

When they reached the doorway, he heard Cutter, from his spot under the table just a couple of feet away, let out a very short, muted sound.

Recognize him from last night, do you? Or just reacting to the evil?

Rafe made eye contact with Flood and nodded as he stepped back to let him pass. He thought about making the typical welcoming gesture of waving him into the room, decided he couldn't stomach it and didn't. Flood looked back at him for a moment, then his gaze flicked to Ducane. When those muddy brown eyes came back, Rafe could almost see the thought process going on. Flood had clearly linked him and Ducane, probably as the same sort. Quinn had said from the beginning the man might be pompous, self-important and evil, but not stupid. He also noted Cutter's presence again, a bit warily, but kept moving into the room.

Ducane gave Rafe a nod, even acknowledged him with a quiet, almost respectful "Crawford" as he passed.

Charlie never even looked at him. Which was just as well. He went back to playing sentry. All business. Unmoving. Unfeeling.

It was that damned gray suit.

She remembered how Hayley had insisted they all have both formal attire and expensive-looking business attire, and at the time it had made perfect sense; the work Foxworth did required them to blend into all sorts of environments. She'd okayed the expense without a second thought, because of the sense it made.

But that dark gray suit that matched his eyes perfectly rattled her.

And don't you dare think about him in that tux.

"—in the purple."

She suddenly tuned back in to what Flood was saying. She saw where he was gesturing, spotted the stocky woman in the rather bright pantsuit. "Mrs. Kline," she murmured, glad yet again of the research Ty and Liam had done, giving her images to put with almost every name on the list.

"Yes," Flood said, sounding pleased, she supposed because she'd recognized the woman whose family name was at the top of that most special list of donors, the ones who kept giving with the most digits to the left of the decimal. "Chat her up if you can. Turn on the charm."

Right. As if there's a switch.

Even as she thought it she knew what he meant, because she'd seen him do it time and again. She even knew the stages, spotting and recognizing someone, assessing their value to him, which then determined just how much of that charm he turned on.

She wondered if he'd ever had a genuine, not self-interested interaction with…anyone.

The knowledge that the answer to that was likely *no* made her faintly nauseous. Only the fact that when this was over she could walk away and cleanse herself of the taint enabled her to say sweetly, "Of course, Max."

And while what he'd done to endanger her people was more than enough reason, she knew more about him now. Knew that he was the antithesis of everything she believed in. She wanted to take him down for more than that very personal betrayal. And take him down Foxworth would.

She was going to greatly enjoy it when they did.

Chapter 18

"You did a wonderful job at the fundraiser, Lita dear. And you were spectacular at the party Friday night." He stopped short of rubbing his hands together in glee, but Charlie guessed it was a close thing.

She should have eaten something before she had that Sunday morning coffee. Or else it was just Flood making her queasy.

She pasted on her best smile. "Thank you. I'm glad everything went so smoothly."

She couldn't deny that it had, at least from the Foxworth point of view. More importantly, she was as certain as she could be that neither Flood nor any of his people knew they'd been under observation the entire time.

"It did." He didn't quite crow. "We made a lot of excellent contacts."

That, she supposed, had been the royal "we," since she'd met no one she'd care to contact after this was over. Except maybe the sharp waitress who had replied to her coworker's comments on all the expensive clothes by saying "Money's all they've got."

Truer words. Take that away, and there's nothing left of them.

She knew some would say that was easy for her to say, but those same people would likely be shocked at how little salary she and Quinn made as the heads of Foxworth. Every one of their operatives made nearly as much, and to their minds it was all well-earned.

No operation goes well unless all the parts are oiled, fit right and work together.

She felt the little tremor she always felt when Rafe's voice echoed in her head. She'd asked him once why he liked working on machinery so much—it seemed odd to her, for someone with his particular skills. At first all he'd said was that it kept his mind busy. But after a moment he'd added that the two skills, shooting and mechanics, were correlated in his mind, that the calculations on a long shot were brother to the logic of machinery.

And then he'd said the words that had become a mantra as they built and expanded Foxworth. She'd never told him that. But then, there were a lot of things she'd never told him. Because he'd walked out of her life and never given her the chance. But he'd agreed completely with the goals of Foxworth, and was not only Quinn's trusted friend, but had become one of their best and most effective operatives.

From the beginning the plan had been to deal in goodwill as much as money, taking nothing from the people they helped except their help in turn for someone else down the line. She'd been able to finance that, building on the financial legacy their parents had left them, and she was proud of that. But it had never been done for personal wealth, although they could have taken a lot more out of the portfolio than they did. But she and her brother had agreed long ago that they didn't want or need the wealth and flash.

They didn't want or need the Maximilian Flood lifestyle. In fact, both she and Quinn found it repulsive, and agreed that it would dishonor the upright, principled people their parents had been to use the inheritance they'd left them to live that kind of life.

"Speaking of that," Flood said, "why don't you plan on visiting your friends today, one last time before we leave?"

Speaking of what?

She'd been tuned out again. Lost in memory. For someone who was rarely caught off guard, she'd spent more time scrambling in the last three days than in recent memory. And when she could least afford it. Focus had obviously been the right choice for her call name.

She was the center of this operation, and that she wasn't that often in the middle of it didn't excuse not paying attention. Not to mention his words had sounded more like an order than a suggestion. And that pricked at her already on-edge nerves. "I thought we were—"

"I know, dear," he interrupted smoothly, "but something's come up. I have an unexpected meeting I need to take later today."

She got a grip on her edginess and went for the innocent voice. "With someone helpful?"

"Someone who was once helpful," he said.

Interesting differentiation.

She tried to gauge how far she could go, all the while thinking that if she was going to do this fieldwork regularly she needed more practice. And again she thought of Rafe, who on an earlier case had gone to that steely cold place in his mind when she'd done something as simple as confronting a driver who had been paid to run down their client. Maybe he'd been right, and she should stay in the office.

Still, she decided she could risk poking a little and asked, "And could perhaps be helpful again?" She tried her best to look concerned as she added, "Or are they going to be asking you for help in return?"

Something flickered in his gaze, and she had the feeling the concern had been just the right touch. As if he thought she wanted to protect him, which would put her right where he wanted her, solidly in his camp.

Dream on, Flood. You're the only one I want in a camp. A prison camp.

"I'll find out this afternoon. Now, I don't want you to have to worry about getting a car on such short notice, so Ducane will drive you in the limo."

You really want me out of the way, don't you? It had to mean he didn't want her to see who he was meeting with. Why? Was there some possibility she might recognize the person? She didn't know anyone here, outside of her brother and the Foxworth-related people. She knew she needed to try for more info.

"Won't you need it to get to your meeting?" She tried her best to make it sound as if she were concerned about inconveniencing him, furrowing her brow as she spoke. He apparently bought it, because he gave her a munificent smile.

"No, but I love that you're worried about that."

She smiled. Maybe she was a better actress than she'd ever given herself credit for.

Or maybe Flood was just that in love with himself that he assumed any common courtesy was out of consideration for his own wonderfulness.

But his answer told her some things. That the meeting would be here at the hotel, or that the person requesting the meeting would be providing transportation, or that Flood would find his own way, uncharacteristic as that might be.

And it told her that he didn't feel his bodyguard's presence was necessary, told her that he was confident whoever he was meeting with did not have ill intent toward him.

She just hoped it didn't also tell her Ducane was assigned not only to drive her, but to watch her.

She decided to test that. "He can just drop me off at the ferry, and Heather can pick me up on the other side," she said, using the name programmed in for Hayley's temporary number, figuring if for any reason Flood decided to check on that he'd get a female who knew she was supposed to be Heather if a call came to that number. "I'll check the ferry schedule. When's your meeting?"

That sounded innocent enough. She'd have to know that, right?

"One o'clock," he said, apparently unconcerned.

She called up the app and checked the sailings. "There's a boat leaving at about a quarter till. And coming back—"

"You can take your time. Whenever you get back we'll pack and head for the plane. It's the least I can do for dropping this on you at the last minute."

She smiled at him as widely as she could manage, given she was fairly certain the first thought that had hit her had been correct. That he wasn't being nice, he didn't want her around while he had this meeting. She wasn't sure what that told her, but that kind of caution had to mean something.

"I'll call Heather right now."

As she spoke she pulled out the phone. She half expected Flood to insist that Ducane take her all the way, perhaps secretly ordering him to meet and assess these friends of hers. She wouldn't put it past Flood to run backgrounds and practically audition anyone around a woman he was considering as a good front woman for his campaign for power.

He didn't stop her from making the call. But neither did he walk away to leave her to do it in private. So he was being cautious, but not paranoid. But still, as they'd agreed, they would handle these calls as if they were being monitored, because too much was at stake not to. At least now that the Foxworth team was in the game, she no longer worried about him having her surreptitiously followed, requiring a rental car and a meandering route. She knew nothing would get past them, and if she was being followed, they'd know it.

Hayley answered on the first ring.

"Heather? It's Lita."

"I didn't expect to hear from you so soon," Hayley said.

"I know, but something came up and Max has to make an unexpected meeting with someone—" she put a little bit of emphasis on the words and hoped Hayley picked up that she didn't know who "—today, so he suggested I come see you again before we leave tonight."

"That's wonderful!" Hayley exclaimed. "I wish Marnie and Lea weren't staying in the city tonight, but they have tickets to watch a play."

Charlie had to stifle a smile. Her sister-in-law was amazingly quick on the uptake, so easily letting her know Teague and Liam would be staying in the city to watch Flood's antics, whatever they might be.

"I'd love to see them again, too, but as long as I get to see you it will be worth the trip. Max is so sweet to suggest it." That one about choked her, but she got it out. "He's even going to have his security man drive me to the ferry landing in Seattle."

"Ohh," Hayley cooed, "he must really like you, Lita."

"I hope so. If I take the twelve forty-five boat to the island, would you be able to pick me up at the ferry landing there?"

A valid question, given that the woman she was talking to was in a suite one floor below where she stood right now.

"Of course, we'll make it work. Can't wait to see you again."

"Ditto," Charlie said, soothed by Hayley's easy assurance she would somehow get it done. She supposed Hayley could take an earlier ferry and then just wait on the other side for the one she would be on.

I'm surprised Quinn hasn't asked for a speedboat.

She grinned at that thought and let it show, figuring it fit the moment. But she wouldn't be mentioning the idea, or Quinn would likely agree. Not that they couldn't afford it, but she was a bit more sensitive about big money now that she'd spent a little time around the backroom dealing it accomplished.

After they'd ended the call she gave Flood the remnants of that grin.

"Thank you for thinking of this."

He smiled as if her gratitude were no more than he'd expected. And deserved. She wondered if there was a pill to control nausea that was strictly situational, not medical.

And she also wondered, not for the first time, how her brother and the other Foxworth operatives did it, dealing with the bad guys day after day, without going stark, raving mad.

Chapter 19

"An unexpected meeting?" Quinn asked, stopping his pacing of the central room of the hotel suite.

Hayley nodded from where she sat on the sofa in the main room, stroking Cutter as he lounged beside her like any well-loved pet. "She implied she didn't know with who, and with the way she was talking I'd say the subject was right there, listening."

Rafe's gut knotted in the same moment Quinn frowned. As if he'd somehow sensed it from across the room, Cutter's head came up and the dog looked at him.

"Suspicious?" Quinn said in a thoughtful tone.

"Or simply assuring himself she truly appreciates his kindness," Hayley said with a grimace. "She said something about how sweet it was of him to think of us getting together again, and she sounded so...not Charlie. I think she just said it so he would hear how she talked about him to her friend."

Quinn's expression shifted to a quick smile. "She thinks pretty good on her feet."

"Runs in the family, obviously," Hayley said with a return smile.

"Including you."

Rafe didn't know if in their mutual adoration they'd forgotten he was here, or if they just knew better than to ask for a sane opinion from him when Charlie was involved. He suspected it might be a little of both. And it wasn't that he begrudged them, not at all. It was just that sometimes they seemed so complete that simply being in the same room with them felt like an intrusion.

"All right," Quinn said then, in the brisk tone that meant back to business, although he had one more compliment for his wife. "That was a good live call, about Teague and Liam. They can keep their cover of hotel employees going a while longer, but we'd likely be recognized after the party."

Finally he looked at Rafe, who shrugged in understanding. "And Ducane would recognize me. Sorry about that."

"Sorry we've got someone good enough to be famous years after he left the service on our team? Hardly." Rafe grimaced at the word *famous*, but Quinn kept going, the decisions now coming rapid-fire. "We'll keep the suite for Teague and Liam's use. Rafe, since you're the most recognizable to Ducane, you and Hayley take your car and head to the other side on the first ferry you can make and wait for Charlie. Better take Cutter, too, since he's probably as recognizable as you are, now."

Rafe said nothing, just nodded.

"What are you going to do?" Hayley asked.

"I'll make a costume change, as it were, and get on the boat ahead of Charlie so I can watch her board and make sure she isn't being followed. I'll leave our car on this side so I can be on foot and free to move at all times. Hayley, on the other side you can wait for her in the normal area where people wait for arrivals."

He shifted his gaze to Rafe. "You take a position with a visual on the ramp where you can watch the walk-ons disembark, and look for the same thing. Once we're sure she's clear, we four will head to headquarters and connect with Teague and Liam on comms and see what the subject appears to be up to."

Again he only nodded. Quinn had a great tactical mind, so he rarely if ever questioned his calls.

As they started to gather their things to put the plan in motion, Hayley spoke, as if she were musing aloud. "I wonder if his meeting is with some big donor who couldn't make it to the party or fundraiser."

"More likely someone who doesn't want to be publicly connected to the...jerk," Rafe said as he put the formal wear and the suit in the garment bag Hayley had opened and hung on a door. If it had been up to him, it would have gotten stuffed into a backpack without much care, so it was probably a good thing the bag was here.

"That could well be," Hayley agreed. "Not like the subject is a genuine public servant."

Quinn snorted. "He doesn't care about serving, people or the law. He only cares about power. And he was in DC long enough to see who truly has it."

"And that money, like what he's here raising, is the way to buy it," Rafe muttered.

"Exactly," Quinn and Hayley agreed in unison. And they smiled at each other in that pleased way Rafe always saw when they were so perfectly in tune. Which was most of the time.

Okay, maybe he did envy them a little.

Charlie wasn't sure what to do. Which usually only applied to her in one situation, one involving a certain Marine turned Foxworth man. But while the man behind the wheel right now was also former military, she had none of the emotional entanglement to deal with, so she was able look at him more clearly. He had that same demeanor her brother, Teague and, yes, Rafe had, but once she had tamped down those emotions she realized he resembled Rafe more. Not so much physically, but in the haunted sort of look in his eyes.

He had the same sort of almost tangible alertness, always aware of surroundings, the kind of what she called mental radar that made him good at his job. Good enough for Flood to hire him. It was the kind of thing they looked for when considering adding someone to Foxworth. The kind of thing that radiated from her brother.

And from Rafe.

She yanked her mind back to business before it could stray down that overused path. The wireless transceiver that was back on her ear courtesy of the—again, thankfully plain—gold earrings was live, so she knew Quinn and the others would hear, although Rafe and Hayley had shut down the voice activation for the trip on the ferry, since they'd be staying outside in the car with Cutter, and it got a bit noisy out there.

She thought about the exchange Cort had had with Rafe, and wondered if she could—and should—give that a nudge.

Deciding she'd never have a better chance, she asked, "Do you miss the Marines, Cort?"

They'd been driving along in silence, so he seemed surprised when she spoke. Just as he'd been surprised when, after she'd again insisted on sitting up front with him, she'd told him she wasn't comfortable treating him like a taxi driver. But he'd conceded. Which gave her a clear view of that near-constant spinning of that simple gold ring on his left hand.

"In some ways, ma'am."

"Ma'am? Ouch. Now I feel old."

He gave her a startled glance. "I meant it respectfully."

He sounded almost worried. What did he think, she was going to complain to Flood and get him fired? Was it his assessment that she already had that much influence with the man? That was interesting. And perhaps encouraging.

"You're obviously not old," he said then, and a bit of that worry crept into his voice.

"Not that getting old is a bad thing," she said, in an exaggeratedly similar tone, as if she were afraid she'd offended.

Again he glanced at her, and she made sure he saw her grinning. And he let out a half chuckle that was obviously relieved.

"You're…"

"Nice?" she suggested, still grinning as he cut himself off.

He'd acted as if he'd forgotten for a moment that, from his point of view, he was talking to his boss's…whatever he thought she was. He had to know they weren't sleeping together, because he'd done a security sweep on her room in the hotel suite when they'd first checked in, and she'd made it pretty clear with a couple of comments. She was playing this game for keeps, but that didn't mean she wanted people to think she was the sort who'd jump into bed with a man like Flood just because he was a power broker. Or because he was, to some, good-looking. Personally she found him more than a little over-the-top. And even if that appealed to her, the cold calculation that always seemed to be in his eyes would have clinched it for her.

"Yeah," Cort said, not looking at her. "Nice."

She didn't have Hayley's knack for hearing what people didn't actually say, but she still got the feeling that, had he been free to say it, there might have been a "What are you doing with him?" attached to that.

I'd like to ask you the same thing.

She knew she couldn't, but maybe…maybe she could turn that around. And neither Quinn nor Hayley had said anything to stop her yet.

"How did you end up working for Max?" She felt a little chill as she had to stop herself from saying Flood—or "the subject"—which would hardly fit her role.

He gave a one-shouldered shrug and didn't look at her. "I needed the job. His people offered it."

"Max didn't interview you?"

"He asked…one question." There was a long, silent moment that, on instinct, she let spin out. Then Cort spoke again, in a very different tone of voice. "He asked if I'd ever killed to get a mission done. I said yes. He said, 'Good.' And that was the interview with him."

Something about that tone tickled at her brain, but she kept analyzing the very telling exchange he'd just described. She wasn't surprised. She'd always known whoever had sold them out had to have a callous, self-centered attitude. But she had to admit she was surprised at how effective his cover persona was.

Or maybe how blind his voters were.

It was when she hit that point that what she'd heard in Cort's undertone coalesced into a word. *Warning.* He'd been warning her, or rather Lita. He'd related that story, something that Flood would no doubt be very unhappy that he'd done, to warn her that Flood was not who she thought he was. He'd taken a calculated risk, for her sake.

His hands shifted on the steering wheel, and she caught the glint of the ring on his left hand.

"Your wife is a lucky woman," she said quietly as they reached a stoplight.

His head snapped around. Since they were stopped he didn't look immediately away, and she saw his surprise replaced by a look of pain so harsh it made her own heart quail.

"Lucky? She's dying, so no, not lucky."

She couldn't completely smother her gasp. His earlier words echoed in her mind. *I needed the job.* The job? Or the money that Flood was no doubt willing to pay for someone who would kill to protect him if necessary? Money for his wife's care? According to what Ty had found, he'd left the military before he would have gotten any retirement from his service. Maybe to come home when she was diagnosed? If nothing else, this explained the constant fiddling with the wedding ring.

"That's why he's doing this." The voice in her ear was barely a whisper, but she knew it had been Rafe.

"Agreed," her brother said.

"I'm so sorry," she said to Cort, meaning it with all her heart. "I had no idea."

The light had changed, and he must have seen it out of the corner of his eyes, because he turned his gaze back to the road ahead.

"No reason you would." His voice was gruff now.

"I wish I had. I'd have at least been more…tactful."

"You were being…"

"Nice?" she suggested again, but in an entirely different tone than before.

Again he flicked her a quick glance. She wasn't grinning now, not after this, but she was smiling. Sadly, letting a bit of the regret she felt show.

He didn't speak again until they were at the ferry landing. He'd insisted on finding a parking space and walking into the terminal with her. When she had paid her fare and was ready to head for the boarding area, she looked up at him, ready to thank him. But something in his expression made her wait a moment again.

"You are nice," he said suddenly, as if he'd been trying to hold it back. "Maybe too nice. For his world, I mean."

And suddenly she had a decision to make, how much to say, what to say that would leave this door open, but not give too much away. He'd risked this job he so badly needed to warn her yet again, which told her a great deal about him.

"You're very observant," she finally answered. And then, just as she turned to go, she looked back and said with full sincerity, "Thank you, Cort."

She could almost feel him watching her go. And her last thoughts before she took her first step onto the big green and white vessel were that she'd been partially right. Their circumstances might be tragic, but Cort Ducane's wife was lucky to have him.

And that Foxworth needed to look into that situation.

Chapter 20

Rafe, Hayley and Cutter had caught the first ferry after the decision was made, before Charlie and Ducane had even left the hotel. That would put them in position well before Charlie made her crossing.

"This'll give you plenty of time to scout out your spot," Hayley had said as they drove down the ramp on the home side, as Rafe thought of it. "We'll have to turn around and come back on the arrivals side when Charlie's ferry gets close."

For a woman who'd never even thought about such things before Quinn had dropped into Hayley's life, by essentially kidnapping her, she was definitely a pro now. And a crucial part of Foxworth.

It had occurred to him then he'd never told her that. Not that she didn't know, but she'd never heard it from him. And after all the times she'd gone out of her way to let him know how much she valued him and his contributions to the team, it seemed rather petty that he hadn't.

Surely he could manage to say that much, at least? It would probably come out sounding boneheaded, but still, he should try, shouldn't he? They'd gone to monitoring only on comms when they'd gotten on the noisy boat, so it wasn't like anybody'd hear his stumbling effort. So he did try.

"You went from knowing nothing about what Foxworth does to being an essential part of the team so fast... I don't think I've ever seen anyone learn as fast as you have."

He knew by the way she reacted, with a startled look, that he should have said it long ago.

"That's quite a compliment. Especially coming from you."

He gave her a wry smile. "I believe you once told me that more than a sentence at a time from me was a compliment."

She grinned, that expression that always made Rafe thankful Quinn had found this woman who so completed his life.

"I did," she said. "And it's true. I take it as a measure of trust."

"It is," he said.

"And maybe someday, you might even trust me about other-than-work things."

Well, that was a shot over the bow he hadn't expected. He was very glad they'd turned off voice activation. His gut was telling him any answer he tried to make would get him in trouble, so he stayed silent, focusing on driving as if they were back in the city instead of this place where encountering five cars on the road counted as heavy traffic.

He heard a movement from the back seat and Cutter's head appeared between them. And Rafe would swear the look the dog gave him was a bit disgusted.

Cutter was different, a law unto himself, and even among the Military Working Dogs he'd served with, Rafe had never seen his like. It had taken him a while to trust the dog as the others did, but he'd proven himself time and again, and now he trusted the dog completely. Tactically, anyway.

The problem was that other talent he seemed to have. How could he trust that when Cutter kept trying to shove him and Charlie together?

They had found their parking spot and settled in before Charlie's ferry had even left the dock. And it hadn't been long before Liam's voice sounded in his ear. "Four here, going voice activated again. All copy?"

"One copy, ready to roll." At the sound of Quinn's voice, Hayley smiled.

"Two copy," she said. "We're in place."

Rafe acknowledged he copied just before Teague chimed in to say the same.

"Focus," came Charlie's voice over the earpiece, spoken softly, as if she were telling herself to do so. Since she'd be inside the ferry cabin, extraneous noise wouldn't be such an issue.

Rafe mentally ran through what he and Hayley had worked out on their own ferry ride. Hayley would stay by the car in the line where people waited to pick up walk-ons, as someone normally would, while he took up his position opposite the ferry landing. From there he could see the foot passengers offloading through the long balcony egress, as they called it.

The plan was that Charlie would disembark the traditional way, but he would also keep an eye on the lower level, where some people tried to use the same route as the vehicles, just in case. He would use the camera with a telephoto lens that was in the permanent gear locker in the trunk to watch the stream of people, as he often did in such public circumstances, simply because it was less suspicious than watching with binoculars. And would make him harder to recognize for anyone who might be following her and could remember him from last night, or the party.

When Charlie had started the conversation with Ducane, his voice was clearly audible since they were in the same vehicle. He had listened to the conversation, at how she gently worked at Ducane, getting him to say some things he probably never would have. And he felt certain now that he'd been right: the man might be working for Flood, but he didn't like him much.

He'd felt a jolt when Ducane said his wife was dying, making any bit of irritation at how easily Charlie lured the man vanish instantly. And Hayley had gone immediately into action, pulling out her Foxworth phone and beginning to text. Since she could just speak to anyone on the team, it had to be someone else.

"One, we're pulling away from the dock," Quinn said, snapping Rafe out of the memory of that sad conversation and back to the present. "So far, no sign of a tail."

"Agreed," Charlie said. "I'm going to keep moving. And silent."

"Yes," Quinn agreed.

They had planned this as well. It would be much easier to spot a tail if the tail had to move to keep her in view. True, they were on a boat, but it was a big one full of people, and she could lose someone if she really wanted to. Especially with Quinn there to run interference. The silence was another precaution, just in case she was being followed. They didn't want anyone Flood might have managed to sic on her thinking she was talking to anyone.

"I'm having Ty look into the situation with Ducane's

wife," Hayley said. "Maybe we can give him another way to go."

Rafe turned his head to look at his boss's wife. She saw the movement and met his gaze. "Prove my point, why don't you?" he said softly.

The look she gave him then had him wondering if maybe he should try to talk more, more often. An idea he never, ever thought he'd have.

When the big green and white vessel came into view in the distance, he headed out to the place he'd picked, lugging the big camera. When he got there it was still too far out to really see faces, so he gave it another few minutes, then tried again.

He spotted Quinn first, on the upper level, leaning casually on the railing while other people were already lining up at the ramp. He looked as if he were simply waiting for the crowd to thin out before he headed for the passenger ramp himself. Rafe didn't see Charlie yet, but he knew Quinn must have her in view.

Once the boat had docked the pedestrians started to move. Knowing Quinn had the exit covered, Rafe focused on the line of people already off the boat and headed either toward the town's main street or the parking area below him. It was a bit difficult with the partially enclosed walkway, but with the powerful telephoto lens he saw well enough. He saw none of the other people they'd had photos of, but that didn't mean Flood didn't have someone they didn't know about.

He spotted Charlie simply by the way she moved in the instant after Quinn said, "Focus is off the boat."

"I have her," Rafe said, keeping any hint of another spin that could be put on those words out of his voice. He wasn't so successful at keeping it out of his head.

He watched her as she pulled out her cell phone and put

it to her ear, as if making a call to whoever was going to pick her up, as many others were doing.

"Focus, I'm clear," she said into the transceiver. "Nobody looked twice at me."

Ha. Any guy with a pulse was looking at you. And more than twice.

"Focus," Hayley said, "Two is on the way to meet you." A decisive bark echoed in his ear. There was a pause before Hayley added, a grin almost audible in her voice, "With an escort. We'll be waiting at the door."

"One en route as well. Five, status?"

"Heading back. Focus still in view." Somehow that half step of distance he gained using the assigned code name let him speak evenly.

He emerged from the trees just as he spotted Hayley and Cutter—leashed at the moment in this place that required it—at the door to the passenger terminal. A moment later Charlie was there, greeting her sister-in-law like the friend she was supposed to be meeting, holding the cover to the end. But it wasn't all a cover, he knew that. Knew that Charlie and Hayley had bonded, both over their love for Quinn and an appreciation for different but equally sharp minds.

And then Quinn was there, and they headed for the car. His car, for which Hayley had the keys—no fancy electronic fob for his old beast—since he'd left to take up his overwatch position. He started that way, having to pause to let other vehicles pass in the parking area as arrivals began to leave. A large SUV passed, blocking his view. When it was clear the other three and Cutter had already reached the car he always thought of as camouflage. Not simply because it was an every-other-car-on-the-road model, but because the tired-looking silver coupe was a sleeper. It might look like it barely had enough gumption to get out of the way, but he kept that engine tuned and ready, and more than a little souped-up. It might look tired, but it had energy to burn. It would beat any—

His thoughts stopped as if he'd plowed that car into a brick wall. Because Quinn, Hayley and Cutter had just piled into the back seat. Leaving him the driver's seat. And Charlie the passenger seat right next to him.

His next stride wobbled a little, and for once it had nothing to do with the old injury to his leg. Jaw set, he kept going. It was only a half-hour drive back to Foxworth headquarters, he could do this. And with luck they'd be discussing tactics, where to go from here. He wouldn't have to say a word, or even look at her.

He was a row of parked cars away when Quinn's voice said, "Three and Four, we're off the boat. We'll keep comms live, but there's that dead spot for about three minutes."

"Four, know it well," came Liam's voice, sounding just as sour as he would expect the tech-reliant Texan to sound.

"Three, copy," Teague said, sounding amused. "Activity kicking up here. Will report anything of interest."

By then Rafe was at the car, and he got into the driver's seat. Hayley had already put the keys back in the ignition so he started it up immediately, with satisfaction at the low, steady purr of the motor.

He glanced at Quinn in the rearview mirror. "Any change?"

"No. Back to headquarters."

He nodded and pulled out of the line of cars. He was glad of the traffic in the at-the-moment busy lot, because it gave him an excuse to keep his gaze elsewhere than on the woman beside him. Too bad it wasn't so easy to ignore the whiff he got of whatever perfume she was wearing.

Something rich smelling, that he didn't like nearly as much as the lighter, breezier scent she used to wear.

And that he'd known up close and personal.

He heard rather than saw Cutter shift his position in the back seat. The dog plopped his head on the center console, just far enough forward that Rafe could see his head with his peripheral vision. Automatically he reached out to scratch behind the dark ears. And his hand collided with another that had apparently done the same.

He had the crazy thought that he would have known it was Charlie even if he couldn't see her, just from the shock that went from his fingers straight to his chest. It was all he could do to just remove his hand and not to yank it back as if he'd touched a searing hot engine.

She did yank her hand back. And instantly went back to looking ahead through the windshield. The dog let out a long, weary-sounding sigh.

"I admire your perseverance, dog," Quinn said from the back seat, his tone wry.

"He's never given up before, and I don't expect he will now." Hayley's tone, by contrast, was almost cheerful. Or amused.

Personally, he didn't find anything the least bit funny about any of this. And judging by Charlie's rigid posture and determined staring, she felt the same way.

At least we agree on something.

They'd been on the road back for nearly fifteen minutes when Teague's voice sounded again. "Three to One, pic incoming. Request ID, if you know him."

"Copy," came Quinn's response from the back seat, now hitting both ears simultaneously.

It couldn't have been more than thirty seconds before Quinn spoke again. "Where?"

There was no mistaking the change in his tone, and it

was sharp enough that Rafe looked at him in the mirror again. He had that intent look that matched the edge.

"In the hall near the ballroom. He looked familiar, but I couldn't place him."

"I can," Quinn said flatly. "He is—or at least was—an aide to a certain former governor. One we suspected but couldn't prove helped hide the body."

Rafe went still. Ogilvie? An aide to the former governor they'd helped take down for murder? The disgraced man who, just over a year and a half later, was hiding out in his basement, still managing to stall off a trial, no doubt calling on every lawyer and judge he'd purchased over the years, using all the dirt they knew he'd collected on others, for any tactic that would keep him out of prison?

"There's more," Teague added, his voice telegraphing tension.

"Go." Quinn's voice was clipped now.

"The subject's aide was with him."

Flood's man Brown, meeting with Ogilvie's? They were the same ilk, so it shouldn't be a surprise, but Rafe was still a bit stunned.

"Well, that makes this a whole different ball game," Liam, still on the other side, drawled over the earpiece.

Indeed it did.

Chapter 21

"Do you suppose," Hayley said in a musing tone, "that the governor called the subject for help? He's running out of ways to stall his trial."

"Gee, after only twenty months?" Liam drawled.

Rafe grimaced at the truth there. The guy should have been in prison long ago. But then, there were a lot of people he thought should be in prison that weren't.

"Could be," Quinn said with a nod. "The subject and his influence is the level of help he'd need."

"Any connection between them before now that we know of?" Teague asked on comms.

"No, but I didn't look for that. I'll start digging now," Ty said. "If you're done with me for the moment, that is."

Quinn nodded. "Go for it. We'll be monitoring you, but we're back on house comms for now. Three and Four copy?"

Teague and Liam chimed a copy, acknowledging they'd be the only ones on the earpieces for now, so if they needed someone at headquarters, they'd have to run up a flag first.

"And Data?" Quinn said. "Great work."

Ty flashed a grin before the screen went dark. For a moment it was silent in the room, and on the earpieces, which they now pulled out.

"Well," Hayley finally said, "hasn't this gotten even murkier."

"Birds of a feather," Rafe muttered. "Politicians."

"And he's a consummate one," Charlie said, to his surprise not giving him the side-eye for speaking at all.

She reached for the remote control Quinn had set down on the table. Rafe already knew they had the same system back in St. Louis, but he would have guessed it anyway from the way she handled it, quickly calling up a recorded video that again lit up the screen.

"Ty pulled this off a news site's archive. It's a press interaction that happened the week after his wife was killed. It's what gave us the idea for who Lita should be."

The video image was shaky at first, then settled. Maximilian Flood stood on the steps of some impressive building before a gaggle of reporters who seemed to radiate adoration.

So much for impartiality.

But he had to admit the guy was pretty. Even more on camera than in person, which he figured meant…something. If nothing else, the guy knew how to use that charisma he had.

"There is nothing," Flood began, "that can describe how I'm feeling right now. My wife was such a determined, brilliant woman. My life will never be the same without her."

Now there were some carefully chosen words…

The reporters began shouting questions at him, which seemed tasteless under the circumstances, but Flood didn't seem to mind. He answered some about the tragedy of the accident, then quickly turned it political with a declaration he would be making traffic safety a cornerstone of his policy push. More questions were called out, including one asking if he would ever marry again. Rafe marveled at the tactlessness, just a week after the woman's death, but any sympathy was destroyed by the sad smile that looked a little too practiced, and the not-so-surreptitious wipe at his eyes.

Rafe studied him. If he hadn't chosen politics he could have made it in Hollywood. But Hollywood was openly fake. Politics hid the fakeness, but changed the world. And in this man's case, not for the better.

"I doubt I could ever find another woman like my Alondra," Flood said, a catch in his voice that matched the sad smile. "If I ever even try again, it would have to be someone who understood how I'm feeling now."

Charlie hit the pause button. "That's when Lita Marshall was born. Or rather, Ty built her."

"Good call," Quinn said.

Hayley made a face at the screen. "He's very good at this."

"Good enough to get away with what he did for three years," Quinn said, distaste clear in his voice.

"But no longer," Charlie said, satisfaction in hers.

"We owe Ty big-time for this one," Rafe said.

"Yes, we do," Charlie and Quinn said simultaneously. The brother and sister laughed at each other, and for a moment the mood lightened.

There was no way, Rafe realized, that Charlie would deny the great work Ty had done just to argue with him. Anything else, maybe, but not the value of any of the Foxworth people. She didn't even deny his own worth to the Foundation, and she hated him.

"So that clip was four years ago," Charlie said. "This was four days ago."

She pressed the play button on the remote. The scene switched, Flood again, this time against a backdrop Rafe recognized as Lambert Field, officially known as St. Louis Lambert International Airport. The rest was the same, a gaggle of reporters tossing questions out at Flood. Only this time the smile wasn't sad, it was wide, white toothed and engaging. And he ended the brief session with a statement no one had even asked for.

"Today I'm happier than I've been in years. And soon I hope to introduce you to the woman who's made that possible."

"Nicely played, sis," Quinn said.

"Congratulations," Hayley said. "Thankfully, for that not being really true."

Charlie laughed. "Thankfully, indeed. Many's the time I've had to fight throwing up, just being close to him."

Rafe spoke before he could stop himself. "At least you're out now."

Charlie turned to look at him then, her vivid blue eyes puzzled. "What?"

He realized Quinn and Hayley were looking at him as well, and wondered what was wrong. Of course she was out. One of them, Teague or Liam, disguised as hotel staff, could get her stuff if she was worried about it, but she had to bail, and now.

Still no one spoke. His brow furrowed, he shifted his gaze to his boss. "She can't go back now. If Ogilvie and Flood are talking—and you know he's at this meeting— then there's a chance Flood will find out who she really is."

"*She* is sitting right here." He looked back at her just as she practically snarled out, "Do you really think he hasn't checked me out, and that Ty didn't lay the groundwork well enough to withstand that?"

"Do you really think Ogilvie hadn't pried into Foxworth deep enough, trying to save his own ass, that he didn't find you?"

"Even if he did, he'd never connect me to the name Lita Marshall."

"Never mind the name, do you think he never found a photograph of you? That he won't eventually see you and make the connection?"

"What could he have found, my old college graduation picture? Because that's about all that's out there."

He knew that was true. If nothing else, Charlie had never wanted to be in the limelight, and avoided it as much as possible. But that didn't change the bottom line, not for him.

"And you look just the same," he said.

She stared at him. He stared back. He was vaguely aware neither Quinn nor Hayley had said a thing yet, but at this instant it didn't matter.

"Why, Mr. Crawford," she said, far too sweetly, "if I didn't know better, I'd take that as a compliment. But I do know better, so I have to assume you're just being an ass."

She didn't add "As usual," but it rang in the silence as if she had. He didn't care. Only one thing mattered right now. But she had to realize it would be beyond foolish to go back, it would be downright dangerous.

"Don't be stupid. Flood is one step away from knowing who you really are."

"Considering how stupid Ogilvie is, more like ten steps."

"If Ogilvie's after Flood's help on his case, what could be better than warning him you're Foxworth?"

"There's no reason Ogilvie would know or guess. He's never seen me in person. And even if he had, it was never like this." She made a gesture that seemed to encompass herself from head to toe. "This is as much a disguise as if I were wearing a mask. I don't ever go to this much trouble."

But you used to.

A memory hit him like a punch to the gut. Charlie, the evening they'd gone out on a date for the first time. Her eyes had been bright and vivid, emphasized by whatever makeup she'd skillfully applied, and her hair had been a dark, shining, sleek mass that went down past her shoulders. She'd been wearing a silky bright blouse the same color as her eyes, a short black skirt and heels that brought her mouth—luscious and tempting with a shade of lipstick he had no word for—within easy reach.

He'd about had a heart attack the moment she'd opened the door.

The memory made his voice both harsh and fierce. "You're not going back there."

For a moment she simply stared at him. But he could almost see the anger boiling up in those eyes. He should have known better. He did know better. Charlaine Foxworth did not respond well to autocratic commands.

"Shut up, Crawford." She somehow made the barely-above-a-whisper demand as much of an order as his words had been. "I already told you, you gave up any right to boss me around long ago."

A movement and a loud, oddly pitched howl made them both jump.

Cutter, on his feet and now between them, looked up at them both with the canine equivalent of a glare. He'd never heard the dog make such a sound before, something that sounded both mournful and angry.

"You're right, Cutter."

Quinn's snapped-out words had the same sort of edge. He was on his feet, which told Rafe how out of it he'd been; he hadn't seen that either the dog or the man was about to move until it had happened. Hell, he'd barely been aware that Quinn and Hayley were still there, seeing and hearing it all.

"Rafe, you're with me. Hayley, don't shoot her."

"Tempting though it may be," his wife answered, and Charlie looked the slightest bit abashed.

He followed Quinn outside, where a blast of cooler air hit him. He needed it. He'd gone too far, slipped the leash, and likely had reached the point where his usefulness was outweighed by the irritation factor of putting up with him. He once more hadn't been able to keep that lid on when she was around, and he was about to find out the price. He'd feel humiliated if he wasn't wondering what the hell he would do if Quinn cut him loose.

Quinn turned to face him, and he inwardly braced himself.

"I have never seen you lose sight of the mission before."

Because he never had. Until now. Until her.

"And I never would have expected it," Quinn went on, "on this of all missions."

That one hit hard. *Stabbed with the truth, Crawford?*

This of all missions indeed. To take down the man who had nearly helped orchestrate the death of them all. Three years they'd been hunting him, he'd lost track of how many false starts there had been. Until now.

Until Charlie found the real one, the man who'd sold them out.

And he, the man with a reputation for cool, the most patient of the most patient faction of the military, had lost all of that.

He said nothing, because he had nothing to say. No words could change this. Just as it seemed no amount of time could move him past this. His reaction in there had been gut level and automatic. He knew perfectly well—

and better than anyone except Quinn—how Charlie would respond, and yet he'd said it anyway. In the form of an order that would get her back up like nothing else could.

Because, as she'd said, he had no right. He'd thrown that away. That he'd done it for her sake didn't matter. She didn't know that, and never would. The reason behind that was a secret he'd take to his grave. He could handle her hating him. He hated himself, after all. He deserved it.

He couldn't handle her knowing why he deserved it.

With one of the greatest efforts of his life, including those on the battlefield, he met Quinn's gaze. "I'll save you the trouble and quit, if you want."

Quinn blinked. "Quit? What the..." His boss—and the man he admired above all others—shook his head sharply. "You're not quitting, damn it. Get your head out of your ass, will you?"

"I..." Words failed him. As they so often did.

Quinn rammed his fingers through his hair, then put his hands on his hips. "I don't know what happened with you two. I only know you've known her as long as you've known me." Suddenly, unexpectedly, Quinn reached out and grasped his shoulders. "You're family, Rafe."

Rafe blinked this time. How often had he thought that, that the Foxworth's were the family he'd never had? Even before he'd been foolish enough to fall for Charlie, he'd felt...included. As he never had before. But he'd always thought it was just him. Just a fanciful idea he had, that would never occur to them.

"She's set on this, and she's right. She's the best chance we have of taking this guy down." Quinn's fingers tightened, almost dug into his shoulder muscles. "I don't care what happened between you. I'm trusting you to set it aside when it comes to protecting my sister."

Rafe stared at the man who had given him this life, who

had given him the chance to put his skills to work in ways that only helped people, who had given him a place to belong when he never thought he'd have that again.

The man who had trusted him with his life and the lives of those he loved more than once.

Rafe knew in that moment he would keep that trust. He'd do whatever it took not to lose this man's respect and high esteem. He should have known he couldn't quit. Not on Quinn Foxworth.

And especially not when Charlie was in danger. He would never be able to tolerate not being there.

You gave up any right to boss me around long ago.

Was she saying he'd once had that right? That the indomitable Charlie Foxworth would have once granted him that? The idea jolted him to the core. But it didn't rattle the one thing he was certain of. He needed to be involved, to be close, even if it was so close his skills were of no use.

He needed to be close enough that he could step in front of a bullet for her.

That was what family did, wasn't it?

He spoke quietly, carefully, making it clear he meant both the assent and the respect.

"Yes, sir."

Chapter 22

Damn Rafe for planting that seed.

Charlie spent the entire trip back to the city wrestling with what he'd said. Not just the thought that someone connected to Ogilvie might figure out who she really was and tell Flood, but the fact that he'd demanded she not go back simply because of that narrow possibility. The fact that he'd demanded at all.

The very idea that he thought he had the right.

That was almost enough to distract her from the task ahead. She had to force herself to, ironically, focus. She had to play this as if nothing had changed, as if this were just a vacation, as if she appreciated the chance to see more of her "friends," as if she were still just as impressed with Flood as she'd made him believe she was. Still, she'd contacted Ty before they left and told him to replace her actual photo wherever it might be out there with a "newer" one that wasn't really her at all, that looked close enough to be believable yet with at least one noticeable difference. Knowing Ty, he'd have that done before they got to the other side.

She hadn't put the wireless transceiver back in her ear yet. She needed to think, and this ferry ride was going to be her only chance.

Of course the fact that Rafe was on the boat just yards away didn't help. He didn't even need to be in sight, just knowing he was here somewhere had her in an uproar. And wouldn't all the people who said Charlaine Foxworth was the toughest woman they'd ever known, that she was smart, savvy and above all cool under stress, laugh to see her now? In a stirred-up mess because one man was somewhere on this nearly five-hundred-foot-long boat.

She got the full measure of how distracted she was when a woman in the row that backed up to hers and one seat over spoke.

"We're live again."

Charlie barely managed not to jump. She knew it was Hayley's voice but had to force herself not to look over her shoulder to be sure. She turned her head just enough to see that Hayley, dressed today in casual leggings and with her hair up in a perky ponytail, looking very little like the stylish woman who'd attended the party, had her phone up to her ear, to make it seem as if that's where the comment had been aimed. They had obviously risked this because she hadn't responded to a roll call on the system.

Embarrassed now, she put the earring back on and settled it into place. Funny how just about every episode of embarrassment she'd suffered in her entire adult life could somehow be traced back to one person.

She thought about muttering "sorry" into the transceiver, but since Rafe was no doubt live and tuned in—he would never miss a check-in—she did not.

"Focus is here," was all she said.

"Copy," came her brother's voice back. "Three reported subject's security has left the hotel, headed for the garage."

Did Teague never miss anything? "You think the subject isn't coming? He's sending him for me?"

"That's our guess. And according to Three he doesn't look happy about it."

"Reduced to a chauffeur, I'm not surprised," Charlie said.

"Just got some info on him from Data." Since that came from Hayley, who was still sitting less than two feet away, she heard it with both ears. "Or rather, on his wife. She's here in the city, in hospice care. Stage four cancer, last treatment option failed."

"No wonder he needs what the subject's willing to pay," Quinn said, sounding grim. "Five, Focus, you two have the best chance with him, so if the opportunity arises…"

She didn't like the linking even with call names, so it was an effort to keep her voice neutral when she said, "Yes. I'll keep working on him."

"Copy," Rafe answered, his tone seemingly unconcerned by the juxtaposition. *Why would he be concerned? He made his decision long ago.*

Her cell phone rang. "Hold on, the subject is calling."

"Ah. The official explanation," Hayley said.

"Probably," she agreed. "Answering now," she added by way of warning before she swiped to answer the incoming call, mentally prepping herself to put on her best happy voice. She put the phone to her free ear.

"Max? Is your meeting over already?"

"No, I'm sorry, Lita dear—" he was starting to say it as if it were one word, Litadear "—we're running long. I'll send Ducane to pick you up."

Or keep an eye on me?

"Are you sure you don't need him there?" She tried her best to put worry into her voice.

"I need you safe more," Flood said, so practiced she would have sworn his concern was genuine if she hadn't known better.

"All right," she said, although thanks to her newly planted paranoia she wasn't certain it was. "That's sweet of you," she added, and it almost gagged her.

"I'm afraid we may have to delay our departure until tomorrow," Flood said. "Will your boss be all right with you being away a little longer?"

He sounded so troubled she almost bought it. Wondered what he'd say if she said no. *My boss is unbending and occasionally tyrannical. And nothing like the accommodating, easygoing woman you think you know.*

She'd only been that once in her life. Only once had she ever been willing to accede to another's wishes, just for the joy of being with them. Only once, and she knew to her bones she never would again.

"I'll call and ask, but I'm sure it will be all right." She decided to go for the empathy play, since it was his favorite. "This is the first time off I've taken since my husband… well, you know."

"Of course I do, honey," he said, his voice fairly dripping with well-practiced compassion.

"I know. You're so understanding, because you've been there, Max."

"I think it's partly why we work so well together," he said, sounding now as if he were reassuring her. "Now, sadly, I need to get back."

She went for a lighter tone for her much more serious question; they needed to know what this meeting really was. "Did this turn into a negotiation? If it did, I feel for them. I've seen you at work."

"In a way, it has," he answered, sounding pleased now.

"And it will come out as it should. I'll see you soon, Lita dear."

For a long moment after the call ended, Charlie stared at the phone in her hand with distaste. "I feel like I need a shower."

"He does drip a bit," Hayley agreed wryly. She had stayed in her seat, and Charlie had tilted the phone to be sure she could hear Flood's side of the conversation.

"Curiouser and curiouser about who this meeting is with," Quinn said. "Especially after his aide met up with the gov's."

"Three here," Teague said. "All I've been able to find out is if the meeting is happening here at the hotel it's not in a publicly accessible space. And the subject isn't waiting in his suite. He's down in the coffee bar, socializing."

"Four here. I'm trying to get into the hotel records, to see who may have rented a new room or suite just for today."

"One, I copy," Quinn said. "We should be on-site in about an hour."

Assuming the boat doesn't sink.

The phrase that formed in her head startled her. She wasn't normally a pessimist, but this case was getting to her. They'd been hunting this mole for three years, had thought they'd been close at least twice before, and instead had discovered their then-target was, while a despicable human being, not the one who'd sold them out.

And this was the first time she'd ever run with a gut feeling instead of facts, figures and solid intel. That kind of information had sent her to the party where she had met Flood, but it was the chill that had enveloped her, the sudden involuntary tensing of every muscle the first time she looked into his eyes that had convinced her this was their true quarry at last.

She'd never told anyone, not even Quinn, about that,

even though her brother had more than once admitted sometimes he just had to go with his gut. She was a facts and numbers person, not an instinct and gut-feeling person.

Until now.

But then, her gut had been in turmoil ever since that day when she'd done that video meeting with the Northwest crew on their last case. She hadn't meant to blow up—she never did—but seeing Rafe sitting there, never even looking at the screen, at her, she'd just lost it. She'd turned an official briefing into something personal, in front of clients. To the point where her imperturbable brother had put an abrupt stop to it.

That was when she'd known she had to deal with this once and for all. And she'd been planning to do just that when Ty had come up with the lead on Flood.

Life is what happens while you're making other plans...

She didn't remember who'd first said it, but she knew the truth of it, now more than ever. She'd always been able to bury herself in planning, researching, crunching the numbers. She loved her work, she loved and believed in Foxworth's mission, but outside of that...life had gone on, often without her.

Rafe had barricaded himself behind an impenetrable wall of brusque reserve. She had barricaded herself behind an equally impenetrable wall of work and withdrawal. All begun on the day he'd walked out of her life forever.

And she still didn't know why.

She bit the inside of her lip, hard. *Focus! That's your call sign, but it's also an order, as of now.*

By the time they reached the dock, she thought she had herself convinced. And like some of the actors she'd seen while working backstage, she mentally prepared herself for the character she must now become again.

"Five has overwatch. He'll be last off, with the car and Cutter," Quinn said.

She knew her brother was worried that they didn't have anyone to cover from the ferry landing side, since Teague and Liam were needed at the hotel. And there, too; they had the front doors and garage area covered, but there were other exits. This office might really need another body here, along with that speedboat.

"Two, stay on her," Quinn continued. "I'll get off first and scope out the terminal, and her ride. Hold back until I report."

"Two, copy," Hayley said.

Charlie knew the couple had been noticeable at the party and the fundraiser, so were keeping a low profile. Although she herself thought there was little chance Quinn would be recognized by anyone they were watching, even if they had seen him at the party. He'd skipped shaving, and today had on worn jeans, a T-shirt, zip-front sweat-shirt and a Mariners baseball cap. No one would connect this rather scruffy guy with the elegant man in the tux from the party.

She was on her feet and moving before her mind could stray to images of that other unexpectedly elegant man in a tux.

The man who even now watched over them all.

Chapter 23

Rafe had to call up every bit of his much-vaunted concentration to shut out everything except the job at hand. This time it was to keep them all safe, as it usually was. Lately, at Hayley's insistence, he'd been up front more on cases, even handling a couple on his own. And they hadn't been disasters, although he was fairly certain they would have gone more smoothly if someone else had run them, or if the whole team had been on the job.

But the outcomes had been right, and the good guys were still standing and breathing, so he counted them as wins.

The whole team's on this one, and you're still antsy as a prairie dog who's spotted a coyote.

He knew why. Just as he knew he should never have blown up the way he did. Now, or the case before this one, or a couple before that. But when Charlie was involved, all his should-haves seemed to fly out the window. Along with his common sense.

Back then, he'd spent what seemed like days on end telling himself over and over that she couldn't want him, not this dynamic, brilliant, gorgeous woman who could have her pick of any man she wanted. But all that was blown away when they touched, blown right out of his mind. Because when they touched they didn't just strike sparks.

Together, they were an inferno.

With an effort he pulled back from that precipice. He watched as the woman he couldn't get out of his head got up from her seat and slowly, casually started toward the line of people ready to disembark. He saw Hayley do the same, keeping a short distance behind but still where she could reach Charlie within a couple of strides; Quinn had taught her well.

He moved forward, to where he could see toward the dock, yet still keep the two women in his peripheral vision. He quickly spotted Quinn, already off the boat and headed down the covered ramp to the terminal, eyes scanning the crowd. As soon as he knew Quinn had the front covered, he took up a place in line behind the women, but close enough that he could still see them both, his height an advantage now. As was, apparently, the icy stare he'd been told he had. Nobody objected but rather quickly stepped aside when he hustled by some slow walkers to keep the two in his line of sight.

When they hit the terminal, Hayley veered to one side and he to the other, as they'd planned. Charlie kept going straight, scanning the crowd for her ride. There were only three or four people facing the oncoming tide of passengers, and Ducane stood out like a misplaced statue, tall, steady and radiating whatever it was that made people also give he himself a wide berth.

It's something you and Quinn both have, that air of competence that could turn deadly, if necessary. It's why people—at least the ones who are awake—react to you the way they do.

Hayley had told him that back when they'd been re-hashing the case that had begun all this, the case that had nearly gotten them all killed, but had brought her and her impossible dog into their lives. The case they were so close to finally bringing to an end.

"I have Focus in sight from the landing," Quinn said in his ear. "And the…chauffeur." Rafe grimaced inwardly, guessing how a man like Ducane probably felt about being ordered to essentially be just that, a driver for the boss's girlfriend. His stomach knotted automatically at the thought, and he tamped it down just as Quinn added, "Five, get the car."

"Copy."

They'd planned this out, too, that Quinn would watch until Charlie met up with the driver. She would stall Du-cane as long as she could, strolling through the terminal, stopping for coffee, giving him and Rafe time to get to the car to follow them to the hotel. And as much as he didn't want the balance upset, Rafe had to admit another body to play chauffeur for them would be handy about now.

"Or you need to learn how to drive, dog," he muttered to Cutter, who was on his feet in the back seat, clearly knowing things were about to start. The animal let out a low, huffing sort of sound, and Rafe nearly laughed at him-self when he realized he was putting the words *You think I couldn't?* to it.

The dog's skills—of all kinds—aside, Cutter had done more to give him back a sense of humor and whimsy than anyone ever had. After all, it took a sense of humor to ac-cept the fact that he'd had a paw in matching up not just their clients with their soulmates, but everybody on the

Foxworth team. Except him, of course, but that was only to be expected.

But with the others, he couldn't deny the dog's part in all of it. His skill in knowing people who belonged together was right up there with his scenting and tracking capabilities, his instincts about suspects and situations, and his ability to go from friendly, tail-wagging pet to ferocious fighter in a split second.

But neither he, Quinn, Hayley nor Cutter could do much once Charlie got into that car alone with the person Flood had sent.

There was no rushing getting on or off a ferry unless you were in an ambulance. You went in the order and to the lane the crew directed. In this case, one of the raised, outside ramps which made for a good view but wasn't much help to him right now. He sat tapping a finger on the steering wheel as Cutter let out a low, impatient woof from about an inch behind his head.

"I know, dog," he muttered.

He tried to tell himself that the chances of Ogilvie's man seeing Charlie and recognizing her were slim to none, but it didn't matter. Because for him, any chance, no matter how slim, was too much. But he also knew Quinn had been right when he'd said she was their best shot at Flood, and that she was—stubbornly—determined to be part of it.

And a stubborn Charlie Foxworth was a force to be reckoned with.

Charlie knew perfectly well why this man unsettled her, that he reminded her of Rafe. But she knew he wasn't really like that infuriating man. After all, he'd married his love, and was clearly devastated that he was losing her. She felt such a qualm that she vowed whatever Foxworth could do to help they would do, no matter how this turned out.

But right now, she had a trek through city traffic to get through, and that meant time to do something constructive. Like pry, looking for the spots to aim at.

With no small effort, she put everything—and everyone—else out of her mind. All that mattered right now was finding out how much—or how little—this conscripted driver knew. And doing it in a way that wouldn't give anything away.

This time Ducane didn't resist her getting in the front seat. She hoped that meant he was comfortable with her not riding in back, or maybe it just made him feel less a hired driver.

"Thanks, Cort," she said. "Although doing this seems a waste of your skills."

He gave her a sharp sideways look. She smiled, and he seemed to relax a little. Charlie pondered what to ask next. She knew she'd have to be careful, since from the viewpoint of Flood and his crew, she had no way of knowing exactly who Flood was meeting with. And they could be wrong about that, too. Just because the man Teague had seen had once worked for the disgraced former governor didn't mean he still did.

Eggshells. Just remember you're walking on eggshells.

"It's such a change," she said, nodding back toward the ferry, "coming from that side back to the city."

"I've never actually been over there," Cort said, glancing back toward the sound.

"It's different," she answered. If the situation had been different, she might have waxed more eloquent, because she was truly beginning to see the pull the place had.

Rafe says it's as far as you can get from a desert without living on an iceberg.

Quinn had told her that, back when she'd been trying to talk him out of staying.

She corralled her memories once more, thinking more than ever that Focus had been the right call name for her. She'd made a career and built Foxworth on her ability to do just that, but now...

"Are you from Seattle?" That seemed innocent enough.

"No. I'm from Tumwater. That's down south," he explained.

And very close to the capital of Olympia. Not for nothing had she studied the map before getting here. She thought back over the research Ty had done. Hadn't Ogilvie himself also claimed the distinctively named town as his home? Hadn't he even gone back there, after they'd taken him down? Was he perhaps a friend? Had that been how Cort had gotten the job, through Ogilvie to Flood?

"I think I've heard of it," she said, going for her best trying-to-remember tone. "Didn't somebody famous come from there?"

"Olympia Beer," Cort said with the best smile she'd seen from him.

Charlie laughed, but inside she was thinking how hard it must be for him to be away from his wife right now. She gave herself an inward shake, telling herself she couldn't let sympathy divert her course.

"Focus, this is Data," came Ty's voice in her ear. "The gov left that town before your guy was born, and your guy was still in the military when he came running back."

And that is why you got that big raise, my friend.

"Hometowns aside," she said to signal she'd gotten the message, "how did you get roped into playing taxi driver?"

"I don't mind. It's better than listening to—" He cut himself off sharply.

"Relax," Charlie said with a smile. "All that political yammering bores me to tears, too."

That got her another wide smile. Cort went silent then,

his expression looking as if he were thinking. Thinking hard. She occasionally glanced into the side-view mirror, but only once caught a glimpse, several vehicles back, of what she thought might be her brother's dark blue SUV that he'd left on this side. She mused for a moment about the vehicle juggling that was apparently part of life here, mainly so she wouldn't be thinking about the vehicle she hadn't seen even a trace of, Rafe's silver coupe.

They'd nearly gotten to the hotel when, stopped at a red light, Cort looked at her.

"I know you're…involved with Senator Flood. In a relationship with him, I mean."

Something in his voice made Charlie answer very carefully. "I don't know if I'd call it that. It's too new. For me, at least."

"Oh." Again he went quiet. But when they arrived at the subterranean parking structure and pulled to a halt at the entrance to the hotel, he turned to look at her again.

"Look, don't take this wrong, but…be careful." Charlie tilted her head, waiting, hoping her silence would draw more out of the man. "I only meant," he started again, clearly worried now that he'd gone too far, "things aren't always what they seem."

"I think with politicians, that's mostly a given," Charlie said dryly, and a look of relief flashed across Cort's face. "Heard some things, have you?"

"I… Some."

"That happens, when to them you're just a tool to be used and ignored otherwise." She knew that one had hit home by the flash of irritation in the man's eyes. And that made her decide to take a calculated risk. "They are a pretty ruthless bunch," she said.

"Yes." Cort sounded relieved, as if he were glad Charlie

understood. "They tend to assume they can get away with anything. It's like they think they're…"

"Invulnerable? Untouchable?"

"Exactly," Cort said.

Charlie kept her gaze unwaveringly on the man's face, watching for any reaction at all as she said, "I think they're where the phrase 'Getting away with murder' originated."

Those bright green eyes widened. Not in shock, but almost in relief. As if he were indeed relieved that he didn't have to explain what he'd meant. It wasn't concrete evidence, but Charlie's brain and gut were in agreement; it was as close as confirmation as they would get. This meeting was with Ogilvie.

Flood was in a private meeting with a murderer.

Chapter 24

So Flood was meeting with Ogilvie.

Rafe knew there was still a chance that the presence of Ogilvie's man at the hotel was a coincidence, but after hearing this his gut screamed it was the truth.

Just as Charlie's apparently did.

It was hardly a surprise, a murderer and a would-be murderer having a meeting. Given what Flood had done in the Reynosa case, facilitating the death of that witness and if necessary the Americans protecting him, meeting with a man who'd successfully done the same with an opposing candidate was nothing unusual.

The question was, what did Ogilvie think Flood could do for him? He already had a team of attorneys who'd managed to keep him out of prison for well over a year, nearly two, by doing that legal dance they did so well, using any and every delaying tactic known to the profession.

They'd known from the beginning that the destruction

of his reputation and future prospects, and perhaps a slap on the wrist from the courts, might well be the only price the former governor would ever pay. And given the man's pride and what had been grandiose future plans, perhaps it was enough.

But it also had become obvious to anyone with a functioning brain that he was stalling, desperately. Because Brett Dunbar's case had been rock-solid, and no matter what they threw at him the detective never wavered. The man had more integrity than they could ever destroy, and they had tried. In the court of public opinion, the most important from a slippery politician's point of view, he'd already been convicted. And it had cost him everything he treasured most.

Funny, Ogilvie had succeeded in having someone murdered, Flood had tried and failed, yet in this moment Rafe wanted Flood more. Ogilvie had been a case, yes, but Flood was…personal. If the cartel he sold them out to had had more notice, or been more efficient on foreign soil, they would all be dead. And none of what Foxworth had accomplished in the three years since would have happened.

Then there was Cutter. He never would have gotten to know the incredible animal that even he, the most pragmatic of realists, had had to admit was special. Uncanny. And a few other words he never in his life would have expected to be using about a dog.

The dog he now knew would be his, if something horrible happened to Quinn and Hayley. And if the worst were ever to happen, there was nothing that would convince him to go on more than that dog. Which Quinn and Hayley obviously knew.

And here and now…there was Charlie. Making this case even more imperative. And yeah, personal.

He heard the sound of a car door opening, then a few

seconds later heard it again. He supposed the man had gone around to open her door for her, since she thanked him.

"You'll be going to see to Max, now?" she asked.

"Actually, no. I'm to wait here until he gets back to the hotel."

Back? Rafe straightened sharply. And in his ear he heard Teague swear. "He slipped past us."

"You couldn't cover it all." Quinn clearly wasn't happy, but just as clearly didn't blame the two men trying to cover the entire hotel.

Rafe listened to the background noise change as they went inside. Then again as they reached the elevator, with at least two other people. There was no further conversation between them, other than a brief exchange where Charlie told Ducane he didn't have to take her all the way to the door, and him replying those were his orders.

The background changed again as they stepped out of the elevator, clearly alone now. But still no exchange of words until they reached the door of Flood's suite. Rafe heard the sound of rustling, then the click of a door unlocking.

"Here we are," Charlie said, "so mission accomplished."

"Yes, Ms. Marshal."

"I really can't get you to use my first name, can I?"

There was a brief pause before he heard a low, respectful, "Have a good day, Ms. Marshal."

There was the sound of the room door closing. "So, here I am, all alone," Charlie said, as if to herself.

"Four to Focus, it's still clear," Liam said. "I slipped in when you were in transit and swept the room."

"Thanks, Four," she said, normally now.

So Flood still wasn't having his own suite monitored. Rafe wasn't sure if that was because he was confident of his cover, thought no one would dare, or just made sure nothing suspect was ever said in the rooms. He'd half expected him to at least have Charlie's room bugged, but apparently not, because Liam's little gadgets weren't just top-of-the-line, they were groundbreaking. And Foxworth's alone.

Did that mean he trusted "Lita" that much already? Or did he simply have that much faith in his facade and assume she would never see through it? Or would never look, because he was such a prize?

Underestimate her at your peril.

One corner of his mouth twitched as he thought the words. Because if nothing else, and despite all that had happened between them, he had never, ever doubted that Charlie would not be easily fooled. It was why he'd known that in time she'd see him for what he was, and that if he didn't walk away, eventually she would.

And if she ever found out the truth, she'd hate him for it.

She already hates you. But at least she doesn't know how much you deserve it.

"He was relieved. I could see it in his face, he was relieved I had the measure of the man," Charlie said now.

"So how long before he starts to wonder why you're with the bastard?" Quinn asked.

"He already knows I'm being…cautious."

I know you're…involved with Senator Flood. In a relationship with him, I mean.

I don't know if I'd call it that. It's too new. For me, at least.

He shoved the memory of that exchange aside as he pulled into the parking garage beneath the hotel. Went back to a question that had occurred to him earlier. And asked, without aiming the question at any one person, "So sending him to get Focus… Was he worried about her, or was it about getting him out of the way?"

"I'd say both," Hayley said. "But probably more keeping him in the dark. The subject only hired him a couple of months ago, so he probably doesn't trust him enough to have him know the whole truth, at least not yet."

"Good call," Charlie said, sounding a bit sour. "Even he has to know you can only buy so much loyalty. And I could see by my chauffeur's expression that deep down he knows he's scum. He just doesn't know how bad he is."

"And he doesn't have the option to walk away like he once might have had," Hayley added. "Not with his wife's situation."

"So, y'all, can we guess why the subject would want him gone at this particular moment?" Liam's drawl became exaggerated when he was being sarcastic.

Rafe knew of one reason, and it wasn't Charlie's— Lita's—welfare. It was because Ducane was from here and would likely recognize the disgraced former governor by both sight and name.

"One and Two, we're back on-site," Quinn said, reminding him he hadn't done that.

"Five, same. With…" He realized they had never really given Cutter a call name.

"We could use Fuzzball," Hayley said, in that tone that was just a little too sweet. "That way we'd have Focus, Five and Fuzzball, all together, one happy family."

He didn't miss the point she'd made, leaving the other "F" out of the combo. Normally he'd let it ride, but as was usual for him when it came to anything connected to Charlie, he couldn't. But he could try for humor, as if it meant nothing. Couldn't he?

"Four, are they ignoring you?" he said.

"Leave me out of it," Liam came back quickly, almost pleadingly.

Rafe wanted to roll his eyes and let out another word that

started with the same letter, but they were live on comms and he couldn't, wouldn't.

He heard a sound he immediately recognized as a Foxworth phone signaling a text message, but since it had come through the earpiece he didn't know whose phone it was, other than not his. A moment later Quinn spoke, answering that question.

"Data thinks he knows where they are. He found a car rental arranged by the hotel concierge, at about the right time, and in the name of the subject's aide. He got into the vehicle's GPS and has the location where it has been stationary for a couple of hours. In Tacoma."

"Which is conveniently about halfway between Seattle and Tumwater," Hayley said.

"Data's already going into our old files, in case the gov is still driving the same vehicle he had back then, to see if he can get into it, too," Quinn said.

"Focus, are we paying him enough?" Hayley asked.

"He says more than," Charlie answered, smiling at the question. "But that may be because of the big raise I just gave him."

"Good," Quinn said, "because he just came back with results already. Apparently it's the same car he had on our case."

Couldn't afford a new one with all the legal bills, I hope. Rafe's thought again told him how personal this one was; he usually didn't get vindictive, once the client had been taken care of.

Of course, this time the client was Foxworth.

"And he says he's done with the photo, too." Hayley this time. "New one is in place at all sites that had the old one. I looked, and it's good. Very close, but she has short hair and a bigger nose."

It took him a moment to figure out that she'd acted on

what he'd said when they were…fighting. Again. Always. She'd shown no sign then that she thought he might have a point, but yet she'd taken action. He wasn't sure how that made him feel.

"Since nobody's here at the moment, I'm going to look around a bit."

Charlie's voice came through as nonchalantly as if she'd said she was going to look out the window. Rafe had to clench his teeth to keep from blurting out an order not to. Just because Flood was apparently in Tacoma didn't mean someone else wouldn't show up at any moment. They didn't know for sure where Brown was, for one, and until they knew that for certain, she damn well should be more careful.

But he'd been recently reminded of how well she took autocratic orders. Especially from him.

"They're moving." Quinn's voice broke in on his thoughts. "Leaving Tacoma. According to Data, each headed back the way they came. Focus, according to traffic, you've got half an hour, thirty-five max."

"Copy. No papers left behind that I can see. I presume anything crucial is in that lockable case he makes his aide lug around."

Silence stretched out, although he could hear some rustling. As if Charlie were moving things, doing a real search. And if someone Flood had left behind walked in on her…

"Well, now I know that in private he's a slob," came her voice, with a wry note in it. "This bedroom's a mess."

"Probably used to having people pick up after him," Hayley said, in much the same tone.

Rafe heard the exchange clearly, registering the likely truth of Hayley's guess even as he tried to deny the blast of relief he felt that Charlie truly hadn't known this about their target.

Another long stretch of silence except for a bit more rustling. When they reached the half-hour point, he was wondering what else she could possibly be doing.

"Pockets and drawers are a bust as well. I'm going to—"

"Three to Focus, get clear. You've got incoming." Teague's voice was sharp with warning.

The split second before she said, "Copy," felt like much longer.

"It's the aide," Teague said, and Rafe wasn't really surprised Flood had left Brown behind to watch things. Probably including his Lita. "He's on the phone, heading for you pretty fast."

The silence before she said, "I'm back in my room," felt like the longest of his life. "Is he still on the phone?"

"Yes," Teague answered. "And at the door now."

"Hold traffic, please. I'm going to try and listen before he realizes I'm here."

Rafe heard a slight click, guessed it was Charlie opening her bedroom door. Then, in the background, he heard a male voice, in what was clearly one side of a conversation.

"—remember that, with the governor. And over there is where they found the body?"

There was no sound of a reaction from Charlie, but Rafe's gut knotted up enough for both of them. She needed to get out of there, but he knew she wouldn't. She was just too damned stubborn.

Then came the words that clinched it, for him, anyway.

"You think it's the same Foxworth we ran afoul of? Yes, I'll look into that right away."

The faint click told him she'd closed the door. And that she knew they'd heard what they needed to hear.

They knew now that Ogilvie had told Flood that the

Foxworth Foundation had been instrumental in taking him down and destroying his career and reputation. And that their Northwest office was in the very place Lita had gone to visit. The same area where Ogilvie had buried the body of the political opponent he'd had murdered.

From there it was a short jump to connect them to his own failed effort three years ago. It was a fairly distinctive name. So no matter how low a profile they tried to keep, thanks to the media and the internet, enough information was out there that Flood would eventually be able to verify the same Foxworth had foiled the cartel in their effort to murder the one man brave enough to testify against them. Ironically, only the fact that Vicente had, in the end, testified and the cartel had been taken down had allowed Flood to survive and keep his position—and the buckets of cash they'd paid him to get his government colleagues to look the other way.

But most of all, what they had just heard was tantamount to an admission that Flood had indeed been the one behind that fiasco three years ago. That he truly was the mole they had been hunting all this time. They'd had little doubt left, but that little bit had been blasted away now.

And now they had to assume he'd soon know for sure they were the same Foxworth. The ones that stood against everything he dealt in: bribery, collusion, influence peddling…and selling out his own country. Not to mention soliciting the murder of American citizens.

And if Flood—or Brown—dug deep enough, long enough, he might just find something. Ty had replaced the recognizable photo, but the internet was forever. And although the chance was slim, any chance was too much for Rafe.

He knew Charlie would say Flood could never put it together in time to stop them. He also knew the timing didn't matter, not to him. Because once Charlie was in Flood's crosshairs, all that was left was to pull the trigger. He had no doubt the self-preservationist Flood would do just that. Quite literally if necessary.

It was one thing when he or Quinn or the others risked their lives. They were trained for it. Charlie's genius was in other areas, involving numbers and finance. And Rafe knew, as they all knew, that if they lost Charlie, they'd lose the very foundation of Foxworth, the one person who enabled them to do what they did, to fight the fight they fought, to do the good they did.

They should pull her out. Except she'd never do it. This was as close as they'd gotten, as they would likely ever get. She might be a numbers person and not a field operative, but she would never quit, not on this. Even if it meant risking her life.

As for what he personally would lose if Flood succeeded...

Nothing you didn't already throw away, Crawford.

But he would not let it happen. If it meant he had to take Flood out himself, so be it. After all, that's what he did. Why they kept him around.

The fact that he could end up in prison himself did not escape him. But he didn't care. Not when it came to this.

Not when it came to Charlie.

And what that said about him was the one thing he couldn't face.

Chapter 25

Charlie arranged the scene carefully, seating herself at the room's small table, with her feet up on the second chair, and the tablet she'd bought specifically for this trip—she wasn't about to bring a laptop Flood or his minion might be tempted to snoop into—open to a reading app and showing her halfway through a current bestseller she frankly didn't think much of.

But she wasn't reading. Her mind was racing as she stared unseeingly at the words on the screen. They couldn't suspect she was connected to Foxworth, at least not yet. And there truly wasn't much out there about her, her distaste for the limelight had seen to that. And Ty had now changed what few pictures of her were out there. Sure, somebody could dig into the Wayback Machine and find the originals, but it would take time for the idea to even occur.

So she had time. She didn't have to bail, not just yet. But maybe soon. She had to find the proof they needed before that happened.

The tap she'd expected came on the bedroom door. "Yes?" she called out.

It opened, and Brown stood there. She gave him her best smile. "Alec, hello. Is Max back?"

"On the way," the man said, and she didn't miss the way he'd scanned both her and the room as he said it.

"Oh, good. I hope his meeting went well."

"Yes and no. He's a little…edgy, so I'd tread carefully, if I were you."

Thankfully you are not. "Thanks for the heads-up. I know he deals with such big things, it must be nearly overwhelming sometimes."

"Only when he has to do business with people who don't know who they're dealing with," Brown said, and there was no mistaking the acid edge in his voice. The tone reminded her of when she'd overheard that brief exchange before they'd left St. Louis.

We don't want to have to take another chance like we did before.

That was an emergency. It required extreme measures.

Brown had had the same edge in his voice then—although Flood had been calm to the point of being blasé with his answer—as he had now, and she had no idea why either time. And she didn't like not knowing.

Ogilvie had clearly told Flood about Foxworth's involvement in his downfall, and they had to assume Flood had remembered the name from his own experience, even if it hadn't involved him firsthand. But had Ogilvie told him because Flood had great influence, or because he knew about Flood's prior encounter with them and so they had a common enemy?

Her best guess was that Ogilvie had been asking for Flood's help with his defense, perhaps asking him to look into Foxworth in an effort to discredit them and their part in his arrest.

Good luck with that. It wasn't ego that made her think that, it was the simple fact that Foxworth ever and always made absolutely sure of their footing before they took aim and fired, as Quinn put it.

"He's told me you've been with him for years. I admire your loyalty," she said to Brown, wondering what tale Flood had spun to so completely win over the man. Or perhaps they were both cut from the same cloth, and that's all Brown needed to know. She had the feeling that if she ever heard them discussing long-term goals, their aims would probably turn her stomach. "Are you sorry he left the Senate?"

Brown looked at her for a moment, as if pondering if he should answer. Finally he shrugged and said, "He can get more done this way."

By circumventing the process? I'll bet.

She watched him go and for a moment simply stayed where she was, her mind racing. So many pieces had tumbled together in the last hour she wasn't sure where to start. How on earth did Quinn and the others make decisions when they were in the field and had to act fast, had to make those decisions on the fly, and sometimes without much concrete information or evidence?

Once more her mind flashed back to when Quinn had told her he'd found Rafe and wanted to hire him. Before she'd seen the tall, rangy, impossibly appealing—to her, anyway—man their childhood friend had become.

"Do we really need...a sniper?" she'd asked, then immediately regretted it; after all, the man had saved her brother's life by being just that.

Quinn, knowing her well, had cut through to her real doubts. "He made decisions, to pull the trigger, that ended with him killing people. Right decisions, in combat, against an enemy, as he was ordered. And that doesn't bother him. But he made two bad ones, in his mind, anyway. I disagree, but the fact that they haunt him to this day tells me what I need to know about him."

"Bad decisions?"

"Once it was based on faulty intel on where a couple of terrorist leaders were holed up. He thinks he should have guessed it was wrong. The real bad guys came up behind them and killed a couple of the team before he could shift and take them out, and he blames himself."

"But if that's what the intelligence he was given said…"

"Exactly. Not his fault."

"What was the second time?"

"Following an order to shoot he suspected was a mistake, that it was the wrong target, but he followed it anyway. Turned out to be a woman trying to get away with her child. Kid wasn't hit but the mother was."

She remembered even now how awful that story had made her feel. And learning later that the mother had survived she was sure hadn't changed Rafe's reaction much. A memory had popped into her mind, of the skinny, lanky boy they'd once known, quiet even then, but ever and always watchful. And even then, those stormy gray eyes of his had made her feel as if he were seeing more than just what was before him. That had never changed.

And once he'd seen what he needed to see, he'd make his decision and take the action he'd decided on. Even as a kid, he'd done that. And now, here she was struggling with making the simplest of decisions, like what to do next.

She didn't think Brown suspected her of anything, not really. Flood had warned her when he'd first introduced them that the man required a great deal of time and experience with someone before he would trust them. She'd merely nodded and said, "Sounds wise."

And had meant it, which Flood had clearly seen because he'd given her that approving smile that reminded her of nothing less than a school teacher smiling at a pupil who'd given a right answer. It wasn't the first time she'd sensed he was testing her, but that was when it had first occurred to her that he was, in essence, schooling her. For a life with him? Or simply how to not cause him any problems?

"Three to Five, you're on scene?" Teague's voice in her ear brought her out of her assessing. Irritation sparked through her when she realized she was holding her breath, waiting for the response, the sound of Rafe's voice.

"East side." She took a breath. "With… Fuzzball sidekick."

"You sure you're not the sidekick?" came Liam's drawl.

"Pretty sure I am."

For a moment Charlie just stood there, marveling at the simple, teasing exchange she'd just heard. Hayley had told her that Rafe tolerated Liam better than anyone, probably because the young Texan simply refused to get ruffled or irritated at his taciturnity. She'd once known that Rafe. Once upon a time, he had unbent with her enough to make her laugh out loud with his wry and unexpectedly humorous observations on just about anything.

Once upon a time.

And it had been as fleeting, or as unreal, as the fairy tale those words implied. Three months of a bliss she'd never expected to find, a kind of joy she'd thought had died in her when her parents had been blown up by a terrorist bomb, an interlude that had made surviving worth it.

And he had thrown it away.

The bottom line never changed, no matter how often

she thought about it, or how long she managed to go without thinking about it.

"—spotted his security just outside the main entrance. Waiting for the subject no doubt, but Data says he's still a good fifteen minutes out, maybe more with the traffic he's seeing. Might be a chance to work him a bit."

"Copy. En route."

"With the sidekick?" Liam asked. "Always a good ice-breaker."

"With Fuzzball," Rafe confirmed, then added, "If I leave him in my car, he's likely to drive off with it."

She smiled, but with a small sense of shock at the continued joking. And then a feeling of warmth. Clearly he felt comfortable enough here to let the humor that had once so startled her emerge. Despite it all, what had happened—and not happened—between them, she had never wished Rafe ill, even though she didn't understand why he'd done it.

Did you never think that maybe he thought he wasn't enough for you?

Quinn's words echoed in her mind now. And the answer was still the same. It had never occurred to her that he'd walked—hell, run—away because he didn't think he was enough for her.

She knew she had a bit of a reputation. Yes, she was smart, and didn't think it was ego but only fact to add a "very" in front of that. She was very good at what she did, and had always had to work at having patience with others who didn't or couldn't see what was so obvious to her. She'd found a way to deal, by trying to find out what others were good at, like her brother's tactical skill, dedication and courage, or Ty's tech genius, and focus—that word again—on that.

With Rafe, when they'd connected after all those years since childhood, she'd started out knowing that he was among the very best at what he did. What she hadn't known, had never expected, was that he made her pulse race and her heart give an odd little flutter every time she saw him. And when he'd eventually let that sense of humor show, she'd been beyond charmed, she'd been head over heels. And that was something that had never happened to her, before or since. Nor would it ever again. She wouldn't be a fool twice.

But she would find out why.

Chapter 26

Rafe saw Ducane's gaze shift from him to Cutter, then back again. Damn it, the guy's eyes really were an unusually bright green. He steadied himself inwardly, knowing he was going to have to use a tactic he rarely did. He was going to have to talk to the guy.

"He yours?" Ducane asked.

"My boss's." He let his mouth quirk slightly. "Both my bosses, actually."

"You've got two?"

He nodded. "Best people a guy could ever work for."

Ducane frowned. "So you don't work for the hotel?"

"Only temporarily. Helping out. Along with my side-kick here." He nodded down at Cutter.

"Seen dogs sort of like him," Ducane said, studying the animal, who looked back at him steadily.

"Only less fluffy?" Rafe suggested.

Ducane smiled at that. And as if the smile were a cue, Cutter stepped forward, nudging the man's hand. As most people instinctively did, Ducane bent and moved to stroke his fingers over the dark head. Rafe immediately shifted his gaze back to the other man's face, waited a silent moment, then saw what he'd expected, that look of bemused wonder.

"Almost scary, isn't it?" he said quietly.

Ducane looked up, met his gaze. "What…?"

"I don't know what it is he's got, only the effect it has." He gave a half shrug, then dived ahead with a truth he'd given up denying early on when it came to this dog. "Sometimes, I'm not even aware I'm feeling bad until he does that and makes me pet him."

Rafe heard a sound in his ear, but it wasn't a word and he couldn't be sure who'd made it.

"So you're saying he knows, even if you don't?" Ducane asked.

"Exactly."

"So he's what, some kind of therapy dog?"

"Not just that. Name anything you'd want a dog to be, and he's it. Soothing, intuitive, devilishly clever, goofily funny and, when necessary, deadly serious."

In the pause while Ducane absorbed this, Hayley said cheerfully, "Nice. Cutter in a nutshell."

"Serious like when he was playing guardian at the gate the last couple of days?"

"Exactly. You do not want to cross him when he's working."

"Ex-MWD?"

"Don't know. He just kind of dropped in out of nowhere and stayed." *And we've all been the better for it.*

Ducane looked back at him. "So, these people you work for, you really…like them?"

"I do. And admire and respect them." He studied the other man for a moment, then went for it. "Everything and everyone you wish others would stand and fight for, they do."

Ducane's expression only flickered for an instant, but Rafe knew what he'd seen. Distaste. So he knew his own boss was far less than that. Maybe he even knew he was the exact opposite, fighting only for himself. But did he know how little Flood cared about anyone else who might get hurt—or killed—in the process? Did he know he himself would be jettisoned easily and without second thoughts if Flood so decided?

"Nice," Ducane said.

"If you're in a bad situation because you had no choice, or you're in the right but up against impossible odds or unbeatable forces, they'll find a way to make it right. Maybe not the way you imagined, but in a way that's undeniable."

Ducane was listening intently. "What if it's a situation that…can't be fixed?"

"His wife," Hayley said instantly, warning him to tread carefully.

"They're not miracle workers, although sometimes it seems like it. But they will take whatever it is and make it as easy as is possible."

"What if it's…inherently unbearable?"

"Then they'll help get you to the other side." He purposely said the "you" as if he meant it specifically, as he indeed did. "Even if it's only to remove every other worry you have."

Ducane let out a harsh sound that was half laughing, half despairing. Rafe recognized the tone, he'd heard it in his own voice, back before Quinn had found him and pulled him out of it. Teetering on the edge of despair.

Rafe wished he could ask Hayley for help. She was the genius at reading people, at knowing when to push and when to back off. Even as he thought it, her voice came through his earpiece.

"Give him something, something you have in common."

"Merland," Charlie said suddenly, unexpectedly.

Rafe was stunned for a moment. He'd almost forgotten he'd told her about the officer who'd passed on intel without vetting it, that had led to the deaths of two men he'd been handling overwatch for.

That he still felt responsible for.

But she was right. It was a door, and it felt like the right one, with this man.

"I had to take an order from an incompetent ass once," he began, then grimaced before going on. "Well, more than once, but this time it cost the lives of two good men I was responsible for. When I got back to base, I wanted more than anything to hunt him down and send him to join them."

Ducane's gaze sharpened. "Did you?"

"No. He wasn't worth ending up in Leavenworth for. But I did stand as a witness against him, and got to watch Mr. High-and-Mighty-Privilege go down in flames and shame. It was worth it. The boss doesn't always win. Even with power behind them."

Ducane shook his head slowly. Rafe saw the despair creeping into his expression. In that moment Cutter moved again, and the anguish faded a little as the man stroked the animal. After a moment, clearly steadier now, he looked up at Rafe again.

"What if that job for...that person, was the only one that would pay what you needed?"

Ducane wasn't even trying to hide it now; this was personal, this was him and he was letting it show.

A new voice came through. Gavin. "You've got his attention, Rafe. Now offer him the bait, but slowly." If anyone would know about that, it was Gavin de Marco. They'd called out the troops to help. For which he was grateful; this was not the pond—or swamp—he usually swam in.

"Talk to him the way someone would have to talk to you, to get you to listen," Quinn put in.

Like you did, when you pulled me out of the pit?

Quinn had been utterly calm back then, not pushing but merely offering another path, and promising he would be there every step of the way. Without the background he and Quinn had had together, the basis of trust, he'd have to be a little more careful, but…

"Is he really the only one?" Rafe asked Ducane.

The man let out an audible breath. "I needed to move fast. There were…things I had to do, to pay for." He seemed to realize suddenly how that could sound, and quickly added, "Nothing illicit, I just… It was personal."

"So your employer was the only one you could find in a hurry who would pay what you needed."

Ducane nodded.

"And now that you've been working for him a while, what do you think of him?" The man shrugged, giving a half shake of his head. Guessing he was still wary of saying what he really thought, Rafe did it for him. "Personally, I don't like him much. I don't know if it's the slippery slime of the swamp, or the smell of it that puts me off."

Ducane's gaze shot back to his face. "It clings, doesn't it," he said, almost in a whisper.

"It does. Now my boss, he's solid gold. Even if he was Army."

"He was?"

"Ranger. But I don't hold it against him. Just rag on him now and then."

A brief grin flashed across Ducane's face. Which seemed the right moment to make the final strike. And he found he really, really didn't want to blow this. He felt for the guy, and he wanted to help him out of this mess. Especially before Foxworth took it all down.

"You want out of that swamp, Ducane?"

His expression gave the true answer, but he shook his head. "Can't afford it."

"Don't be so sure."

"You don't understand. There's more to it."

Yes, there was. And it was something he couldn't let Ducane know, that he already knew about his wife. Just as he couldn't speak the name Foxworth, the one thing that might convince the man, given he was local and had probably heard of them during the Ogilvie chaos.

But it also might give away the entire operation here and now, and before they had Flood nailed.

"They're on our street now," Liam warned in his ear.

Over Ducane's shoulder he saw Brown coming out the hotel's main doors. The man glanced toward them, flicked his gaze to Cutter and stared for a moment with his brow furrowed. Rafe's breath caught. Recognition, yes, but... more puzzlement.

It made him uneasy, because they still didn't know why Flood had told Brown to stay here. They'd figured Flood went dressed in ordinary, casual clothes as a sort of disguise, given he was usually dressed up to the hilt, but they hadn't expected him to go alone. The only reasons that made sense were that this meeting was strictly personal, or too clandestine even for the trusted aide, or... Flood didn't trust either his own security or his new lady, and had left the only one he did trust to watch. And if it was the latter, it only meant one thing to Rafe—Charlie's position was indeed precarious.

Then Brown turned away, to look toward the street entrance to the garage. In almost the same instant Rafe heard Liam again. "They're almost to the driveway."

Rafe grabbed the few seconds he had left to hand Ducane a card, on which was printed only a phone number, a special Foxworth phone number, the otherwise blank cards printed for exactly this kind of situation. Then, as he spotted the rental car approaching, he spoke, as seriously and convincingly as he could.

"We can find you a way out of that trap you're in."

Ducane gave a sad shake of his head. "It's hopeless."

Doing something he almost never did, Rafe acted on impulse, reaching out and grasping the man's shoulder as he spoke one last time, almost solemnly.

"Hopeless is what we do best."

Chapter 27

Charlie sat on the edge of the bed, forcing herself to take deep, calming breaths. She didn't need to compose herself because Flood was on his way back, she was ready for that. Eager for it, in fact. She wanted this case over and done, wanted the man disgraced, publicly vilified and hopefully locked up.

No, she needed to compose herself because she'd just heard compelling and undeniable evidence of how much Rafer Crawford had changed since that day Quinn had brought him into the office in St. Louis. He'd been hesitant, uncertain about what his place might be in this foundation his childhood neighbors had begun. And, she'd sensed even then, more uncertain that he could fit in at all.

While you sat there and stared at that tall, lean, powerful guy with the impossible stormy gray eyes and wondered how the gangly kid you remembered had turned into such a hunk of gorgeousness.

She'd never had that kind of reaction before. She'd seen

it before—and uncomfortably often aimed at her little brother—in other women, but had thought herself immune.

Boy, had she been wrong. It had taken her a while to get past always connecting him to that kid she'd known, but reading through the military record they'd pulled, remembering what Quinn had told her about him being the sniper who had saved his life and the lives of his platoon, seeing his name on that world-famous trophy, helped.

But a few times watching him move, looking into those eyes, feeling the incredible warmth when he gave her one of those rare smiles... Yes, those things pushed her way beyond the boy from down the street.

And now she knew just how deeply he was embedded in Foxworth, not only the workings but the philosophy. When he'd spoken to Cort, the pure truth and, yes, passion in his voice had been clear. He not only completely believed in what they were doing, he'd allowed it to show when he approached the man. He'd played it perfectly, and that was something she had to admit she wouldn't have thought he had in him.

Because he'd been such a blunt weapon with you? Because of that you assumed he couldn't deal with anyone subtly or carefully?

She stood up abruptly, knowing she had to prepare for Flood's return. But then what Quinn had said rammed into her mind, distracting her yet again.

...how do you explain the way he reacts around you? The way he reacts to just seeing you on a video call? Hell, the way he reacts when he just hears your name? That's not somebody who doesn't care.

Was that it? Had he been so abrupt, so cold when he'd walked away, because he cared...too much? But if that were true, why had he walked away at all? If—

The sound of voices—including that smooth, well-oiled

one that made her skin crawl—from the main room of the suite yanked her back to reality.

Focus, indeed. Before you blow this whole thing.

"Subject has arrived," she said quietly.

And she settled in to play the part of a woman blind enough to be fooled by the likes of Maximilian Flood. But what she heard when she again quietly opened the bedroom door stopped her in her tracks.

"—saw that Ducane was pretty deep in conversation with that hotel security guy with the dog."

"Was he, now," Flood said, in that tone she'd come to know meant he was adding new factors to his never-ending calculations. Calculations that were always about what impact something new might have on him personally, the rest of the world be damned.

Charlie heard Quinn mutter something and whispered back, "I'm going to try and cover for them." She shut the door behind her quietly, so she could say she'd been on this side of it, not eavesdropping.

"He's still here?" she asked brightly as she walked toward the two men. "I thought maybe he—and the dog—were hired on just for you, Max."

Flood turned to look at her, smiling that smile she didn't believe was any more than one layer of skin deep. "Perhaps they're to be here until we leave."

"That makes sense." She smiled. "Cort knows him, or at least of him. That must be why they were chatting." Both men's gazes narrowed, and she went on cheerfully. "I gather he's rather famous in military circles. Won some trophy or other a couple of times."

The furrow in Flood's brow cleared. "I see. Been chatting a bit with Ducane yourself?"

She let out a little laugh. "Chat? Hardly. He treats me with kid gloves. On your orders, I presume." Flood smiled again. "I did ask him, though. Because the dog caught my attention."

His smile widened. "So you like dogs?"

"Love them," she said earnestly. *Especially that one, who has saved the day so many times. And tries so hard to get through to that stubborn partner of his...*

"Then we'll have to get one, eventually. It's always good PR."

How like him, to think of it that way. Trot the dog out for photo opportunities, then shove him back in the shadows until the next time. But then, that so often seemed the way politicians did it, up to and including presidents.

Of course the bigger point in what he'd said was that "we" part.

"Are you hungry?" he asked. "Would you like to get a late lunch?"

"You didn't eat at your meeting?"

Something flickered in his eyes, as if the thought of the meeting irritated him. "I was not hungry," he answered, and the same emotion sounded in his voice. She was a little surprised he let it show, and hoped it was a sign he trusted her.

"I am hungry," she said, weighing the options. "Heather and I didn't eat, either. We were too busy reminiscing."

He smiled indulgently. "Then let's go downstairs. I hope you don't mind if Alec joins us? We need to discuss the logistics of our return trip."

"Of course not," she said, although the guy made her edgy. As did the words about the return trip. She knew Quinn would have her back until this was done, following them wherever, and that they'd pull in everybody from all their locations if necessary. But she wanted this *over*. Three years was long enough for Flood to have gotten away with this.

"Let me just clean up a bit, then," he said, and headed for his room of the suite.

Charlie took the first deep breath she'd allowed herself since she'd stepped out of the bedroom.

"Nicely done, Focus," Hayley said in her ear.

"Agreed," Quinn added. "Cover for both security man and Five."

"I'm not so sure I convinced the aide," she whispered. "He still looks suspicious. But then, he always does."

Brown was busy on his phone. Not texting, he was doing more reading. But she didn't like the glance he gave her as she wandered that way. She kept going past him, toward the large windows of the suite that faced toward the water, as if that had been her goal all along. But she didn't miss how he turned the phone so she could not get even a glimpse of what he was doing. He'd often done the same with his laptop, either quickly closed what he was working on or slapped the lid down any time she got anywhere close, even though she'd made no effort to see.

Not that she hadn't wanted to spy. The very way he acted made her curious. She herself was careful, but Brown carried it to the point where the word that popped into her mind was paranoid. Maybe that was his job, to be paranoid on behalf of his boss. Flood didn't come off that way. Maybe this was why—he had his aide do it for him.

She stared out through the glass, across the buildings of the city, and the expanse of Puget Sound beyond. At home if she looked out a window toward water, it was the Mississippi in the distance. From the office it was the Gateway Arch. Ironic, she supposed, that she worked in the shadow of that monument called the Gateway to the West, yet so rarely headed that way. But now she was here, less than a hundred miles as the crow—or the eagle, as Hayley would put it—flies from the Pacific, and she couldn't deny the pull of it.

She saw smaller boats here and there, and to the north two

of the iconic green and white ferries, passing each other on their journeys east and west. She found herself envying the people on the westbound ones, knowing where they would land, not too far from the Foxworth Northwest headquarters.

What is it about this place? Quinn, then Rafe... What kind of hold did it get on people?

It was a puzzle. Especially since she, the quintessential big-city girl, was feeling it, too.

The restaurant in the hotel wasn't crowded, although she had the feeling if it had been there would have been a table found for them, anyway. Most places that catered to people of Flood's standing made sure there was always a prime spot available.

Throughout the meal, she felt as if she were trying to pick her way through a minefield. Flood seemed on edge, and Brown more so. But Brown had always been worse at hiding his feelings. Finally she worked up her most concerned expression before asking, "Did your meeting not go well, Max? You seem a little glum."

His gaze narrowed for a moment, but then he shook his head. "Just something unexpected," he said.

Considering the man never went into a meeting without knowing exactly what was going to happen and how he would turn it to his advantage, this was a rather amazing admission. As was the fact that he let any concern show at all.

Quinn seemed to have the same thought, because she heard him mutter in her ear, "Didn't think he allowed the unexpected."

He didn't expect any of you to survive the cartel, either. It was all she could do not to smile at the thought. But she put concern in her voice when she spoke.

"Will it be a problem for you?"

And that quickly he was back to his polished self. "I won't let it be. I'll have a solution before we leave."

"If you need to stay longer," she began, almost hoping he'd say yes. She wanted this to go down here, on her brother's home turf.

Not because Rafe was here.

Her words got her a wide smile. "I may. There are… some details to work out. And someone awaiting a decision from me."

That sparked her sometimes overactive curiosity, but she said only, "That's fine. I've been thinking I'd like to see more of the area, so I'm sure I can stay occupied while you handle what you need to handle."

"You're so understanding, Lita dear."

Oh, I understand. More than you know. But you will. Soon.

As they finished the meal off with some rather fluffy coffee drinks, he surprised her. "We should see some of the sights now. You feel up to a walk?"

She hadn't expected that. And if she had to bet, she'd say they'd encounter some sort of news media outside. Flood would want to make one last splash before he left. Perhaps that was what Brown had been working on upstairs, leaking that the Senator would be strolling around downtown.

She managed to smile. "Of course. Any place in particular?"

"Since it's not far, less than a mile, I thought we'd walk down to the Great Wheel."

She tried her best to act as if she'd just brightened up. "The Ferris wheel? Sounds lovely. Isn't the aquarium near there?"

Flood laughed. "I should have known. My lady does have a soft spot for the creatures of the world. Of course, we can do that. It's very close by. I'll call for Ducane to accompany us."

"Let me just run up and change into walking shoes," she said, getting to her feet in an effort to show eagerness.

Flood started to rise. "No, dear, finish your coffee. I'll just do this quickly so we can get going. I read that they have sea otters! I love sea otters."

That seemed to decide him, and he was still smiling as he sat back down. But when she reached the door of the hotel restaurant and glanced back, Brown was getting to his feet. She moved quickly to be out of sight, and then headed at just short of a run toward the elevators while talking.

"Focus, I think he's sending Brown to follow me. Can someone stall him?"

"Got him." Rafe's answer was short and almost lazily certain. He said something else she couldn't hear, and she realized he must be talking to Cutter.

"One, copy. Focus, what's up?"

"Brown doesn't have that locked case with him. I think it's still up in the suite. Now I just need somebody who can pick a lock."

"Four here, I think that'll be me," Liam said, and she could almost hear his grin.

"Go," Quinn said. "Three, watch the approach."

"Copy," Teague said.

"Focus, I'll meet you there," Liam said.

She made it to the elevators, found one that was waiting on the ground floor, stepped inside and quickly pushed the button for the suite's floor. In the couple of moments it took for the doors to slide shut, she saw Brown round the corner, and less than two strides behind him came Cutter, then Rafe.

Try and get past them, Mr. Oh-So-Cool Brown.

Because despite everything, there was one thing she was certain of: if Rafe Crawford was determined to stop you, you'd be stopped.

She knew that firsthand.

Chapter 28

"Got it."

Liam's voice held a touch of triumph even through the earpiece. Rafe considered it well-earned, given he'd gotten into that locked case in just over a minute.

"Yes, I rented the damned car, but there was no accident, and no damage."

Brown, the caretaker of that case, was glaring at him now. And his voice had taken on an edge that matched. To which Cutter reacted with a low sound that was more awareness than threat, but Rafe didn't think Brown realized that. Which was fine with him. He smiled inwardly as the man took a half step away from the dog.

He heard Liam again, a semi-profane exclamation. Then some rustling, and a few clicks.

"A few irrelevant papers, and a flash drive," Charlie said, instantly making sense of the sounds in the background, Liam pulling his ever-present small laptop out of his pack.

Custom built by the man himself, Rafe guessed the thing could run the country if he cut it loose.

He put on his best businesslike voice, letting only a tinge of irritation through, as he thought any qualified security man might at having to deal with something like this.

"I'm sorry, sir, but the rental company says there is. If you'll just step over to the concierge desk, I'm sure this can be straightened out quickly."

"I don't have time for this," Brown snapped. And looked as if he regretted his tone when Cutter made that sound again. "Is that dog of yours under control?"

"That dog will do exactly what he's supposed to do, exactly when he's supposed to do it," Rafe answered, with a smile that succeeded in making Brown look nervous. He left out the part where Cutter sometimes made that decision on his own.

"Five, you're enjoying this too much." Quinn, who had stayed in place to monitor Flood, sounded as if he were smiling himself.

"Hoping you have to take him down?" Teague suggested from his position near Flood's suite, to warn if anyone seemed headed that way.

He couldn't deny he was enjoying it. Brown was exactly the kind of self-important jerk he enjoyed taking down a peg or three. But the real goal was the most self-important jerk of all, the one who had nearly gotten them all killed with his treachery. And for that, Rafe would rein in the urge.

Liam spoke again. "It's encrypted. It's going to take a few minutes longer. Five, keep stalling."

Rafe thought fast. "Come with me, please, sir. I'm sure the concierge will be at her desk and we'll get this straightened out in no time." He put the slightest emphasis on the "at her desk." And Hayley didn't miss it.

"Two will make sure she's not," she assured him.

"Do you know who I am?" Brown demanded.

Ah, there it is. The punctured ego. "I know you're the man who rented and returned a seriously damaged vehicle, and the man who didn't report said damage. There are a couple of laws involved there."

"Are you threatening me?" He sounded so incredulous Rafe nearly laughed.

Promising, jackass. Promising. "Of course not, Mr. Brown. I just know you wouldn't want this to somehow rebound on your boss, so you'll want to get it straightened out right away. Perhaps they have the wrong information, or a record got switched." He gave it a beat. "Unless of course, there's something you're not telling me?"

The man was clearly furious, but gave in. They started back toward the lobby, Brown pulling out his cell phone as they went.

"No calls until this is resolved, I'm afraid," he said, putting everything he could manufacture of regret into his voice. It wasn't much.

"You can't stop me from using my phone! You're not a cop."

Cutter definitely growled this time. Rafe smiled. "Do you really want to play that card, Mr. Brown?"

"This is ridiculous. We'll have your job when this is over."

"Now who's threatening who?" Rafe asked mildly.

That seemed to shut him up, temporarily at least. They kept walking, although he was going much slower than the clearly angry Brown wanted to. Indeed stalling.

Then Hayley's voice came through again. "Two to Five, you're clear."

When they turned the corner from the elevators back into the lobby, he saw that the concierge desk was indeed vacant.

So did Brown, and he turned on Rafe quickly. "I do not have time to wait around to straighten out what is obviously a clerical error. The senator has plans, and I have to be there."

Plans like walking his new lady around in public to be followed by a gaggle of media? Not enough headlines this weekend already?

He clamped down on his temper. "I'll find out where she is."

He estimated Brown would last maybe three minutes before he threw caution to the wind and stalked off in a snit. He reached out and picked up the phone on the desk and faked a dial. Asked the dial tone for an ETA, then hung it back up.

"She was with another guest. She's on her way now," he told Brown. It wasn't true, of course, Hayley would keep her occupied, somehow, until they got an all clear or the woman insisted she had to get back.

He figured this had bought them another maybe five minutes at most. He had to hope Liam was as good as ever with that tech crap.

Even as he thought it he heard the young Texan exclaim, "In. It's downloading now."

A moment later Charlie spoke. "Looks like financials of some sort. There's a lot."

"Copy, Focus. I'll have Data stand by. I'm headed toward the elevators to send as many as I can up to the top so he'll have to wait. Five," Quinn added, "try not to kill him."

"Mmm," Rafe murmured, mentally adding, *Tell that to your dog.*

Brown lasted another two minutes. "I have to get upstairs." He glanced at Cutter. "I'll stop by here on my way back to meet Senator Flood."

Rafe let the name-drop echo for a long moment, watched the man's puzzled expression as he again didn't react to it.

"One, every elevator's headed up."

That would only buy them an extra thirty, maybe forty-five seconds. But it might be enough. Or it might not. And Charlie was up in that room. He didn't want to think what might happen if Brown walked in on her and Liam with that case open and the laptop madly copying all those files.

He couldn't order—he knew better than that, despite his occasional gut reaction—her to leave, even though Liam would be better equipped, and armed, to handle the situation. Quinn could, but he couldn't suggest it with Brown still right here, glaring at him again. He couldn't do it until Brown actually left, anyway. It had to have occurred to Quinn, though, so maybe he would—

"Did you hear me?" the now thoroughly irritated man demanded.

In that moment Liam yelped. "Got it. We're clearing out. Less than a minute.

He breathed again. "Did you say something worth hearing?" he asked.

On that the man turned on his heel and strode away. Cutter watched him go, nearly trembling with eagerness to go after him.

"Sorry, buddy. I know you wanted a bite," Rafe told him, not even caring at this point if Brown heard him.

He watched as the aide impatiently slapped at the controls on three different elevators. Saw him back up to where he could watch the indicator lights on all of them at once.

He seemed more than just irritated. He seemed worried. It was normally Hayley's bailiwick, to recognize that, but in this case it was obvious even to him. And he wondered why. Wondered if perhaps he was regretting having left the case up in the suite, even locked. And Rafe didn't like what that had to mean.

"Five, I still have eyes on him. He's beyond edgy." He hesitated, but when it came to Charlie's safety, there could be no hedging. "He doesn't want her alone with that case. He doesn't trust her."

"One, copy. Question is does he not trust her specifically, or does he just not trust anyone?"

"Two also copies. My guess is a little of both. My question is, how much of the suspicion is his own and how much is the subject's?"

Leave it to Hayley to nail it down. But was Flood really that good an actor? Because if the demeanor of being head over heels for Charlie was fake, it was a damned good fake.

Or maybe you just can't imagine any man not *being head over heels for her...*

"He's a career politician," Quinn said dryly, as if that answered everything. As perhaps it did. Personally he thought the words career and politician should be mutually exclusive, but apparently the example George Washington had set had been too hard to follow.

A pair of elevator doors slid open. Brown dived for them. "He's got a ride."

The doors slid closed. Ten agonizing seconds ticked by where the only sound he could hear was the hammering of his pulse. Then Liam. "Clear." Rafe breathed again. "Focus on her way down, Four on the way to base. Files will be on the way to Data within five."

Liam heading for their own suite meant they'd be down one on surveillance, so Rafe had already made the decision to stay where he was until Charlie was back down to ground level when Quinn gave the order for him to do just that. Then he'd keep eyes on her until she was back in her brother's sight line.

I don't care what happened between you. I'm trusting you to set it aside when it comes to protecting my sister.

Quinn's figurative slapping some sense into him rang in his head. And now that it was real, now that it was happening and she needed that protection, he knew it had never really been in question. If Charlie was in danger, he would do what he had to to protect her. No matter what.

He heard the faint chime of an elevator arriving. Cutter was back on his feet, looking toward the sound. The door slid open and she stepped out. Cutter's tail began to wag. He gave a little tug on the lead, clearly wanting to go to her. *I know the feeling, dog.* But he held the animal back.

She spotted him immediately. More likely them, since she was smiling and that had to be for Cutter. She started walking toward them, with that graceful, purposeful walk that had always seemed to imply—to him, anyway—that she had important places to go and even more important things to do. Because Charlaine Foxworth was indeed a force to be reckoned with.

And yet all he could think of as he watched her, dressed in a sleek pantsuit that somehow managed to be sexy rather than just utterly businesslike, and was a deep greenish blue that somehow made her eyes look the same shade, was of those days—and nights—long ago, when looking into those eyes as he was buried in that lusciously sleek, curved body had been closer to heaven than he had ever expected to get.

And closer than he would ever get again.

Chapter 29

Charlie smiled widely when one of the two otters—both female, according to the sign—who, after a burst of play with her companion was now lolling on her back in the water, turned her head to look straight at Charlie. She hadn't been lying about that, she did think they were among the most adorable creatures on the planet. And when this one moved its paw almost as if waving to her, she couldn't help laughing out loud.

Flood, as usual, was over with the knot of media people Brown had arranged. She could hear him, but did her best to tune him out; he was using that voice and tone that she hated, that pontificating tone that made it clear who was the important one of the group.

She glanced at Cort, who had come over to stand a discreet couple of feet away from her, apparently at Flood's instruction. As usual, he was alert and scanning the crowd regularly, but now he was smiling. Whether at the otter or her response to it, she didn't know. Or, really, care.

"Can't help it," she said to him. "They're just too darn cute."

"They are, Ms. Marshall."

She thought about asking him how his wife was doing, but didn't want to nip the conversation in the bud if he was relaxed enough to maybe actually talk. She tried to think of something else, hoping all the practice she'd had with the laconic Mr. Crawford would pay off.

She glanced toward Flood, who was shifting the discussion to his pet political projects.

"Amazing how they turn out just to hear the same old, same old."

"I never try to understand the workings of the media mind," he said with a grimace.

She laughed again. "I knew I liked you, Mr. Ducane."

He almost smiled. She saw him fighting it.

As the otters went back to playing, rollicking and rolling in the water, she heard the inevitable begin from that small gathering, the questions about Flood's late wife and his new love. Ducane shifted subtly, so he was more directly between her and the media as some began to notice her, apparently recognizing her from the few photographs that had already hit.

"I appreciate that," she said to her guardian, very quietly.

He gave her a glance, as if he hadn't expected her to notice, but only nodded.

Eventually the otters, after all that play, seemed to have decided it was time for a late afternoon nap. They were now both floating quietly on their backs, eyes closed and paws resting on their chests.

"Now, that looks peaceful," she said.

Ducane's eyes flicked toward Flood, then to the otters, then to her. "Yes," he agreed. Then, after a moment's hesitation, he asked quietly, "Does it bother you? When they talk about his wife?"

"No," she said, honestly. "From what I know, Alondra was as lovely as her name." *And too good for the likes of Flood.*

The smile broke through this time at her words. "Do you know what it means?"

"Alondra? No."

"It's Spanish for lark, my mother's favorite bird."

"That's lovely. You speak Spanish?"

He nodded. "My mother was born in Puerto Rico."

"What's her name?"

"Solana. It means sunshine."

"Nice as well."

She studied him for a moment. This was the most conversation she'd gotten out of the man, and she couldn't resist pressing on, hoping that somewhere would be the key that would help him get free of Flood.

"May I ask how you ended up Cort?"

Again the brief smile. "It's short for Cortez. My mother's maiden name."

She smiled back, liking that. "And your father?"

"Straight back to Great Britain for generations, before one of them ventured here and wound up in South Carolina." His mouth quirked. "Spelling got a lot simpler along the way."

"Lucky for you," she teased.

"Very," he agreed.

Charlie was pleased to see him grin, a full-on grin. He seemed like a different man, at least in this moment less rigid. Less haunted. And she renewed her determination that Foxworth would find a way to help him. He didn't deserve to go down when Flood did because of something out of his control that had put him in a desperate state.

"You two having a nice time?" It came from just a couple

of feet away; apparently the media interaction had ended. Flood's voice, with the tiniest edge of accusation in it, shattered the easy mood.

Charlie didn't miss the flash of tension in Ducane's eyes. And Hayley's voice sounded in her ear, saying, "Focus, I do believe he's a tiny bit jealous."

That Cort would dare to smile at me? Okay, grin, but still...

But she needed to defuse the situation, quickly.

"Oh," she said, as brightly and airily as she could, "we were just laughing at these poor otters, napping afloat after getting tired out after playing all afternoon. Not a bad life." *If you don't mind living in a zoo...*

Either her tone or her words seemed to work, and Flood relaxed. He slipped an arm around her, and she managed not to recoil, instead converting the urge to pull away into leaning in. Ducane had moved back several steps and turned his attention to the other aquarium visitors.

Thinking a bit of flattery might not be amiss, she added, "Unlike you, Max. You always seem to be working."

"That's how things get done," he said. "But I'm ready for an evening off. Dinner here at the hotel tonight, I think. Alec and I need to go over some things for tomorrow."

"Have you made that decision you mentioned yet?"

"I believe so, yes."

"I have faith in you, Max. You'll do what's best." *For yourself, and to hell with anyone else.*

Quinn's voice came quietly through the transceiver. "Careful, Focus. It's getting close to leaking through."

Charlie gave an inward sigh, knowing her brother was right. It was getting harder all the time to hide her distaste for the ilk in general, and her loathing of this one in particular.

"I think you need to go shopping," Hayley said. "For female things, because you're extending your stay."

There was no doubt about it, her sister-in-law was a genius. She needed a break from the man, and this was the perfect way to get it. And was exactly what she told Flood, in almost those words. Saw him cringe just slightly at the phrase "female things," which showed her one more aspect of the man.

Using the term *man* loosely.

"I'll send someone with you," Flood said.

"You don't need to, Max. I think I'll just walk down the block to that shop next to the cell phone store. They should have what I need."

"I'm not comfortable with you out there alone." With anyone else it would have been an expression of caring. With Flood she had the feeling it was wanting her watched at all times.

She thought for a brief moment, about what "Lita" would do. She went for her best shot. "I'm not comfortable with taking staff away from you, when you're clearly in the middle of something important."

"Ducane can accompany you," Flood said. "Since we're staying in, we won't need him."

She'd been hoping for that, another chance to assess and maybe wear down the man who clearly didn't think much of his current employer. But she frowned as if she didn't like the idea, which made Flood smile in turn, no doubt because she didn't jump at the chance to be with the good-looking guardian.

"All right," she finally said with an audible sigh. "If it will put you at ease."

"That's what I love about you, Lita dear. You're willing to compromise."

On everything but payback, you monster. She smiled

even as she thought it, and there was genuine pleasure in it as she thought about how they were going to wipe that phony benevolence off his face.

Quinn's voice as he spoke in her ear told her he'd followed her line of thought perfectly. "One to Five, pull out of the hotel and be ready to meet with Focus and friend. Put a little more pressure on him."

"Five, copy." Rafe's voice, ever cool.

"Take your sidekick," Hayley said. "He could tip the scales."

"Agreed," Rafe said.

It was amazing—and wonderful—the utter faith and confidence the Northwest office had in their canine operative. Especially when Rafe agreed with it, so easily. He was the most skeptical man she'd ever met when it came to anything inexplicable by either logic or math or the proper tools. And yet he obviously believed, as they all did, that Cutter had…some unexpected capabilities.

When he joined her, it seemed Cort was back in quiet mode, saying nothing, communicating mostly with nods as they walked toward the shop on the corner. She wondered if that moment when Flood had almost snapped at them had scared him, since he so badly needed this job.

Or if it was something else.

"Are you all right, Cort?" She used his first name intentionally, and it seemed to startle him.

"I… Fine. I'm fine."

"Something's obviously bothering you. Or," she added, watching his face, "you've decided I'm not worth talking to."

That got a low half chuckle out of him. "You're the only one in this crowd who is worth talking to."

The moment he said it he looked as if he regretted it. She was pondering how to keep it going when that all too recognizable awareness shot through her. She looked past Cort and down the street.

She spotted Cutter first, heading their way. With a tiny lean to the right she saw Rafe, and he did not look happy. A little jolt went through her at the idea he might be jealous. Genuine jealousy, not Flood's kind. She couldn't deny she liked the idea, but she wouldn't let it interfere with the mission. She knew Rafe wouldn't, either.

Not this mission.

Chapter 30

"Thanks for the compliment," Charlie said, sounding beyond rueful in Rafe's ear as she waved him back with a subtle hand signal. "And I get your point. I have to admit, the best thing that has come out of this trip for me was the chance to see friends I haven't seen in a while."

Rafe slowed his pace, now that he was close enough to get there in a couple of long strides. Cutter didn't agree, but only gave him a side-eye as he slowed his own pace to match.

"Trouble in paradise?" Ducane asked.

Rafe halted and pretended to look in a store window, reminding himself the guy had a dying wife and wasn't likely to hit on his boss's…girlfriend.

"It was never paradise," Charlie answered. "Not even close."

Ducane went very still. Looked as if he regretted having said it. Charlie hesitated, then Quinn spoke in his ear. "Five? Opinion?"

He knew what his boss meant. Was Ducane close to breaking? Should she push him? He couldn't go with his gut right now, because his gut was never sane when it came to Charlie. So he risked a look, focusing on Ducane, seeing the tangle of emotions in his expression. Thought he saw not just regret but edginess, even a sort of concern.

Hell, maybe he was getting better at being...emotionally observant.

"Go for it," Rafe said.

"Focus, copy? Five, stand by to step in. If we have to break cover, it's worth the risk."

Rafe agreed. This was an in they couldn't afford to pass up. Charlie responded to Quinn's order by going on with Ducane.

"I'm starting to think Max isn't who I thought he was." *He's actually exactly who I thought he was.*

Ducane started to speak, stopped, then said in a very circumspect tone, "I couldn't speak to that, Ms. Marshall."

"I'm sorry. I shouldn't dump my worries on you. You have enough problems. How is your wife?"

"Not good today." It was gruff, rough, and Rafe felt like a grade-A jerk for his reaction to the man's simple friendliness toward Charlie. The guy had a wife he clearly loved, and he was losing her.

"I'm so sorry. Is she here? In the city?" Out of the corner of his eye he saw Ducane nod. "You should be with her," Charlie said firmly.

"Can't afford time off."

"Then let's go to her now."

Rafe turned in time to see Ducane give her a startled look. "What?"

"We'll go now, while Max is busy. I'll just find something to read while you visit."

Ducane was gaping at her now, any thought of watching the surroundings or other people clearly blasted out of his mind.

"You…you'd do that?"

"Of course."

Rafe found himself holding his breath. He sensed a tipping point, the only question was which way would the man fall?

"You," Ducane said after a moment, "are too good for him."

"I know why I'm changing my mind, but what makes you think that?"

"Because he's not the altruistic guy he presents himself as. He's just an influence peddler."

Charlie took an audible deep breath, then plunged ahead. "Yes. He is. You're right."

Ducane blinked and drew back. His brow furrowed. Rafe usually never got involved in this aspect of their cases, but he felt as if he could relate to Ducane, at least enough to have an idea about how to reach him.

"Don't give him time to dwell on that," he said quietly, knowing she'd heard him by the way her head tilted just slightly toward the ear with the transceiver. And because she immediately did exactly what he'd said. *First time for everything…*

"How much do you know about when Governor Ogilvie was removed from office?"

Rafe had turned to watch carefully now, sensing Ducane was intent on the conversation. And there was a note of sheer puzzlement in his voice when he answered Charlie's question.

"Not much." He grimaced. "It was about the time my wife was diagnosed. I do remember cheering for that detective." He gave Charlie a sideways look. "I didn't like

Ogilvie much. Never expected him to turn out to be a murderer, though."

Charlie gave Rafe a sideways look in turn. And a small nod. A clear signal.

"See to him," Rafe murmured to his companion as they started toward the other two, and Cutter gave a very small *whuff* of acknowledgment.

Ducane looked startled all over again at Rafe's approach, and he didn't give the man any time to process it; he had the feeling the best way to breach this wall was to simply blow it up as fast as possible.

"That last-minute meeting your employer—I'm not going to call him your boss—had was with Ogilvie."

Ducane's brow furrowed again. "How do you know that?" His gaze shifted to Charlie. "You told him?"

"No," she said quietly. "I didn't have to."

Again Rafe didn't give him time to process. "We think Ogilvie wants his help with the case against him."

Ducane's mouth twisted wryly. "As if anything could help that—" He bit off something Rafe guessed would have been profane. Then, looking from Rafe to Charlie and back again, he asked slowly, "Just who is 'we'?"

Rafe looked at Charlie then, who looked uncharacteristically undecided. Quinn's words went through his mind again. *If we have to break cover, it's worth the risk.* So he took the last step.

"Ever hear of the Foxworth Foundation?"

"Yeah, they helped that detective who took Ogilvie out. And once I heard some people at the hospital talking about how they helped them, that they—" He stopped suddenly, staring at Rafe. "Are you saying…you're with them?"

"Yes."

Ducane kept staring. Then, slowly, he said, "What you

said…about being prouder of what you do now… That's Foxworth?"

Rafe nodded.

"I…can see why. So what, you're still on Ogilvie, to make sure he doesn't find a way to slime his way out of murder charges?"

"We are, but that's not why we're here now." Rafe studied the other man for a moment before saying, "Right now, we're looking to take down a traitor who sold intel that nearly got our whole team killed."

"Whole team?"

Rafe nodded. "Including him," he said, with a gesture at Cutter. Taking it as his cue, the dog stepped forward. Ducane reached down to stroke the dog's head. Even as many times as he'd seen it—and experienced it himself— he still marveled at the effect the dog had. He let it happen in silence and took the chance to grab a glance at Charlie.

She was looking straight at him. Approvingly. Something he hadn't seen in a very long time.

Ducane straightened, and Rafe looked back at him. "I don't envy the guy you're after."

"Already knew that," Rafe said.

It didn't take more than three seconds for Ducane to get there. His eyes widened. He started to speak, but Rafe cut him off before he could say the name, just in case; their connection to Ogilvie was common knowledge, this was not. Yet.

"Yes. Your employer."

"You mean he's the one who sold you out?"

"He is," Rafe said firmly. "But we're still working on proof that will stand against someone in his position."

Ducane let out a low whistle. "Good luck with that."

"We're hoping for a little more than luck."

It was the first time Charlie had spoken since Rafe had joined them. Ducane turned his head to look at her.

"You're part of this?"

"She's the reason Foxworth exists," Rafe said, meaning it. And when Charlie shot him a startled yet gratified glance, he decided it was worth that little release of emotion he'd allowed into his voice.

"Let me reintroduce myself, Cort. I'm Charlaine Foxworth."

Well, there they were, Rafe thought. Charlie-like, she hadn't just broken their cover.

She'd blown it up.

Chapter 31

"Why are you all trusting me with this? You don't even know me."

Charlie leaned back in her chair and didn't respond. It was Rafe who had the rapport with the guy right now, if only because the man knew who he was. And admired him, was perhaps even a bit awed. And Quinn clearly realized it, too, because he also stayed silent.

They were back in the suite they'd kept as a temporary headquarters. Teague and Liam had confirmed Flood and Brown were still secluded in their own suite, and with their help she, Rafe and Cutter had come in through a back entrance and arrived unobserved. Quinn and Hayley, they said in her ear, were on their way.

Cutter, who was sitting beside Cort's chair, leaned his head against the man's leg. And once more she saw the results, saw the man start to truly let down his guard as he stroked the dog's soft fur. And Rafe gently used that to get him to open up. Odd, how she'd become the watcher, and Rafe the communicator.

But the biggest surprise—to her—was how well he was doing it.

"We know enough," Rafe said. "We do our homework, Cort. We know your background, your military record." She glanced over in time to see Rafe flash a brief grin. It was clearly aimed at Cort but it was her breath he took away. "Nice job, by the way, getting the officer you punched to admit he deserved it."

Cort looked startled, but then, slowly, he smiled. "He wasn't a bad guy, for a lieutenant. He just got a little mouthy now and then."

And that quickly they were at ease, two vets who knew in a way she never would what that life was like. She'd never seen Rafe like this, and she wondered if it was because she'd never been around him when he was this at ease, or if he'd come so far since he'd walked away from what they had.

What she'd thought they had.

"We also know," Rafe said, very quietly, "the straits you're in right now. Why you need the job badly enough to work for someone you don't like or respect. We can help. It's part of what we do."

Cort stiffened despite Cutter's presence. Charlie saw him glance her way. "I didn't tell him that, either," she said.

"Foxworth already knew?"

"We've been monitoring everything since we came on scene at the party Friday night."

"Monitoring? As in…you've got us all bugged?"

"No. Just us. But our system picks up conversations." Rafe gave a wry smile. "You don't take down a sitting governor without covering all the bases. Same applies to someone like…our subject, as we refer to him."

Cutter whined slightly and nudged Cort. His hand went back to the dog's head, and she saw it yet again, the calming.

"Let me tell you why we're determined to take him down, too."

And Rafe did, using language she supposed would ring familiar, Marine to Marine.

"We've been searching for who sold us out for three years," Rafe ended with. "And now that we've found him, we have to prove it."

"He's insulated like he was still a senator. Maybe more," Cort said. "I don't know what I could do."

And that easily, Rafe had done it. Because Charlie had no doubt Cort was solidly in their corner now.

"It's more what you don't do," Rafe said, and although she was watching Cort, she felt his gaze shift to her.

"Don't blow her cover?" Cort said.

"Exactly," Charlie said. Then, with a grimace of distaste she added, "Unless I ask you to."

"I'm surprised you've lasted this long," he said.

"Word of advice," Rafe said, almost solemnly. "Don't ever underestimate her."

The words and the way he said them kicked her pulse up a notch. Then Quinn's voice announcing their arrival came through her earpiece about thirty seconds before the door opened. Cort turned to look, warily, so she smiled at him. And the smile widened when Gavin came in right on their heels. Cort gave the famous attorney that look she knew well, the one that said they recognized him but weren't quite sure why.

Quinn came over to them.

"Meet my boss," Rafe said, bringing to mind how he'd so carefully referred to Flood as Cort's employer, not his boss. "Cort Ducane, Quinn Foxworth."

"My brother," Charlie explained at Cort's reaction to the last name. "And the tactical mind behind everything we do."

Rafe introduced Hayley to Cort. She quickly went over to the table where they'd been sitting and put a shopping bag and her purse down on the floor, grabbing her phone as she straightened. She held the phone out to Cort.

"Here," she said. "Use this to call the hospital billing department."

"What?" Cort asked, startled.

"Just call them for the status of your wife's charges."

Cort glanced at Rafe, another sign of the tentative bond. Rafe nodded. The other man took the phone, and after another moment of hesitation, dialed the number he apparently knew by heart. A simple fact that made Charlie ache a little. This was a good man, caught by tragedy and thrown into a bad situation. And she felt a tremendous satisfaction knowing Foxworth would get him out of part of it, at least.

A couple of minutes later Cort had ended the call, set the phone down carefully on the table, and looked at Hayley.

"You did this?"

"Foxworth did." She smiled at Charlie. "Thanks to our financial genius."

"You paid off a six-figure bill. So I'd help you?" Cort looked bewildered.

"No," Hayley said gently. "We hope you will, but that's why we paid it off now, before. We didn't want you to think we were holding that offer over your head, didn't want you to feel coerced into helping us. It's done and paid, no matter what you decide to do."

"I...don't understand."

"It's why I told you I'm prouder of what I do now than of anything else," Rafe said, very solemnly. The words warmed Charlie inside as Cort's head snapped around to stare at him.

"I know the feeling." Gavin's words, spoken with quiet feeling, made the man look that way. Cort's brow furrowed.

"And meet Gavin de Marco," Charlie said, not even trying to suppress her smile as the famous name registered and Cort's eyes widened in shock. "He runs legal interference for Foxworth when necessary."

"You...work for them, too?"

"I do." He glanced at Charlie. "Quinn thought I might come in handy, if this all goes down over here in the city."

"Glad you're here, my friend," Charlie said, meaning it.

Cort stared at them all, one by one. And Charlie saw the moment when he broke, when he accepted.

"I'd like to feel the way you all do," he said wearily.

"We'll see what we can do about that," Quinn said, briskly now. "But right now, you two need to get back. Liam says the subject is starting to wonder where you are."

Charlie stifled another grimace. Then drew back slightly as something occurred to her. "I was supposed to be shopping."

"I know," Hayley said, grinning. She bent over and grabbed the small shopping bag she'd come in with. "Here. Girly stuff."

Charlie took the bag and looked inside to see a package of tampons, some skin lotion and a small bottle of what happened to be the only perfume she usually ever wore, the heavy stuff Flood preferred notwithstanding.

Because Rafe loved it enough to actually say so once...

She shoved away the memory and the crazy thought that somehow Hayley had known that. She looked at her brother instead. "Thank you," she said.

Quinn shrugged. "I didn't do it, Hayley did."

"Exactly. Thank you for bringing her into the family."

She hugged her sister-in-law, who was smiling widely now, then looked at Cort, who immediately got to his feet.

She saved her last glance for Rafe, and accompanied it with a quietly spoken, "Well done." Rafe looked surprised, which told her rather more than she'd wanted to know; he still expected her to jab at him.

They were nearly back to Flood's suite when Charlie looked up at the man beside her. She didn't think she was imagining that he looked less loaded down. Nothing could ease the pain he was going through, but at least they'd been able to remove something that was making the heavy burden even worse. Even if it netted them nothing, she would count the expenditure worth it for that alone.

But in fact, it netted them results much sooner than she would have dared hope. Because less than half an hour after they'd stepped back into Flood's realm, when Cort came to tell her they were ready to head down for dinner, he whispered something else to her.

"I heard him say something to his aide that seems… curious. He said he thought he and Bradford—that's Ogilvie's first name, right?—could reach a 'mutually beneficial accord.' And I'm wondering what could be mutually beneficial."

She got what he meant immediately. "As in what could the gov, stuck in his mess, possibly do for someone like our subject?" Cort nodded. "That's a very good question. One, you copy that?"

"Affirmative," came Quinn's voice immediately. "Definitely curious."

Cort blinked. "You really meant that about monitoring." When she nodded, he looked at her more closely. She reached up and tapped at the guilty earring. "Oh."

She laughed and followed him out to where Flood and his minion were waiting.

Rafe was pacing the suite. Big as it was, and even with Teague and Liam still out watching Flood's suite, he wished it was bigger because he wasn't wearing himself out nearly enough. Cutter was watching him go back and forth, and he knew from the dog's close attention that the moment the animal felt he was pushing it too far, he'd be herding him to a chair.

"Mutually beneficial," he muttered to himself.

He'd taken out his earpiece, thinking he couldn't stomach Charlie making nice with Flood. He was starting to worry about how long she could hold him off. And to what extremes the man might go.

He kept pacing. Quinn was over by the windows with Hayley, probably discussing their next move and what they would do if they couldn't end this before Flood was ready to leave and head back east to his rat hole. Rafe hated even the thought of this going on another day, let alone weeks.

He walked over to where Quinn's secured laptop sat on the table. It was open, and on the screen were the records Ty had sent, of the transactions run through the offshore account he had backtracked to Flood, since the day it had been set up. He wasn't really focused on entries—that kind of financial stuff was Charlie's bailiwick, not his, as so much was—he was just noting the ridiculous amount of money involved, that Flood apparently asked and got for his influence. And oddly, it hadn't really dropped much since he'd quit the Senate, so he clearly had plenty of influence left.

He stared at the screen, doing more marveling at the fact that this was simple to Charlie, while he was boggled. The numbers he did best with were velocity and range, or maybe properly gapping spark plugs, so this stuff was beyond him.

But then he was back to that phrase that was nagging at him. *Mutually beneficial.*

What could a disgraced former governor, who killed his

political opponent and was eventually going to go down for it, offer a mover and shaker on Flood's level?

His eyes were fixed on the screen, but he wasn't really seeing it as he wrestled with what didn't make any sense. He didn't know how long he'd been standing there when he felt the nudge of a cold nose against his right hand. He snapped back to reality and looked down at Cutter. He gave the dog a scratch behind his right ear.

"I'll bet you could figure this out faster than I could, buddy. It might as well be in…dog, for all the good it does me."

He looked back at the screen ruefully. Only this time his gaze locked on two entries, just three days apart. Sizable entries. He'd noticed them before, but only the numbers, which had made him shake his head. But now he backtracked on the spreadsheet line to the name on the entry. And suddenly, those spark plugs he'd just thought about started to fire.

"When was Flood's wife killed?" he asked, without looking at either Quinn or Hayley.

"Four years ago," Quinn said.

"Date, exactly."

His peripheral vision caught Hayley checking her phone. "March 27," she said a moment later.

Like a teetering pile of blocks finally collapsing, the pieces fell.

A large payment dated March 25 of that year.

A second even larger payout dated March 28, three days later.

Both payments allocated on the paperwork for something called the Lark Project.

The exchange rang in his head as if Charlie and Cort were standing right beside him. The exchange about Alondra, Flood's wife's name.

It's Spanish for lark, my mother's favorite bird.

The Lark Project.

Mutually beneficial.

Cutter let out a low, worried sound, no doubt at the sudden, shocked stillness as Rafe stopped breathing for a moment.

"Rafe? What is it?" Hayley asked.

"You spot something?" Quinn had come over to stand beside them.

He took in a deep breath. This wasn't his thing, he could be wrong. Way wrong. He could be making the proverbial mountain out of the hill their mole had built.

But he didn't think so.

He looked up at the two people he was so proud to work for and with. Hesitated, until Cutter nudged his hand, as if in encouragement. That tipped him over the edge.

"I think I know what Ogilvie could do for him." He grimaced. "Or more like, not do. As in talk."

Quinn frowned in puzzlement, but he and Hayley both waited quietly.

"I think…" It finally came out in a burst. "I think he paid to have his wife killed, and Ogilvie knows it."

Chapter 32

"It all fits." Rafe heard Charlie whisper it, trusting Liam's device to pick it up. "I overheard the aide referring to that meeting, saying something about they'd better go see what he's got."

"And we know that's how the gov works," Quinn said.

Charlie's voice came faster now. "And I overheard something else, back at the beginning, about some chance they'd had to take, extreme measures the subject said, because it was an emergency."

Rafe's gut knotted again. He was even more certain now.

Gavin inserted the earpiece Hayley had given him before saying, "This is how the governor has managed to stall his trial so long. He's got a lot of dirt on a lot of people."

"Two of a kind," Charlie muttered. "Good job, bro. Er, One."

"Not me. Five put it together."

She didn't react to that at all. Rafe figured she was probably shocked; putting mechanical pieces together was more his style. But he didn't care if she was surprised, all he cared about was one thing.

"Focus, you've got to get out of there," he said.

"Out?" She sounded almost offended. "We haven't nailed this down yet."

"The gov could recognize you. Pictures of you with him are popping up."

"Five's got a point," Liam put in. "He probably did his research on Foxworth well before Data planted the new images."

Mentally tossing the Texan thanks for the support, Rafe searched for words to convince her. But she spoke first. "Look, it all fits too well, and I wouldn't put murdering his wife past him. But I don't think he'll break the way Ogilvie did when confronted. We need proof."

"Agreed," Quinn said, and Rafe stiffened as he stared at his boss. Quinn gave a slow shake of his head as he added, "And he covers his back better, because he's smarter."

"The bar was pretty low there," Hayley said, easing the tension a bit in that way she had.

He heard Charlie start to chuckle, but she stopped abruptly just as they heard a knocking sound. Then she spoke again, this time clearly not to them but for them. "Hello, Alec."

They heard another voice, male, but not clearly enough to catch the words.

"Meet him there? All right," Charlie said, sounding as cheerful as if it were all real. "I'll be ready in just a minute."

"I'll be on you to the elevators," came Teague's voice.

"I've got the garage exit," Liam said.

The comms devices then went silent for the moment. Rafe felt his nails digging into his palms and only then realized he'd been clenching his fists. He hunted for words, realizing that his years of being uncommunicative had a cost. When he really wanted to say something, the right thing, the discarded words weren't there.

He should be the one tracking Flood. He should—

Quinn's phone buzzed. He glanced at it, then went over to his laptop and hit a couple of keys. The screen went live, and Rafe saw Ty.

He began without preamble. "I did some research, and I think we're right. It was buried deep, but the late missus had that accident on her way to a meeting. With one of those guerilla journalist types."

"She was going to blow the whistle on him," Quinn said softly.

"I think so," Ty agreed. "Problem is, I don't know about what, specifically. They managed to quash any public mention, but it was mentioned in an old comment I found on a private message board."

As if anything's private to Tyler Hewitt. Rafe thought it almost numbly.

"Thanks, Ty," Quinn said.

"Just call me Data," the young tech whiz said cheerfully. "I'll keep going."

The screen went blank.

Rafe stood staring at Quinn. Remembered again his words, as close to an emotional order as he'd ever heard from the man. "I'm trusting you to set it aside when it comes to protecting my sister."

What if I have to disobey you to protect her?

His own Foxworth phone rang. For once he welcomed the interruption. He pulled it out, didn't recognize the incoming number. But he recognized the voice before the caller even gave his name.

"Crawford?"

"Ducane," he said.

"Yeah. Look, this is probably nothing, but—"

"Nothing's nothing," Rafe said, rolling his eyes at his own absurd phrasing. "What?"

"My employer just changed his plans at the last second. He had an evening planned with…Ms. Marshall, but now I'm supposed to drive him in half an hour to a city council meeting where he's going to speak." The thought made Rafe's stomach churn a bit, but he sensed this wasn't the real reason Ducane had called. And his next words made it clear Rafe was right. "The thing is, his aide just left with Ms. Marshall, telling her he was going to drive her to the original location. And she didn't seem to know there'd been a change at all."

Meet him there, Charlie had said.

Rafe felt a chill go through him that was almost violent.

Flood publicly on display, no doubt on video as well. A time-stamped alibi with a lot of witnesses.

Charlie alone with Brown, the guy she—and Ducane— thought was more than a little off-center. The guy that he himself had been aware of in the same way he'd be aware of every step in a minefield.

Flood would never personally get his hands dirty.

Brown wouldn't hesitate.

"Hold on," he said to Ducane, moving the phone away slightly. Then he snapped into the earpiece, "Focus, new intel. You're burned. Four, track what vehicle they take. I'll be en route. Cutter, on me."

The dog had already been at Rafe's heels. He started toward the door. Felt rather than saw Quinn's stare. And he knew it wasn't because he'd suddenly started tossing out orders when that wasn't his job.

He looked steadily at his boss. "If you're going to trust me, trust me."

Quinn's jaw was tight, but he nodded. "We'll take the subject. We still need proof, but you know what price is too high."

Rafe had already been determined, but Quinn's trust, his faith that Rafe had accurately assessed the threat and would keep his sister safe, solidified it like granite. He held up his phone, where Ducane was still on the line.

Quinn nodded again. "Tell him."

Rafe went back to the phone as he ran for the elevator, laying out their suspicions about Flood's late wife, and that they suspected he had the same in store for Charlie. He wasn't sure how the man, whose own obviously much-loved wife was down to her last days, would take it. The oath he let loose was a clue.

"Cort," Rafe said, for the first time using the man's first name, "how into this do you want to get?"

"How deep do you need me?"

"Stalling your employer as long as possible."

He heard Ducane take a deep breath. "Done."

"Stall as long as you can, however you have to. Text us when you can't delay any longer."

He and Cutter were just coming out of the elevator on the ground floor when Liam spoke again. "Five, it's the same rental they took down south. I should be at the gate before them. Oh, and she's in the back seat."

"Copy," he repeated, noting the difference; when she'd ridden with Ducane as her acting chauffeur, she'd always sat in front with him. She might not be a trained field operative, but Charlie had good instincts. About most things, anyway.

He headed for one of the back doors to the garage, near where he'd parked. Cutter was glued to him, practically brushing against his leg with every step. Knowing he didn't have to worry about the dog, he took care of one other matter.

"Data," he said.

"Here," Ty responded in his ear almost instantly.

"I know you're already recording, but double-check on Focus."

"Done," Ty said after a brief moment.

He spoke again as he and Cutter got into his car. "Focus, stay low and quiet."

"Hope you know where we're going," she said, in a teasing tone clearly aimed at Brown, but the words were meant for them.

"Oh, I know."

Now that they were in the quiet of the vehicle, he could hear Brown's voice. And if he'd had any doubts about the plan, the undertone in the man's voice would have convinced him. He'd heard that sound before, and he knew it meant a man set on his course—and with plans to enjoy it.

Fury burst free inside him. He wanted to stop this right now and blow the guy to bits. Right now he didn't care if Flood went down, even if he had almost gotten them all killed. Right now, all he cared about was Charlie, and that she was in the hands of a man who would likely have no qualms about killing her if it would keep his boss's little fiefdom intact. Cutter made a small sound as he stuck his head between the front seats, and Rafe reached out to stroke the dark head. Oddly, this time he felt not the soothing he'd almost gotten used to, but a burst of energy, as if the dog was as wound up as he was and eager to get on with it.

I'll take you as my backup anytime, dog.

"They're clear of the parking garage, turning south," Liam said. "I got a GPS tracker on it while they were stopped at the exit gate."

Bless you, Liam Burnett. "Five, copy. Keep me updated."

"Affirmative. Still heading south. Normal speed."

Every second counted, and Liam had just bought him enough to get his gear together, and he was armed with everything he might need by the time he pulled out onto the street in their wake. He fought the urge to speed up until he had them in sight; the last thing he needed was to get stopped and have to explain to a cop, who likely wouldn't see past all the armament. Even Gavin might have trouble getting him out of that one.

But worse was the thought that he might not be there in time to protect Charlie.

He wondered what Quinn and the others would come up with to deal with the pompous, too-slick Flood building his alibi. Knowing them—especially Gavin—it would be clever, dramatic and inescapable. But he shoved that out of his mind. He didn't give a damn anymore about what Flood had done to them. He only cared about stopping what he'd no doubt ordered Brown to do now.

He did wonder how Flood thought he could get away with a second dead woman. Then again, he wasn't sure anybody would look askance at the guy, not the way he'd play up a second tragedy in his life. He'd probably use it like a surgeon, something about deciding he was cursed and would have to struggle through life alone.

Not going to happen.

He would not let anything happen to Charlie. How they'd parted, how angry she was at him, didn't matter. Nothing mattered except keeping her safe.

Liam's voice came through again. "Five, they're turning west and…hang on…okay, now south again."

Rafe swore silently as he picked up a little more speed. He'd just spotted the car when Quinn confirmed Flood was indeed still at the hotel, preparing for his appearance at the city council meeting. "Our new friend is doing a good job of stalling. Told the subject media was gathering, so he should probably have the limo shined up for a big arrival. He bought it, and us more time."

Charlie's voice came just a couple of minutes later. "Where are we going? Did Max cancel our restaurant plans?"

"In a way," Brown said, and the way he said it jabbed at Rafe, because he knew in his gut what the man meant.

"Focus, stay cool, I've got you in sight."

At least Brown didn't seem to have any idea he was being followed. He even politely signaled a lane change, then made another turn.

"Industrial district," Rafe suddenly guessed.

"Headed that way," Liam confirmed. "Another couple of blocks."

Rafe had to fight the almost overpowering urge to catch up and take the guy out right here, but the collateral damage could be huge, and that was not what Foxworth was about. He'd meant what he'd said to Cort.

"A warehouse?" For the first time Rafe thought he heard a touch of nerves in Charlie's voice. "And it looks abandoned, with that moving and storage company sign hanging crooked like that."

Good job, Charlie. Because now he knew where they were going; he'd noticed the falling sign the last time he'd been through here.

"Wait until you see the surprise waiting for you inside," Brown said, not even trying to hide that predatory—and pleased—tone now.

"Focus, I'm on-site," Rafe said.

"Well, Alec," Charlie said, her voice back to her steady self, but taking on a drawl that could almost match Liam's, "there are surprises, and then there are surprises."

Despite it all Rafe found himself laughing inwardly. She was something, was his Charlie.

And he didn't even bother to dispute his own terminology as he parked in the shelter of a large dumpster that would shield the coupe from this angle. He got out, pulled on his armored and full of arms vest, grabbed his trusted, exquisitely cared for Remington M40 and opened the door for his furry partner.

Charlie knew why they were here. She was a little surprised, not that Flood would actually order her murder, but that he would do it this way. True, the city wasn't the peaceful, picturesque place it had once been, and in sad fact a murder wasn't all that unusual anymore, but this seemed a bit too blatant for the smooth, subtle Flood.

But not for Brown. If nothing else, the expression of obviously gleeful anticipation would have told her. She thought of Rafe, and how only the number of lives he'd saved had enabled him to live with the number he'd taken. He had never, ever taken such pleasure in what to him was a grim but necessary job. Because he was sane, without some twisted, convoluted ego that took pleasure in ending a human life.

The warehouse had the empty look and hollow sound of a place long abandoned. Their footsteps echoed in the void. They had only gone a couple of yards when she glanced back. And saw the glint of metal in his right hand. Her heart started to pound even faster, but she forced herself to think of a way to warn Rafe.

"Why, what a pretty little popgun in your hand," she said, too sweetly. "Expecting to have to take out some rats?"

The laugh she heard in her ear gave her all the nerve she needed. Brown looked disconcerted, and she counted that a win since the man prided himself on never showing weakness, as he'd put it to Flood more than once.

"Does he really think he can get away with two dead women on his résumé? Or are you supposed to take the heat for this one?"

Brown actually gaped at her. But in her ear Rafe hissed, "Stop provoking him. At least until he's down."

Not if. Until. A given. That's my Rafe.

My Rafe. The simple phrase echoed in her mind, and in that moment nothing else mattered.

"He will be," she said it aloud, putting all the faith she felt into her voice. It also changed Brown's expression from astonished to puzzled at the, to him, nonsensical words.

"As soon as I get in position." Rafe's voice sounded as if he'd heard exactly what she'd intended.

And then Brown grabbed her arm, yanking hard enough that she let out a little yelp of pain. "It's true, isn't it? You're one of those Foxworth people. The ones who brought down Ogilvie."

She saw no point in denying it, but Rafe's warning rang in her head. Especially now that Brown had her jammed up against his chest, so that any bullet that hit him would probably hit her, too. She stalled.

"Foxworth people? You say that like it's a tribe." *As we are, of sorts.*

"I saw that photo Ogilvie had. It's you."

"Focus, we're in place."

She almost laughed in delight at the sound of him, and the thought of his furry partner. And she let a bit of it show when she said lightly, "Ogilvie? Didn't he used to be the governor here?"

"Stop playing dumb."

But I am. Dumb, stupid and a few other things for ever letting that man over there out of my sight.

She heard a faint, metallic click. "Never mind," Brown said. "It doesn't matter now." His grip on her tightened. He jammed the barrel of the gun up under her chin. It would take the top of her head off. "Goodbye, whatever your name really is."

* * *

The instant Brown grabbed her and yanked her to him, Rafe wanted nothing more than to rip the man limb from limb. He fairly shook from the need to tear him apart. Beside him Cutter was dancing, seeming to be full of the same need. He was a man who excelled at one thing, a man whose name they put on trophies and medals for that skill. But right now he wanted to throw it away. He wanted to choke the life out of this predator with his own hands, and watch the life leave his eyes as he did it.

He mentally grabbed for that legendary cool he had lost in that moment. He did one thing better than most, and Quinn—and Charlie—were counting on him to do it.

And never had it been more important than now. Because now it was Charlie.

The moment Brown moved the pistol under Charlie's chin, a vision of what would happen if he fired it flashed through Rafe's mind. He'd seen it before. Had more than one mental video of the bloody, gory, instant results.

Cutter's head bumped him, hard enough to snap him out of it.

Now.

He let his breath out. He felt that calm some called uncanny steal over him. He settled in, mentally calculated the distance, angle, trajectory, and added in the cold barrel of the M40. For a split second he wished for the armor piercing AS50 that could take down a helicopter, but his old friend would get the job done. He planned for any move the target made. Registered on an instinctive level a cross-body shot from Brown would be less accurate than straight, so he had to be forced into that.

He's less than fifty feet away. You'd take him down if all you had was a musket.

When he spoke to the transceiver, his voice was steady.

"Focus, when my partner shows, drop to your left. Cutter... now!"

The dog bolted like a racehorse out of the gate. His ferocious snarl made Brown freeze. He half turned, staring. Rafe knew what Brown was seeing, Cutter racing out of the shadows, fangs bared as he sprinted toward them looking like some predator out of a nightmare.

Come on, Charlie.

She dropped. Brown, fixated on the dog about to jump him, moved his gun hand toward the animal. Target clear. Acquired. Fire. The shot echoed in the empty building. Brown went down. Hard. Then Cutter was atop him, snarling a signal no one could miss.

Rafe slung the rifle over his shoulder in the same moment he started running. If there was any pain from his leg he didn't feel it, he just ran. Brown was screaming at the dog, but he didn't call Cutter off. Because only one thing mattered.

And then he had Charlie in his arms, felt her warmth, her arms around him in turn as she hugged him back fiercely. He closed his eyes. Savored it for a long, sweet moment.

"Status?" Liam's voice suggested in his ear.

He opened his eyes. Somewhat reluctantly he gave Cutter the command to simply guard. And it was Charlie who answered the question. "Focus, we're good. It's over here, thanks to... Five. All yours now, One."

"Copy," Quinn said. "Get here ASAP. We've got a plan to finish this once and for all."

Rafe knew they had to go, but he still didn't want to move. Oddly, he no longer cared all that much about the man who had been one of his top goals for three years.

The only one he cared about was here in his arms.

Chapter 33

Charlie never thought she would willingly pass up watching their revenge on Flood for anything, but if it bought her a few more minutes in Rafe's embrace, she would have.

But her brother's words were an order to Rafe, and she had a job yet to perform tonight, so they needed to get to city hall. Thanks to phone calls from Brett Dunbar and Gavin, plus the weight of the Foxworth name, they were able to clear out much faster than she would have expected, with the understanding there would be a nightmare of details later.

Rafe drove the three miles or so to city hall too fast, but they got lucky with traffic and made it shortly after Gavin had made his grand entrance. In the middle of Flood's grandiose speechifying, as Liam put it.

"And grand it was," Hayley said with a grin. "For almost a full minute you could have heard a pin drop. Flood literally gaped at him. And then the buzz started."

She and Quinn were watching the relayed video on Hayley's tablet in the lobby area outside the council chambers. Cort was with them, and she guessed from the way the man looked at her as they approached that they had told him that Brown had been ordered to kill her.

When they reached them, one of the first things Rafe had done was to look at the man straight on and say, "Thank you," in a tone that warmed Charlie down to the bone.

Cort had looked rather shyly pleased, but then things started to happen fast. Quinn quickly outlined the plan to them. It made sense, and as she watched the feed she knew it would work. The mayor and council were none too happy about this interruption, but on top of Gavin's worldwide standing, they were also very familiar with the Foxworth name, and fear was evident in many faces there. Enough that Charlie started wondering what they'd been up to, to so fear the famous attorney and the organization that had taken the governor down.

But Gavin's name and reputation kept them at bay long enough for them to realize this was about Flood, not them, and they appeared so relieved they didn't even try to stop him as he approached the former senator at the lectern he'd commandeered. It didn't hurt that the brother of the security guard here had been a beneficiary of Foxworth's help once, and so he had been more than willing to make sure he got this assignment and not be in a hurry to restore order.

"I see you recognize the Foxworth name, Flood," Gavin said in that smooth, slightly amused tone that gave the impression he knew more about you than you did yourself. And the lack of the honorific of even "mister," let alone "senator," registered on Flood's face. "As well you should, since you sold them, and federal witness Vicente Reynosa, out to the cartel that was trying to stop him from testifying."

Gasps went around the room. And suddenly the smooth,

casual attorney went into attack mode, rattling off the list of evidence so rapidly the usually smooth-talking Flood got flustered.

"That's not proof!" He practically yelped it. "You can't prove any of this!"

"The first disclaimer of the guilty man," Gavin said with a pitying shake of his head. "Not that it's a lie, but that I can't prove it."

Charlie heard Quinn, both in person and in her ear, tell Gavin they were here and ready. Ty chimed in with the news that several local news feeds had already picked up on the live stream and it was spreading rapidly.

Gavin smiled widely in response. And then uncoiled. "But in fact, that's not what we're here to prove, anyway," he said. "This is not a courtroom, merely an official venue—" he glanced at the now clearly fascinated city officials, the ones Charlie could scarcely believe were allowing this, but such was the power and presence of Gavin de Marco "—the council has been kind enough to lend us. What we are going to present is something more…personal."

"That's what this is, a personal, politically motivated attack," Flood fumed. "Security, throw this man out!"

The security guard made a show of taking out a phone, saying, "Gavin de Marco? I'll check on that."

Charlie was smiling now, the man was so clearly rattled. She glanced at Rafe, who was reacting as well, in a half-smile kind of way that made her want to kiss that mouth.

"What was politically motivated, Maximilian Flood," Gavin said, moving toward the man like the apex predator he was in court, "was the murder of your wife."

Flood's eyes widened, but he came back hard. "I don't care how big you are, I'll have you arrested, de Marco.

And sue you for everything you've got and more. This is ridiculous."

When he spoke again, Gavin sounded like the crack of doom. "What's ridiculous is the facade you've built. What's obscene is the way you played the sympathy card over her death. We know who you paid, when you paid them and how much you paid them to rid yourself of the woman who had discovered the truth about you and was going to go public."

For a moment Charlie thought Flood was going to take a swing at him. Even as she thought it she heard Rafe murmur, "Go ahead, Flood. You'd be in for a shock."

She remembered then that Rafe, too, had seen the man fight.

"And if that's not enough," Gavin said, letting so much disdain into his voice it almost dripped ice water, "there's one more thing you'll have to explain."

Gavin turned and looked at the big doors into the room. Charlie read her cue, and glanced at her brother, who nodded. She started to walk toward those doors, only pausing to glance at Rafe when he stepped in behind her.

"At your back, all the way," he said quietly.

Feeling suddenly invincible, she strode into the council chambers, head up, gaze fastened on Flood. And she smiled, a grimly satisfied smile, as Flood spotted her and shock registered.

Gavin's tone was nothing less than triumphant when he said, "You can only buy so much loyalty, Flood. The man you tasked with murdering her is in the hospital. And he's talking."

Flood turned white and swayed on his feet, having to grab the lectern for balance.

"And the facade crumbles," she said. Behind her, Rafe

laughed. And that warmed her almost as much as the expression on Flood's face.

And so it ended with more of a whimper than a bang.

After a long aftermath, they were finally able to pack up the suite and retreat to Foxworth headquarters for a break while Gavin dealt with the fallout. Rafe was thankful for that; he felt oddly exhausted.

Ty reported that the live stream of the meeting had poured all of Flood's many crimes out to a stunned and rapidly expanding audience. The video had hit the networks after so many outlets had it that it couldn't be stopped or squelched. A couple of city police detectives had arrived; the de Marco name still carried a lot of weight even in those quarters, and their friend Brett Dunbar had made a couple of calls as well, to officers he trusted. Even if Flood were able to wiggle out of the worst of it, the scandal wouldn't be soon forgotten.

And Charlie was giving him that look again. That soft, warm look that did impossible things to his insides. He tried to call up his usual distance, but something about seeing that 9mm jammed under her chin had blasted away every bit of the icy cool he usually carted around.

"Thank you for my sister, Rafe," Quinn said solemnly.

He started to just shrug, but he couldn't treat this as if it were just another case. "That was the most important," he said, his voice a little rough.

"Who would have ever thought Flood would be an anticlimax, and yet in a way he was," Hayley said.

At that Rafe's mouth quirked upward at one corner. "And nothing could tick him off more."

They all laughed, which gave him a strange feeling on top of all the other strange feelings. Some he was familiar with, camaraderie, the satisfaction of accomplishment.

And he liked the fact that Quinn had set up some in-depth interviews with Cort Ducane for next week. The man had stalled Flood just long enough that Quinn could be sure his sister was safe before making their move. Long enough that he and Charlie had gotten there in time for her grand entrance, which Gavin had declared topped his any day.

But the satisfaction faded when, as Quinn and Hayley were getting ready to follow Teague and Liam out the door for some well-deserved rest—they'd been running 24-7 for days now—Charlie whispered to him that she wasn't leaving until they had talked. With some vague hope of outlasting her he'd escaped to his quarters in the hangar.

When Cutter showed up demanding entrance about an hour later, he gave in wearily. He knew too well the dog was immovable when his canine brain was set. And he knew as well that if he resisted, he was going to find out the meaning of the phrase "nipping at his heels" quite literally.

This would be the last time.

Rafe practically chanted it to himself as he walked—reluctantly—toward the back door of the Foxworth head-quarters. It was a little chilly, a portent of fall. His fall, too? He grimaced at the corny wordplay.

When he reached the patio he hesitated, but his companion, that darned, determined, dauntless dog, wasn't having it. He didn't just step behind him and nudge, he shoved. And made a sound just short of a growl to hurry him up.

He stepped onto the patio, even more determined now that this would be the last meeting with Charlie. She would go back to St. Louis and life would settle down here, and he'd be back to his routine of machines that didn't talk back or ask about his damned feelings. Feelings that had been out of control so often while she'd been here. Even down-range under fire he'd never felt as terrified as he had when Brown had jammed that pistol under her chin.

But he counted all the training, all the competition, all the kills before worth it for that single shot. If he never took another, that would be enough.

Cutter shoved him again.

"You're worse than a sheriff dragging somebody to the gallows," he muttered at the dog.

Cutter let out a canine sound that somehow sounded like a very human, "Enough already."

Sucking in a deep breath that he knew wouldn't be enough to steady him for this, he reached for the door and pulled it open.

The movement caught his trained eye first. Then the rest registered and he stared in shock.

"You remember."

Her voice was low, almost husky, and his breath jammed up in his throat. Remember? How could he ever forget? That dress. She was wearing that dress. That blue, silky, clingy thing that hugged every luscious curve and somehow made her eyes glow in the same shade of blue.

That dress she'd worn the first night they'd made love.

Had sex, you mean. The hottest damned sex of my life.

The tactical part of his mind tried valiantly to kick in, asking why she even still owned it years later, why she had brought it here, had she planned this…and noting that she'd obviously had it fixed from when he'd broken the zipper tearing it off of her.

None of it worked.

And then she was in front of him, asking in that same, sultry voice, "Do you ever wonder if it would be the same?"

Every damned day.

If he were the sharing sort, he might tell her that his time with her had set the standard, never to be met again. Not that he tried very often, no matter how many years it had been.

"I don't," she went on, "because I know it will be."

She was so close to him now he caught that sweet scent she'd worn back then. Different from what she'd worn with Flood, which had been heavier, screaming money, this was light, airy, fresh. She'd remembered that, too? Another memory flashed, Hayley and a shopping bag? Had she been in on this? Or had Charlie asked her to get—

Belatedly, it hit him. She'd said "will be." As if she had every intention of this night ending the way the night she'd first worn this dress had.

He knew in that moment he was doomed. If Charlie Foxworth had set her mind on seducing him, she would succeed.

Because when it came to her, all his vaunted fortitude and patience vanished.

Desperately, he made one try. "You don't have to sleep with me just because I saved your life."

She should have slapped him. At least she should have given him a furious, Charlie-like retort.

Instead she laughed. Delightedly. As if she knew they were well past that kind of nonsense. As if she recognized the desperate ploy for what it was. She reached out and cupped his cheek. Her touch seared him until he'd have sworn he felt that simple gesture down to his bones. Bones that seemed to be melting as he stood there.

"Char—"

It was all he got out before she kissed him.

At the feel of her soft, luscious mouth on his, it was as if the years between had never rolled by. The spark struck, caught, blazed. And no amount of his tactical mind saying this was a mistake could overpower the body screaming it was essential.

His will broke, because nothing could withstand a determined Charlaine Foxworth, and he was kissing her back.

New sensations collided with old memories, and the resultant inferno exploded like nothing he'd ever seen or felt.

He wasn't sure he'd survive.

He was sure he didn't care.

On some level, in some rarely used part of his mind that dealt with those feelings he never admitted to, he knew this would make it harder than ever when she, inevitably, was gone. When this ended yet again, for the simple reason that he didn't deserve anything that felt this good.

But a body that overheated at her first touch, hardened completely at that first kiss, didn't care. This was Charlie, and she knew how to blow up his walls. As she was blowing them up now.

When she went for his shirt, it was fierce and determined and very Charlie. And he didn't care if he broke the zipper on that dress, that damned enchanting dress, again.

This was happening. All the hot dreams he'd never been able to rid himself of, all the memories that cropped up whenever he let his mental guard down, were nothing compared to this reality, Charlie pulling his clothes off, touching him, stroking him, only pulling back long enough to step free of the dress that then fell to pool around their feet. He fumbled with the lacy, matching blue bra, but Charlie didn't. She was free of it in seconds, and seemingly of their own volition his hands were cupping her naked breasts. Her nipples were already taut, and when he rubbed them with his thumbs she moaned and he thought he would drop to his knees right here. And when she slid her hands down over his belly to stroke already rock-hard flesh, he nearly did.

"Don't think of anything else but how this feels," she whispered.

"As if I could," he ground out.

They somehow made it as far as the couch in front of the fire, which had come on against the chill he'd noticed outside. He would have suggested the bed in the guest room, but that twelve extra feet was too far. Way too far.

Her fingers tangled in his hair, pulling his mouth even harder against hers. He almost staggered, and for once it had nothing to do with his bad leg. They went down to the cushions, entwined now, her hands sliding over him.

"Hurry," she said breathlessly. "It's been too long."

A lifetime.

Hunger overwhelmed him and his last bit of caution vanished in an explosion of need. He stroked, kissed, tasted, even knowing he could never, ever get his fill. She arched against him, urging him on. And then her hand slid down to guide him into her, and the memories were seared to ash by the fierce fire of the reality. He was buried inside her, her body welcoming him, holding him, and he couldn't stop the blissful groan that escaped him.

As if the sound had triggered her she began to move, arching up to take him deeper, her fingers digging into his hips as if to keep him from escaping. As if he could. As if he would.

Some buried part of him warned this really would be the last time, and his determination suddenly matched hers, a determination to make it something neither of them would ever, ever forget. He drove hard and deep again and again until she cried out his name and clutched at him. This sign of the same kind of need from this indomitable woman was the last match to the fuse, and he barely held on until he felt her body clench fiercely around him and his name broke from her again, this time on a near scream.

Then it overtook him, and as his body exploded with exquisite pleasure, Rafe Crawford felt whole for the first time in years. The first time since the last night he'd spent with her.

He'd thought before he wasn't sure he'd survive this.

Now he wondered how he had survived without it.

Chapter 34

"This is pretty, but I like your hair straight and smooth. That's when it shimmers like moonlight on dark water."

Charlie stared at him as he toyed with the waves she'd worked so hard to get just right. The waves she herself didn't really like, but Flood had. Somehow that figured.

But those words had been almost...poetic. Especially for Rafe. It almost made her change her mind, because she so did not want to shatter this mood, this lovely peace between them.

But she wanted more and more of this, she wanted a future full of this, and to get that, this had to be done. And never let it be said Charlie Foxworth shirked what had to be done.

She steadied herself and said it. "Time for that talk."

She felt him go still beside her. They'd made it to the bed, finally. She'd vaguely noticed Cutter taking up a station at the bedroom door as if to make sure they didn't leave. Or no one interrupted them.

But that thought had slipped away quickly in a burst of renewed heat. She'd wanted nothing more but that fierce, strong body inside her again. Then she wanted to touch and kiss every new scar he'd gained in the years since, and then spend some time on the one she knew so well, the one she'd so often wished she could heal with a touch.

This night had been everything she'd hoped and planned for. Nothing had been lost in the years since, in fact it seemed to have only honed the need until it cut through all restraint. She wanted him more than ever, and she was not going to give up without a fight.

There would never be a better time.

"I want an answer. Now."

In his quieter way, he didn't respond to autocratic orders any better than she did, not when it came to personal things. Quinn could order him into a death trap and she had no doubt he would go, but this...this was a scarier place to him, this place where emotions lived. Where the heart lived.

She didn't give him time to think. Running on gut instinct now, and the new knowledge she had thanks to all she'd learned on this operation, working beside him, she didn't ask, she simply stated.

"Why. That's all I want to know. All I ever wanted to know. Why you walked away." She saw his jaw tighten. Even the cords of his neck tightened. But she kept going. "I deserve that much, Rafe. Just give me a good enough reason for why you did it."

It was a moment before he spoke, and she heard a world of apprehension in his voice. "Not sleeping with the boss isn't good enough?"

She let out a snort of laughter. "Do you really think I'm foolish enough to think I'm your boss?"

He looked straight at her then. "You're everyone's boss.

There's no one at any branch of Foxworth that wouldn't jump to do what you asked."

"Even you?"

His already low, rumbly voice dropped another notch. "Especially me."

"Rafe…" Her voice died away as he looked at her, those stormy gray eyes capturing her with the intensity of his gaze.

"Do you have any idea—" it was barely above a whisper "—how proud your parents would be of you, of what you've accomplished?"

It was so unexpected she was at a loss for words. Something rare enough that it rattled her. She felt her eyes begin to sting, was afraid she was going to cry and turn this into the very kind of emotional morass he hated. *She* hated.

Then his mouth quirked in a very Rafe-like way. "I know, I'm not supposed to be that…emotionally observant."

She recognized the phrase she'd used. It had apparently stuck with him. "Why did you tell me that?"

"Because it's true. And…" He hesitated, then, as if it were a great strain, said, "I needed to."

"There's a difference between being emotionally observant and emotionally available. What you just said was almost the latter."

"Almost?"

"It would take admitting why you felt that need to get all the way there."

He grimaced, looked away. "Just because I don't vomit it all out doesn't mean I don't feel it."

She felt an inward ache, some combination of sympathy and sadness. "Is that how you look at it? As…vomiting?"

"I look at it as pointless," he snapped. "Nobody wants to hear all that."

He didn't say "from me," but it hung in the air as if he had. Her eyes began to sting again, and she had to blink rapidly. She waited a long beat to be sure her voice would be steady, then said quietly, "I do. It's all I ever wanted, to hear that kind of thing from you. But now... I need to. To understand why."

She saw the reference back to his own need to tell her that thing about her parents that had so warmed her register in those eyes. But he didn't speak. He looked away. She'd known his walls were high and solid, but this...

She kept going. Because she had to. Foxworths didn't give up. Especially when the world—hers, anyway—was at stake.

"What could have made you leave," she said slowly, steadily, "without even an explanation? Made you walk away from what we had?"

When he still didn't answer, she knew she had to use the weapon her brother had given her.

"You were what I'd been hoping for my entire life. What could have ever made you think you weren't enough?"

"For you?" It burst from him. "How could you even begin to think I was good enough for you?"

The pure anguish in his tone, something she knew he never let show, broke her. The tears she'd been fighting welled up, and she felt the drops overflowing and then streaking down her cheeks. She didn't even try to wipe them away. She'd wept tears of happiness at Quinn and Hayley's wedding, and that had been the only time she'd cried since she'd vowed she never would again after their parents had died. Until now. Now she couldn't seem to stop.

"How...how could you ever think...you're not?"

It came out brokenly, which was how she felt inside at this confirmation of what seemed so impossible to her.

And for the first time in longer than she could remember, Charlaine Foxworth had no idea what to do.

It was impossible. Charlie was crying. The indomitable, undefeatable Charlie Foxworth was crying. Over…him.

He'd seen some incredible things in his life. He'd seen ugly things, horrible things, and a few beautiful things. He'd never seen anything that hit him as hard and deep as did the sight of her tears. He wanted to speak, to tell her he wasn't worth those tears, but the undeniable fact that she thought he was made his chest so tight he couldn't get a single word out. The pressure built, and built, until he could barely breathe.

He felt something break inside him, something so definite he was surprised the crack hadn't been audible.

He couldn't do this anymore. He had to tell her. He had to tell her, and then she'd understand, not just why he'd left, but why she was a million miles too good for him. He'd tell her and it would be over, this connection between them that had gone from heart high and soul deep but was now stretched so thin it wouldn't take much to snap it.

The truth should do it.

"I…" He had to stop, the tightness in his throat was so bad. It was like a blocked rifle barrel, and if he didn't clear it, whatever rounds he fired were going to blow up in his face.

You're about to finally blow this up for good, anyway, so what does it matter?

He swallowed, then told himself to settle in for the second biggest, most important shot of his life. He stared at his hands, the hands that had such skill when it came to things that didn't feel. They'd delivered death, many times.

But it wasn't his hands that would deliver this death.

Still staring at them, he ground the words out. "I'm not

good enough because I'm the reason a good, decent woman and her unborn child are dead." At last he looked up and met her gaze, made himself look into those beautiful blue eyes. "*My* unborn child."

She stared at him, her expression frozen. He'd shocked her out of the tears at least. For a moment he thought perhaps that was all it was going to take, and in that moment he was almost relieved. If he didn't have to go through it all, then maybe—

"Start," Charlie said with no intonation at all, "at the beginning."

He should have known. He wasn't going to get off that easy. Not with Charlie.

So where was the beginning? He wasn't sure, so he started with the best thing he could think of. "Her name was Laura. She was a civilian aide. She was from St. Louis, too, and we got to talking about that and…"

He trailed off, floundering in the unfamiliar waters. Silence spun out until Charlie said, with just the tiniest bit of snap in her voice, "Points to her if she got you to talk." He winced inwardly. Then, to his shock, she apologized. "Sorry. Go on."

He wasn't sure he could. It was going to take a lot of talking—especially for him—to get through this. He didn't think he had it in him. But something about the way Charlie was looking at him, something in those eyes…

He kept going. "We…got close, for the duration of her deployment. Then she was due to rotate out on an afternoon flight. I was gearing up for a mission, a nasty one, and that…that's when she told me she was pregnant."

"Timing is indeed everything," Charlie said, and he couldn't read anything in her very neutral tone.

"I…lost it. That she chose to wait and tell me then, when she admitted she'd known for at least two weeks. We were loading up, departure set for less than ten minutes on. I had to focus on the mission, she knew that. We…argued. I was pissed, and I didn't try to hide it."

That day had taught him a lot about hiding his anger, and any other emotion that might dare to try and rise up. It was not a lesson he wanted to learn again.

"Understandable." Her tone was just as neutral as it had been. "On both sides."

She said it as if she understood instinctively what Laura had had to explain to him, that she'd been afraid to tell him for this very reason. He sucked in some air, knowing he would need it to go on. And he had to go on, even though it was the last thing he wanted to do.

And the last time this woman would ever want to listen to him.

"She finally agreed to delay her departure until a flight out the next day. So we could…could…"

"Figure out what the hell you were going to do?"

"Yes." He grimaced, then let out a harsh laugh. "I was thinking, *If I survive the mission.*"

He stopped. He couldn't do this. He just couldn't. The images, the gruesome memories were all there, right there, careening around in his brain, as vivid as they had been that day. He couldn't let them out. They would destroy everything, the moment he put them into words. He never had, had never spoken of this to anyone, and he was no more ready to go through it now than he had been before.

Especially to Charlie.

And then she reached out. She took both his hands in hers. His first instinct was to pull away, pull back, but he couldn't do that, either. He wasn't even sure why he was still breathing.

"Finish it, Rafe. Let it out before it smothers you."

This time a short, sharp, bitter bite of laughter escaped him. "If only," he muttered.

But somehow the feel of her fingers wrapped around his gave him...not strength, really, but the courage to go on. It was ironic, really, that the person forcing him to talk was the one he least wanted to tell this to.

He stared down at their hands, entwined. The memories that caused, of those brief months of joy, of that revisited paradise last night, almost swamped him. He felt as if some clawing, biting creature had broken free in his chest, his gut, and it was going to leave him torn to ribbons. And the only coherent thought he had then was that it was no less than he deserved.

So do it. Get it done. Finish it once and for all. And if it finishes you, so be it.

He kept staring at their hands, on some level certain this would be the last physical contact they would ever have. And with an effort greater than he'd ever had to make walking into an enemy's nest, he pulled the pin.

"I survived, all right. But we came back to find the forward operating base a smoking ruin." Her fingers tightened, and he thought he heard a quick intake of breath. He kept on, knowing if he stopped now he'd never finish it. He released the safety lever on that metaphorical grenade. "They'd been attacked while we were gone. Half the people assigned there were dead. Including Laura."

"And your child," she whispered, sounding as if the tears were about to start again.

"Yes." He was hoarse now and didn't even try to hide it. "All because I...because I made her wait. She would have been gone, well on her way home, safe, but I lost my temper and...they both died. Because of me."

He pulled his hands back, knowing she wouldn't want to be touching him anymore. That she let him only proved it. He didn't have to—and couldn't—look at her to know she was staring at him in horror and distaste.

He stood up, he wasn't quite sure how. Nor was he sure where he was going to go, except away from here. Away from her, because he couldn't stand to see the revulsion he deserved in her eyes. She didn't try to stop him, but he heard a painfully choked sort of sound break from her.

"Now you know I was right," he said, his voice sounding as broken as he felt inside. He yanked on the jeans he'd picked up from the floor and turned to go, certain now she'd be glad to see the back of him. Forever.

He nearly tripped over Cutter.

The dog was on his feet, staring up at him with that fierce, amber-flecked gaze.

"Out of my way, dog," he said as he started to go around the animal who had become such a huge part of all of their lives. Cutter dodged back and got between him and the back door. "Do not," he said, "try and herd me."

Cutter growled. He took another step. The growl became a snarl, fierce and threatening. He stopped, startled. The dog's hackles were up, those lethal fangs bared, and for the first time Rafe had an inkling of what it must feel like for all the nefarious sorts they'd taken down since Cutter had joined them.

"Going to go for my throat, dog?" It came out in a whisper. "Go ahead."

He sensed rather than heard Charlie move behind him. Whatever she was going to say or do, he didn't want to be here for it. He changed direction, heading now for the front door.

Cutter launched, barreling into him. The dog hit his right leg just below the knee. It pushed all his weight onto his bad leg. At that angle it gave out. He was going down, hard.

And then there were arms around him, slight but undeniably strong. Holding on. Tight. Cushioning the fall.

Charlie.

She went down to the floor with him. Holding on tight. And now he saw her face, wet with tears that had overflowed. Were still flowing. Charlie Foxworth, the indomitable, unbreakable Charlie Foxworth, crying again. Still. Over him.

He should pull away. He tried. Cutter growled, and Charlie held on. The dog stood over them as they lay on the floor, like some supernatural guardian making sure they didn't escape. He tried again to move. Cutter growled again. Feeling suddenly exhausted, his head and shoulders dropped back to the floor.

"No," she whispered. "You're not leaving me. Not like this." He tried to speak. Couldn't. But Charlie could. "What happened was horrible. And heartbreaking. But it wasn't your fault. Do you hear me, Rafer James Crawford? It. Was. Not. Your. Fault."

He still couldn't find his voice, but he let out a harsh breath, closed his eyes and shook his head.

Charlie raised up on an elbow, and when he opened his eyes again she was looking down at him. "It wasn't her fault, either, except for the rotten timing. She was in an emotional place. Should she not tell you until she got home and you were stuck half a world away? Or maybe not tell you at all?"

His stomach knotted painfully. "I…wondered about that."

"Maybe that was her plan and at the last minute she couldn't do it. I don't know. You don't know. But it doesn't matter, Rafe. You couldn't control that any more than you could stop that attack when you weren't even there."

A tremor went through him, and he couldn't even muster up the strength to try and hide it from her.

"And look at what you've done since, the people you've saved, including me. The lives you've helped rebuild."

"That's...different."

"What's different is it's your work, which you excel at. When it gets dangerous, you're the one they want at their back. And you're always there for them. It's only the personal side you won't risk. You wall it up and lock the door." She paused, as if waiting for him to deny it. He couldn't. Because it was true. "I never, ever thought you'd be a coward, Rafe. But when it comes to your heart..."

He winced. His mouth twisted. "How did you get so smart about people?"

"I've been hanging around my sister-in-law."

He blinked at that. And because Hayley deserved it, he said quietly, "That would do it."

"And there's another thing you should know." He braced himself. "It was you who gave me the words that became a mantra for Foxworth, as we grew and expanded."

He stared at her. What the hell could she mean? When she went on, it was in the tone of someone indeed quoting a mantra.

"'No operation goes well unless all the parts are oiled, fit right and work together.'"

His brow furrowed. It had been a long time ago, but he did remember saying it. Vaguely. "I was...talking about machines."

"And is Foxworth not a well-oiled machine?"

"I..."

"I was planning a trip here, before Flood." That seeming non sequitur made the swirling waters still for a moment. "I wanted to have it out with you once and for all. I couldn't go on like this, wishing I could...not care." Her breath caught audibly, and he couldn't stop himself from looking. Tears were still flowing, from those huge blue eyes down the cheeks of this woman who never cowered, never quailed...never, ever cried.

"Charlie..." It came out like a mangled whisper. She tightened her arms around him.

"Are you going to throw us away?"

"I thought I already had." He sounded like a rusty wheel, but it was the best he could do.

"Because of a tragedy you couldn't have prevented?"

"But she...they..." He stopped, unable to go on because one of her tears had dropped onto his face. It seared him, making his own eyes sting.

"It's horrible," she said again. "And I'm so sorry this world hasn't been blessed with the presence of your child." He stared at her, startled that she chose that to focus on. "But we're here, and we're alive, Rafe. You may have thrown us away, but I never let go."

"You'd be better off if you did."

"No. No, I wouldn't. We love who we love."

He froze. Didn't, couldn't breathe as those words pounded in his head. She couldn't mean what that implied.

Charlie laughed, a rueful yet somehow unrepentant sound. "Oh, yes, Mr. Crawford. I love you."

"You can't—"

"I never stopped. I even think I loved you most when I was sniping the worst."

He took in a long, deep breath. "I just a while ago realized... I kept digging at you because it was a connection, at least."

"It's always been there, that connection. Maybe even since childhood, but certainly since the day my brother brought you into Foxworth. From the moment I saw you...

I knew. You were the one I was afraid I'd never find. And when we were together, it was so right. So very right."

"Too right," he whispered, remembered that feeling, that soaring, joyous feeling. Before all the reasons why it was wrong, why he didn't deserve it, came crashing in. "But you didn't know then."

"Not the specifics, no. But I knew you were…hurting. And Quinn warned me you were too stubborn to admit it." She smiled, rather crookedly, and through the tears it was the most wrenching yet beautiful thing he'd ever seen. "I didn't care. I just knew I'd never reacted this way to any man, ever."

She leaned down suddenly. Before he realized her intent, her mouth was on his. The kiss was hot and fierce, and flooded him with the memories and images of last night, those wild hours in the dark when he'd given it all because he'd known it would be the last time.

And yet here she was, saying she still loved him. And showing him. He was breathless when she finally pulled back.

"You know what I want?" She sounded a little breathless herself.

He couldn't find any words, so only shook his head.

"I want eighteen thousand repeats of last night." He blinked. She smiled. "That works out to every night for fifty years, give or take." Of course she'd do the math. Only Charlie. Only Charlie could make him laugh at a time like this. But his laugh faded when her voice took on that low, husky note again as she said quietly, "And know that I, as you were for me, will be at your back all the way."

There were still no words—he really was going to have to do something about that—but he did answer her. He kissed her. Long and deep. And when at last she pulled back to look at him, there was a gleam in those blue eyes he'd never seen before.

"Now, listen up, Crawford. This will only work if I assume that if you're in one of those moods, it has nothing to do with me. So if it ever does have something to do with me, you're going to have to break through that miasma you live in and *tell* me. You're going to have to do it for us."

She was saying it as if it were a given there would be an us. Us. Them. Him and Charlie Foxworth.

"And by the way," she added, "if you think you're going to walk away again, I think you'd better take into account one more thing."

He had to swallow before he could force out, "What?"

Charlie grinned at him then. "Him," she said, jerking a thumb at Cutter. "And I think you know better than to try and cross him when his mind is set."

He glanced at the dog. Cutter stared back at him, looking as wise as the sphinx whose position he had assumed. There was a world of wisdom and determination in those amber-flecked eyes. Just as there was a world of love in Charlie's vivid blue ones.

He felt muscles he hadn't even realized were tensed relax. Followed by a strange flood of warmth inside, spreading everywhere. The dam had broken, the last wall had been breached. He wasn't sure exactly how, but he knew with a gut-deep certainty that a sea change was upon him. He knew it had to happen, even if he didn't know how.

He had to walk a new path, one he'd never been on before.

And he knew that no one would be better able to keep him on that path than stubborn, brilliant, loving—and forgiving—Charlie Foxworth.

With a little help, maybe, from her brother's dog.

Epilogue

"Do we need to take him to the vet?"

Quinn looked at Cutter a little anxiously. He'd never seen the dog like this, sleeping so much, barely showing an interest in anything going on. Not that he wanted something to worry about, not when he was snuggled up on the couch with his wife's arms around him, but the animal was acting oddly.

"He's eating okay," he went on, brow furrowed with concern, "but…"

"He's fine."

When he looked up at Hayley's words, he found her grinning. "What's funny?"

"He's just exhausted. And I can't blame him. This was a very long haul."

He couldn't deny the three years it had taken them to finally get to the mole who had betrayed them had been long. "At least Flood's going to pay now."

Her grin widened. "I didn't mean Flood."

Belatedly it hit him. "Oh." Slowly, a smile that held the same quality as her grin curved his mouth. "Yeah."

"You are happy about it?"

"That those two knuckleheads finally got it together? Yes. Absolutely I am. I think they're the only ones who could put up with each other."

"Now that they've figured out how," Hayley agreed happily. "With a little help. Can you believe he actually knocked Rafe down?"

He looked back at their exhausted, match-making dog. "I believe he knew exactly how to use that leg against him."

"And," Hayley added softly, "how desperate the situation was. He never would have done it otherwise."

"No, he wouldn't."

She shifted her gaze to his face, and he felt that strange quiver he always felt whenever she looked at him that way. "I hope they're having a wonderful time at the cabin."

He couldn't help the upward twitch of his eyebrows. "Oh, I'm sure they are," he said as he recalled those last moments at the small landing strip in the mountains. He'd flown them there himself and arranged for one of the locals to drive them up to the isolated lodge-style cabin.

"We'll try not to burn it down," Charlie had said, happier than he had ever seen her.

"But no promises," Rafe had said gruffly, his gaze fastened on the woman beside him.

Hayley let out a satisfied sigh. "It's wonderful to see them so happy. By the way, what did you say to him, right as they got off the plane?"

"I told him not to blow their second chance." Quinn smiled. "He reminded me that the second shot out of a rifle is always more accurate."

Hayley blinked. "What?"

Quinn laughed. "It's a sniper thing. They call it a cold

bore shot. The first shot, I mean. It warms up the barrel and leaves carbon behind, and that affects the next shot, makes the path different, more accurate."

She was laughing now. "So was that our inimitable Rafe saying second time's the charm?"

"Pretty much," Quinn agreed, grinning at her now.

She let out an obviously happy sigh. "I was afraid it would never happen for him. For them."

"Me, too." He jerked a thumb at Cutter. "But we should have known he'd never quit until it was done."

"It's not in him," Hayley agreed. "Us first, now all of the Foxworth team, plus all those clients… Not a bad track record, dog."

Cutter's dark ears twitched, and his head came up. But only his head, and he was looking at them sleepily. When he saw them still seated, he plopped back down and seemed to doze back off in mere seconds.

"Do you think she'll really move here?" Hayley asked. "We won't lose Rafe, will we?"

"I should ask you. You're the mind reader."

Hayley looked thoughtful. "I think she liked it here. And more importantly, I think she knows Rafe wouldn't be really happy anywhere else." She grinned then. "I think we're going to lose our live-in security at headquarters, though."

Quinn laughed. "No, I can't see my sister living in that tiny room."

He was quiet for a moment, as he pondered the changes that had already happened, and those yet to come.

"It all makes you wonder where we go from here," he mused aloud.

"There will always be people who need us. So we go and do whatever it takes to help them. As we did this time."

Cutter bestirred himself enough to add a small woof of

agreement, then went back to sleep. Quinn took it as the canine equivalent of "Mission accomplished."

Quinn shifted on the couch so he could look directly at the woman who had changed his life. He reached up and gently turned her chin so that their gazes locked.

"I love you, Hayley Foxworth. You are my life."

"As you are mine, Quinn Foxworth." She reached up to cup his cheek. "And it's a good, good life."

"The best," Quinn whispered, just before he kissed her.

Knowing his people were all happy, Cutter slept on, taking his well-earned rest.

Until the next time.

* * * * *

Catch up with everyone at the
Foxworth Foundation with previous books
in Justine Davis's Cutter's Code miniseries:

Operation Takedown
Operation Witness Protection
Operation Payback
Operation Whistleblower
Operation Mountain Recovery
Operation Second Chance

Available now from Harlequin Romantic Suspense!

Get 3 FREE REWARDS!

We'll send you 2 FREE Books <u>plus</u> a FREE Mystery Gift.

FREE Value Over **$20**

Both the **Harlequin Intrigue®** and **Harlequin® Romantic Suspense** series feature compelling novels filled with heart-racing action-packed romance that will keep you on the edge of your seat.

YES! Please send me 2 FREE novels from the Harlequin Intrigue or Harlequin Romantic Suspense series and my FREE gift (gift is worth about $10 retail). After receiving them, if I don't wish to receive any more books, I can return the shipping statement marked "cancel." If I don't cancel, I will receive 6 brand-new Harlequin Intrigue Larger-Print books every month and be billed just $6.49 each in the U.S. or $6.99 each in Canada, a savings of at least 13% off the cover price, or 4 brand-new Harlequin Romantic Suspense books every month and be billed just $5.49 each in the U.S. or $6.24 each in Canada, a savings of at least 12% off the cover price. It's quite a bargain! Shipping and handling is just 50¢ per book in the U.S. and $1.25 per book in Canada.* I understand that accepting the 2 free books and gift places me under no obligation to buy anything. I can always return a shipment and cancel at any time by calling the number below. The free books and gift are mine to keep no matter what I decide.

Choose one:
- ☐ **Harlequin Intrigue Larger-Print** (199/399 BPA GRMX)
- ☐ **Harlequin Romantic Suspense** (240/340 BPA GRMX)
- ☐ **Or Try Both!** (199/399 & 240/340 BPA GRQD)

Name (please print)

Address   Apt. #

City   State/Province   Zip/Postal Code

Email: Please check this box ☐ if you would like to receive newsletters and promotional emails from Harlequin Enterprises ULC and its affiliates. You can unsubscribe anytime.

> Mail to the **Harlequin Reader Service:**
> **IN U.S.A.:** P.O. Box 1341, Buffalo, NY 14240-8531
> **IN CANADA:** P.O. Box 603, Fort Erie, Ontario L2A 5X3

Want to try 2 free books from another series! Call 1-800-873-8635 or visit www.ReaderService.com.

*Terms and prices subject to change without notice. Prices do not include sales taxes, which will be charged (if applicable) based on your state or country of residence. Canadian residents will be charged applicable taxes. Offer not valid in Quebec. This offer is limited to one order per household. Books received may not be as shown. Not valid for current subscribers to the Harlequin Intrigue or Harlequin Romantic Suspense series. All orders subject to approval. Credit or debit balances in a customer's account(s) may be offset by any other outstanding balance owed by or to the customer. Please allow 4 to 6 weeks for delivery. Offer available while quantities last.

Your Privacy—Your information is being collected by Harlequin Enterprises ULC, operating as Harlequin Reader Service. For a complete summary of the information we collect, how we use this information and to whom it is disclosed, please visit our privacy notice located at corporate.harlequin.com/privacy-notice. From time to time we may also exchange your personal information with reputable third parties. If you wish to opt out of this sharing of your personal information, please visit readerservice.com/consumerschoice or call 1-800-873-8635. **Notice to California Residents**—Under California law, you have specific rights to control and access your data. For more information on these rights and how to exercise them, visit corporate.harlequin.com/california-privacy.

HIHRS23